Philip José Farmer shocked the world of science fiction in 1952 with the publication of his novella *The Lovers* in *Startling Stories*. It told of the romance between a man and an alien parasitic insect which had taken the form of a woman, and with this story Farmer had introduced real sex into a world of science fiction that needed the uplift. More importantly perhaps, *The Lovers* can be credited with introducing the dimension of human feeling to a genre too frequently starved of this. The novella won him a Hugo Award in 1953; his second Hugo came in 1968 for the story *Riders of the Purple Wage* written for Harlan Ellison's famous *Dangerous Visions* series; and his third came in 1972 for the first part of the Riverworld Series, *To Your Scattered Bodies Go*. The series, now completed with the recent publication of *The Magic Labyrinth*, conjures up a fabulous alternative world through which flows a river over 14 million miles long, where all the people that ever lived are resurrected for further quests and adventures beyond death. Leslie Fiedler, eminent critic and Professor of English at the State University of New York at Buffalo, has said that Farmer 'has imagination capable of being kindled by the irredeemable mystery of the universe and of the soul, and in turn able to kindle the imagination of others – readers who for a couple of generations have been turning to science fiction to keep wonder and ecstasy alive'.

By the same author

Philip José Farmer

Jesus on Mars

A PANTHER BOOK

GRANADA

London Toronto Sydney New York

Published by Granada Publishing Limited in 1982

ISBN 0 586 05308 5

A Granada Paperback UK Original
Copyright © Philip José Farmer 1979

Granada Publishing Limited
Frogmore, St Albans, Herts AL2 2NF
and
36 Golden Square, London W1R 4AH
866 United Nations Plaza, New York, NY 10017, USA
117 York Street, Sydney, NSW 2000, Australia
100 Skyway Avenue, Rexdale, Ontario, M9W 3A6, Canada
61 Beach Road, Auckland, New Zealand

Printed and bound in Great Britain
by Cox and Wyman Ltd, Reading
Set in Plantin

Granada ®
Granada Publishing ®

To my mother

1

The great canyon complex of the Vallis Marineris was a black wound on a red body. It ran for 3,000 miles from east to west near the equator of Mars. At its widest it was fifty miles and at its deepest several miles. If it resembled a terrible gash in a corpse, it also looked like a colossal centipede, the legs being the channels winding through the highlands towards the vast rift, and the bristles on the legs, the subtributaries.

From the *Aries*, in a stationary orbit, Richard Orme looked down as if from an incredibly high mountain. A rapidly dying wind was blowing high clouds of ice crystals and low clouds of red dust across part of the complex, obscuring the section that was their goal after four months of voyage. He turned from the port and floated towards Madeleine Danton. She was seated before a viewscreen, her waist belted to a chair, which was bolted to the deck. Behind her floated Nadir Shirazi and Avram Bronski. Their hands gripped the back of the chair while they stared over her shoulders at the screen.

Orme seized Shirazi's shoulder, swivelled around, and steadied himself. On the screen was the exposed tunnel that the satellite had photographed five years ago. Its roof, once a thin shell of rock, had fallen in. A passage ten feet wide, twenty feet tall, and eighty feet long was revealed.

Though the dust storm looked solid from the ports of the ship, the pictures transmitted by the robot rover, which had landed two years ago, were fairly clear within fifty feet. Beyond was a reddish haze.

The tunnel's floor was slowly being covered by dust. At one end it disappeared into the darkness of the part of the roof that had not collapsed. At the other end, vaguely discernible through the dust, was a door. It was of some dark material that could be metal or stone. Its smoothness showed that it had been machine-made.

On the black surface of the door were two large orange characters: Greek letters, capital tau and capital omega. Danton's oval face was expressionless. Shirazi's hawkish features showed an intensity reminding Orme of a bird of prey that has just spotted a rabbit. Bronski's dark handsome face held a smirk.

His own black features, he supposed, looked slightly ecstatic.

Orme's heart was thudding, and its sudden increase in rate would have been monitored about 11.5 minutes from now by Houston if the sensors had been attached to him. But he was dressed in a jump suit. Launch time was two hours away. By then the lower wind should have subsided to a gentle breeze.

'Let's see the ship,' Orme said.

Danton punched in the orders on the tiny console before her. The view lifted up, showing a vague dark mass through the dust, the walls of the mile-deep rift, and then a huge mass; no, only its intimations, a ghost.

The rover was crawling towards it now. Minutes passed while the curving outlines of the mass became clearer. Danton gave a verbal order to the robot to stop. Now they could see the great curving thing that had first attracted the survey satellite six years ago, shocking and exciting all of Earth and resulting in the first manned expedition to the red planet.

'I've seen it a hundred times on Earth,' Orme said. 'And I still don't believe it. A spaceship!'

Nobody answered. They understood that he was just talking to relieve tension.

How long ago was it that the vessel had landed or crashed? A hundred years ago? A thousand? How long had it been before a landslide of rotten stone had covered it? And how many years had passed before some of the rock covering had slid off to expose a small part of the colossus? Or had it been deliberately concealed, the stones piled on it by its crew?

If it hadn't been for the curiosity of an Australian scientist, his 'hunch' that the shadowy thing in the photographs looked unnatural and his persistence, the vessel still might not be noticed. It might have been undiscovered forever. Then the open tunnel had been found, and after three years, a robot had been landed to make a closer inspection. And the whole world was agog.

Richard Orme, born in Toronto, Canada in 1979, had been thirty years old when the IASA had reluctantly announced that the curving mass was indeed artificial. He had anticipated the events that would follow, and he had worked and schemed and fought to be a member of this expedition. A toss of a coin had decided whether he or an Australian astronaut would be the captain and the fourth crewperson of the *Aries*. The loser had smiled and congratulated him, but that night he'd got drunk and been badly crippled in an automobile accident. Though he knew that it was irrational, Orme had felt guilty about it. Part of the guilt came from his elation at having won.

Orme glanced at the chronometer and said, 'Time to start the next phase.'

Danton stayed at the console; Bronski and Shirazi got busy helping Orme to suit up. Then Orme helped the Iranian to get Bronski into his armour. Meanwhile, Danton, in her slightly French-accented English, kept up a steady flow of reports on environmental data and the progress of the preparations. It was not an easy job since the long time-lag transmissions meant that she had to receive and often answer to comments relayed from Earth through the satellite above Houston. She had to keep in mind what she had said earlier.

The whole world was listening at this moment; it would be doing so at every opportunity. The operation should go smoothly because of their many hours of practice landing on the Moon. But there was always the possibility of electro-mechanical malfunction.

9

Finally, Orme and Bronski slid through the hatch into the lander, the *Barsoom*. The head of IASA had been a reader of Edgar Rice Burroughs in his childhood. His name was John Carter, the same as the hero of Burroughs's earlier books about Mars, known as Barsoom by its fictional natives. Carter had first proposed the name and had made the necessary political manipulations to get it accepted. Those who had wanted to name the lander *Tau Omega*, after the two characters on the tunnel door, had lost in the voting by a narrow margin.

After half an hour of rechecking, Orme gave the order for launching. The *Barsoom* departed slowly from the mother ship under a weak jet pulse. Orme felt a warm spot over his navel, as if that psychic umbilical cord attaching him to the mother planet had been severed. But there was no time for any introspection. His mind had to be focused on the objective, the position of the lander in relation to the landing surface, and the constant inflow of flight data. He had to be a machine without flaw; the awe and wonder during descent and the ecstasy of accomplishment could come after the touchdown on Mars. If, that is, there were no immediate problems.

The crew had practised landings on Earth in a much more powerful machine which could handle the heavy gravity and thick atmosphere. It had also practised on the Moon, where the gravitational pull was much weaker than that of Earth's and the atmosphere was practically nil. But the atmosphere here, though relatively tenuous, was still a considerable factor. However, the theory of a Martian landing had been worked out and the crew had drilled so many times under simulated conditions that the reality should be no problem.

For four days the crew of the *Aries* had waited for the winds to die down. Now, finally, the high ice clouds and the lower dust clouds were subsiding. Only a few thin cirri floated along below them, and the surface atmosphere should not present difficulties.

The red orb expanded swiftly. The top of Olympus Mons, a volcano as wide as the state of New Mexico and 15.5 miles high, sank out of sight. The Tharsis ridge, looking like a colossal dinosaur with fleshy dorsal plates, widened and then dropped out of sight. The Tithonius Chasma, more than 46 miles wide and several miles deep, part of the Vallis Marineris canyon complex, broadened.

For twenty seconds, whiteness surrounded them as they passed through a long, narrow and deep cloud of ice. To the east lay a shadow, night on Mars, advancing at almost the rate it did on Earth. It was the bow which shot darkness and a terrible cold over the wastelands. Not that it was warm on the surface. When they landed, they would find the temperature to be +20° C.

Orme turned the lander to face west as the thin but still strong wind began to carry them east. He adjusted the pulses to counter the push of the atmosphere. The *Barsoom* sank, and he noted that the air, though it was becoming thicker, was not moving as swiftly as the higher altitude wind. He decreased the pulses; the raser indicator showed that the *Barsoom* was maintaining its angle of descent. A straight line drawn from the lander would end dead on the point of contact, the floor of the Tithonius Chasma.

Time passed as he poured data into the transceiver. The transmitter would also be sending photographs of the approaching surface of Mars and of the two Marsnauts in this womb of irradiated plastic.

Like a mouth, the rift opened beneath him. The vast mounds of the volcanoes outside dropped, and presently the ship was below the edges of the awesomely towering cliffs. They were still in the thin but bright sunlight of the red planet. Not until the sun was low would the shadow of the western wall fall on them.

Orme, glancing now and then out of the port, could see the metallic curve of the other vessel buried beneath the landslide. Reddish rocks and a finer material, dust, were mixed in this collapse from the weathered material of the canyon wall. There was little wind here, which made Orme's task easier.

Bronski, overcome by emotion, forgot his English and spoke in Polish. This had been his native language; he had not learned French until the age of ten, when his parents had fled to Sweden and thence to Paris. He corrected himself a moment later, saying, 'It *is* an artifact! A ship!'

Orme thought that it remained to be proved that it was a spacecraft but he had no time to comment. Besides, he felt that Bronski was right.

The lander settled firmly on its six pads, and it sank a trifle as its telescoping legs absorbed the shock, then recoiled to lift the vessel. Orme cut off the power and sat for a moment feeling the weak pull of Mars and hearing the silence. Then he said jubilantly, 'Martians, we're here!'

He'd planned a number of short speeches, some quite poetic, but he had finally decided to hell with it. He'd say whatever came spontaneously.

Danton's voice broke the silence. 'Congratulations, commander.'

Orme was startled when Bronski's arms enfolded him from behind and his voice bellowed in Orme's ears.

'By God, we've done it!'

'He's here, too,' Orme said, and he meant it. 'Even if this place does look like the devil's workshop.'

2

Orme unstrapped himself and rose slowly, remembering that
though there was gravity it was not Earth's. He looked
through the port and quickly described what he saw. The
lander was 300 feet from the edge of the landslide, resting on
an area detected from the *Aries*. It was comparatively free of
the rocks that littered the floor of the canyon; the pads had
missed all of them and sat on rock swept smooth of dust by the
recent winds. Through the top port he could see the sky, a
light blue crossed by a few wisps of whiteness. Coming
towards them was the robot explorer, RED II, which had first
seen the two Greek characters on the tunnel door. Danton
had directed it to approach the *Barsoom* closely and transmit
pictures of the Marsnauts as they left the lander and worked
around the *Aries*. These pictures would be transmitted to the
Aries, which would relay them to the satellite and thence to
Earth.

Eight hundred feet behind the explorer, invisible even
from its height, was the tunnel. Orme and Bronski got to
work. After donning their suits and helmets and checking
them, they entered the cramped room of the decompression
chamber and closed the port leading to the interior of the
lander. Orme set a gauge and pressed a button. Within three
minutes the pressure in the chamber had been reduced to that
of the atmosphere outside. Orme opened the hatch and
unrolled a metal ladder. Though he could easily have jumped
down to the ground fourteen feet below, he was forbidden to
do so. The two were to take no chances.

He clambered down the ladder and stepped backward on to
the rock and turned. He felt a headiness which was not caused
by the lighter gravity. He, Richard Orme, a black Canadian,

was the first human being to step upon the surface of the red planet. Whatever happened from this second on, he would be recorded in history as the first man on Mars. The rover, that metallic insect-like machine, was transmitting pictures of the unique event right now. Of him, Richard Orme, the first Earthman to step upon the ancient rock of another planet.

'Columbus, you should be here!' he said, acutely conscious that 11.5 minutes from now, billions would hear this statement. He did not utter his succeeding thought. *And you'd crap in your pants!* The old navigator could never even have dreamed of this.

'Five hundred and twenty-three years have brought us a long way!' he said. He didn't elaborate. There would be enough people on earth who'd understand what he meant and explain it to the viewers.

Bronski came down the ladder then, looked around for a minute, and at a signal from Orme joined him in the work. From a compartment at the bottom of the lander they unloaded a cable, a driller, and a sonar. The latter determined that the landing place was solid rock and thick enough for the anchor. Bronski drilled into the basalt and then disengaged the drill from the power unit. One end of the cable was secured to the part of the drill sticking up from the surface. Orme prepared a cement mixture and poured it down between the drill and the hole.

While waiting for the quick-drying material to harden, they walked to the silvery metal curve protruding from the masses of rock. Standing under the great arc and looking up at it, Orme felt awed. If this was a vessel, and it surely was, then it would be the size of an old passenger liner, say the *Queen Mary*, or as large as the Zeppelin *Hindenburg*. Whoever had built it had had an energy source that Earth lacked. To lift this monster from a planet into space, to drive it through interstellar space and to land here required a power staggering to think about.

How long had it lain here at the bottom of this colossal

14

canyon? Long enough, certainly, for the wall to weather and for chunks of rock to fall down and bury it. And then long enough for some force, perhaps the effect of very strong winds over a long time, to remove the rocks that had covered this part of the vessel.

But it was possible that this exposed section had never been covered. The survey satellite had photographed it many times, but no areographer had noticed it until Lackley, the Australian, had had his 'hunch'.

Or, perhaps, some beings had started to remove the rocks and something had interrupted their work.

At this thought, a chill ran up his spine and over his scalp. Involuntarily, he turned around to look behind him. There was, of course, no group of Martians advancing silently towards him. He laughed.

'What's so funny?' Bronski said.

'Nothing in particular. I laughed because . . . it doesn't matter. Joy, maybe. Here. Get the kit out.'

He turned his back to Bronski, who removed a box from the cylinder on it. This was a minilaboratory designed for making chemical-physical tests. Bronski put the box on the ground, opened the lid, and he and Orme went through the process with a swiftness owing to long training. When they were done, Orme gave his report.

'The door looks like metal. As you heard through the audiometer, the interior is hollow. It rings when hit with a steel hammer. Even a diamond won't scratch it. Nitric acid leaves it unmarked. I don't want to use a laser beam on it because air might damage the contents. Providing there are any. Whatever material it's made of, it's unknown to Terrestrial science.'

Bronski replaced the box in the cylinder, and they walked back to the *Barsoom*. The cement was hard. In this atmosphere, where the pressure was equal to that ten miles above Earth's surface, the moisture quickly left the cement. It had boiled off in a vapour invisible in this twilight.

Orme used a tiny jack to draw up the slack and make the cable taut. Now even a 250-mile-an-hour wind, which wasn't likely at the canyon bottom, would not be able to push the lander over.

Nadir Shirazi, who was spelling Danton now, said, 'How do you two feel? Do you want to rest before you go to the tunnel?'

'I'm too excited to stop now,' Bronski said. 'I'd like to push on.'

From the compartment which had held the anchoring material, they removed a telescoping aluminium ladder and a box of explosives. Orme carrying the box, they walked to the edge of the tunnel. The rover followed them, its main scanner keeping them in view for the two in the *Aries* and the billions of people on Earth. Orme put the box down and opened its lid. Bronski lowered the ladder down into the tunnel. With a powerful lamp he'd taken from the box, Orme played a beam of light along the tunnel. At the left side of the two men, the rover followed the light with its antennas.

Orme had seen the interior of the opening many times by courtesy of the rover. But now that he was seeing it with his own eyes, he felt the same thrill as when he'd first witnessed it in the Houston laboratory. At the far end was a mass of rock, pieces of the fallen roof. These presumably covered another door. Along the length of the floor were other stone chunks, large and small. At the other end was the upper part of a door, its lower quarter behind more pieces of rock. Red dust covered the rocks. But its thinness indicated the roof had caved in recently.

What had caused the collapse? No one had a theory which could hold up under any rationalization. The tunnel was too far away from the nearest cliff for any rocks to have fallen on it. Anyway, there were no large rocks inside the tunnel or near it. To the west were some huge boulders, but these had been trundled down the canyon floor by water in some very remote past.

One scientist had proposed that a small meteorite had

shattered the roof. But the area around here was free of any impact craters, small or large. And it seemed too much of a coincidence that a rare meteorite should happen to strike this very narrow area and reveal what would otherwise never have been discovered.

Orme steadied the beam on the orange characters in the dull black door. Tau Omega in majuscule writing. But had they been made by one versed in Greek? Were not the letters so simple that they would have been used by other sentients? T and Ω would naturally occur to anyone who was originating an alphabet. If indeed these characters were alphabetical. They could just as easily be letters in a syllabary, or in an ideogrammatic system such as the Chinese used. They could also be arithmetical symbols.

Orme gestured to Bronski to go down the ladder. If he wasn't to be the first man to step on to Mars, he at least could be the first to touch the door in the tunnel.

The rover was on the edge of the opening now, one scanner on Orme and the other following the Frenchman. When Orme saw that Bronski was off the ladder, he dropped the box to him. Bronski caught it easily, and Orme went down the ladder.

Bronski had climbed up the small pile of rocks and was examining the door by the time Orme reached him. Orme picked up a stone about the size of his head and heaved it up and out of the tunnel, first making sure that the rover wouldn't be struck by it. Bronski came down from the top of the pile to help him. In about five minutes the way to the door was cleared. In the light of the four-legged lamp, which had been set on the floor, Bronski removed the box from the cylinder on Orme's back. The tests revealed that the door was of a steel alloy.

'It's set within the opening very tightly,' Orme said. 'Obviously, it's an air-pressure seal, designed for just what happened, the collapse of a section of tunnel.'

Unlike the shell of the supposed spaceship, the door was

thick. There was no hollow echo when he hit it with the hammer.

'We could try to blow it out,' Orme said. 'But I think it'll be easier of we go to the roof of the next section and dig down.'

They got out of the tunnel and returned to the lander. Orme was beginning to get tired, which meant that Bronski should be even more fatigued. Orme was only five feet eight, but he weighed a muscular 190 pounds on Earth, with no excess fat. The slender Bronski was quick, but he could not keep up with his captain.

Orme suggested that they eat while taking a rest and perhaps even grab a nap. The Frenchman refused.

'I'm still too keyed up.'

Carter, however, from his command post in Houston, ordered that they attach the monitors. After reading the indicators, he said, 'You guys will have to recharge your batteries. You're really tired.'

By the time the message came through, they had eaten. For an hour they rested in their reclined seats. Orme used alpha-wave techniques to get to sleep. Even so, it took twenty minutes, according to the monitors, before he succumbed. He would have sworn that he'd been awake the entire period.

Twenty minutes later, they were back at the tunnel site. Eighteen inches beyond the door, Orme cut a hole into the tunnel roof with a small laser-tipped drill. When it broke through, the explosion of enclosed air drove the tool up out of the hole. But Orme, expecting this, was standing to one side. Even so, the drill was almost jerked out of his hand.

He set to work at once to drill five more holes, all in a circle with a diameter of three feet. He could have connected the holes with the laser and cut a complete section to drop down into the tunnel. But he had to conserve power, so he planted gelignite charges in the holes and touched off the explosive at a distance with a battery. The circular section went up in smoke and larger fragments of rock. They rose higher than they would have on the home planet, the smoke disappeared more quickly, and the dust settled more swiftly.

'If there's an automatic sealing system, and it's still working, then the end of that tunnel will be shut off,' Orme said. 'And we'll have to open a door. But that will mean that the next section will seal. We don't have the materials to go through many doors.'

The tunnel, if it continued in a straight line, would go into the canyon wall. By now the shadow of the western wall was over them, and it was getting colder. They were comfortable in their suits, bulky though they were and with much equipment strapped onto them. Inside each was a flask of water which they could suck up through a tube by bending their heads inside the helmet down and to one side. They still had half a flask left, and they could urinate into a bladder attached to the front of one leg.

Nevertheless, John Carter ordered them to quit for the night after they'd taken a reading to determine if the tunnel did enter the cliff.

'You can conserve the power in your lights if you work in daylight. And we can observe you better.'

Orme didn't want to agree, but he had to. After validating that the tunnel did go beneath the cliff, he told Bronski they had to get back.

'Tomorrow we'll put in a full day. We'll be refreshed. It was the landing that took everything out of us. Even though we exercised on the *Aries* during the trip, we aren't in tiptop shape. Null gravity is insidious; it weakens you after a long time.'

Bronski said, 'Yes.' His tone indicated that he knew this and Orme knew that he knew it. But it was better to talk repetitions and banalities than to listen to the silence. The stars were out now, shining more brightly than in Earth's thick atmosphere. Being at the bottom of the canyon was like standing at the bottom of a well. The stars they could see looked baleful, as if they didn't like the presence of these two aliens.

Orme knew that his reaction was due to his fatigue, the feeling of insignificance in relation to the towering wall, the eeriness of the entire situation, the feeling that somewhere down there were beings who could be menacing. Just how, he didn't know, since Earth people represented no danger to Martians – if they existed – and there was no reason he could think of why *they* should believe two aliens to be dangerous.

But the buried spaceship indicated a very advanced technology, and the tunnel seemed to mean that the people who had landed had dug into Mars. If they had managed to survive underground, and they must have been there a long time, why hadn't they emerged to repair the ship? If, that is, the ship had been wrecked?

There was no use worrying about such things. Tomorrow or the day after or a week or two from now would bring the answers.

Nevertheless, he was glad to get back to the lander. Though it wasn't the most comfortable or roomy of homes, it was still, in a sense, a piece of Earth. He had no trouble falling asleep, but, in the middle of the night, he woke with a start. He'd thought he'd heard something hard rapping against the double hull. He got up and looked through the ports but could see nothing except darkness on all sides but one. Stars still moved slowly across the open roof of the canyon. The rover was a vague bulk which he would have thought a boulder if he hadn't known it was there.

Then, as he watched, a light sprang from it, a beam that moved down into the tunnel and then lifted and described a 380-degree arc. After two minutes, the light went out. Once an hour, as ordered by Danton, it became activated and swept the area with visible light, infrared, and radar. If anything moved for miles, it would sound an alarm in the lander and in the *Aries*.

His sleep the rest of the night was untroubled. The alarm, triggered by a radio wave from the *Aries*, awoke him with a start. It was still dark outside, but the sky was paling above the top of the canyon. After the necessary reports, checking the equipment, and breakfast, he and Bronski climbed down on to the ground. On the way to the base of the cliff, he looked at the grey curve sticking out of the rubble. If they ran into a dead end in the tunnels, they would start removing the rocks from around the spaceship. Or, if they didn't find a port or some means of easy entrance, after so many days of labour, they would try to cut into it with a laser.

On Earth, removing the rocks, some of which were rather large, would have been impossible without a crane or much blasting powder. Here, two men should be able to lift any boulder he'd seen in the pile. But Shirazi and Danton might have to come down, too, to help.

As he went past the rover, he waved at it. Though it looked like a science fiction version of a Martian, it was familiar, and hence friendly. Another reminder of the home planet.

A moment later he looked back. The rover was following him as a dog follows its master. Danton, on duty now, had ordered it to accompany them. When he and Bronski descended into the tunnel through the hole they had made the day before, the rover extended a flexible arm at the end of which was a light and a camera. It would keep an eye on them so that the two in the *Barsoom* and the whole world could watch their progress – or lack of it.

Orme shook his head. It wasn't like him to be having such pessimistic thoughts. He was as optimistic as a person could be and still be sane. But there was in everyone a layer of darkness that no amount of psychological testing could reveal. It was too deep. It was unknown even to its possessor unless certain situations occurred to reveal it. This was one of them. But he wasn't going to let it overcome him. Once he got busy, he'd forget it.

Orme, in the lead, was almost within reach of the door, which should give entrance to another section of tunnel. If he had been a step closer, he would have been knocked down, perhaps badly crippled or killed, when it shot open.

It was as if a charge of TNT had gone off in the section beyond. He was lifted up and half-turned over by the explosion of air from the tunnel behind it. He glimpsed light there, had a vague impression of some kind of domed machine, and then he struck the ground.

Half-stunned, he lay helpless for a minute or perhaps more. He was not really aware of where he was or even who he was. Before his senses rallied, he was seized by people in spacesuits, the dark faceplates of their helmets masking their features. But they were human-sized and had two arms and two legs and five fingers. Two of them lifted him up and half-carried him towards the big wheeled machine. Danton's voice was yammering in his ear. 'What's going on, Richard? Richard? Are you there?'

As he began to come to, he thought, *You can see me, can't you?* but he did not reply for a minute. Then he mumbled, 'I'm okay. There's some things . . . no . . . people . . . like people . . .'

He was shoved into the open door of the machine and set firmly down in a chair. Something passed across his chest. A moment later, he knew that it was a metal band that confined his arms.

Bronski was dragged in, struggling, and he was placed in a chair in front of Orme. Past the rows of chairs were two chairs before a control board. The driver and another person had to sit there. The big curving screen in front gave a 150-degree view, allowing Orme to see what some of his captors were doing.

He said, 'Madeleine, they're placing six metal strips across the doorway. Now . . . they're putting six horizontal strips across the vertical. They seem to be glued on. Now . . . they're gluing on a screen to the strips.'

The rover's arm was still sticking down through the hole. But it was a figure seen in fog through the finely meshed screen.

'Now they're spraying something over the screen. What

they're doing, they're putting up a kind of temporary door, I think, so they can pump air back into this section. Can you read me, Madeleine?'

There was no answer. The barrier was blocking off radio waves.

The workers returned to the rear of the machine where, he supposed, they stored their tools in a compartment. Then they climbed in and took seats, the door was shut, the machine turned around and headed towards the opposite door. It sat for perhaps ten minutes, and suddenly the door swung open. The machine rolled into another section just like the previous ones except that it had overhead lights.

Orme thought that Nadir and Madeleine must be going crazy by now. And on Earth, where the first photographs by the rover and the voice recordings would be coming in, people would be in a frenzy. He said, 'God, let these . . . people . . . be friendly. Let them also be Yours.'

3

Avram Bronski said, 'This may be the most luxurious prison cell in the solar system.'

They were in a four-room apartment cut out of the rock high up on one side of the immense cave. The walls were panelled with a light reddish-brown wood-like material. The ceiling was stone but painted with murals depicting scenes of domestic animals. No 'Martians' appeared in them nor were they represented in the framed paintings on the walls. These paintings were either abstract art, still life, or of buildings or creatures that either existed there or were from mythology. Some looked like dragons; one was a whalelike seven-horned beast bursting out of a sea.

Bronski, who had been doing some private speculating, had explained that the law against representing any living creature in painting, sculpture, or in any form whatsoever, had been modified. But he thought, if he were right, that it was still forbidden to make images of sentient beings.

'Though not in holographic communication,' he said. 'And, since their medical science seems to be highly advanced, they must use pictures of the human body in textbooks and replicas of organs and so forth for the students. I don't have the slightest idea whether or not they dissect corpses.'

The holographic TV sets in the apartment could be dialled to see and hear the correct time. After three days' confinement, Orme and Bronski had learned to read the numbers necessary to understand the system. Bronski, who on Earth was a famed linguist in addition to being a premier areologist, had mastered the words associated with the symbols. They had correlated their own chronometers to the local time. But they didn't think they'd be going any place soon, so time was of no special concern.

One of the few things they'd ascertained was that the tau and the omega on the tunnel door were not of Greek origin. That language was spoken by a few here, but the arithmetical symbols on the TV sets came from a place far from Earth.

Orme got up off the chair and walked to Bronski. Together they stared at a scene that had become familiar by now, though it hadn't lost its fascination. Their prison was about one hundred feet up on one wall of the vast hemisphere cut out of solid basalt. The base of the wall opposite was an estimated thirty-five miles away. The apex of the dome seemed to be a mile and a half high.

From where they stood, they could see seven enormous horseshoe-shaped openings and twenty-one smaller ones. These must lead to passageways opening into other hollows. They believed that this hollow was only part of a gigantic underground complex.

Except for the floor of the dome, the stone was sky-blue. This was not the natural colour of basalt, so it must have been spray-painted or treated with something else. Whatever the method used, the dome looked just like the heavens above Earth on a cloudless day.

About one hundred feet below the highest point of the hemisphere hung a sun-bright globe. A half-hour before 18:00 in the 'evening', it began to dim. By 18:00 it was shining feebly, as if the sun had turned into the moon. This was the only light aside from that coming from the windows of houses, until 06:00, when the 'sun' began to wax.

The luminary didn't seem to be hanging from a cable though it was difficult to see past the brightness. But if it was suspended without attachment, it was held up by some sort of antigravity device. Until now Orme and Bronski had been sure that antigravity machines were possible only in science fiction; that is, unless you labelled stairs, ladders, elevators, balloons, airships, airplanes, and rockets as such.

So far, the luminary was the only thing they'd seen without visible means of support. The people they saw either walked or rode horses or horse-driven buggies and wagons or bicycles or the few wheeled-powered vehicles.

The cavern floor was neither level nor curving downward to form a horizon. Instead, it had a gentle gradient upward from the centre in all directions, ending at the wall. Water flowed from holes at the base of the wall and formed winding brooks, creeks, and two rivers. The latter were each about three-quarters of a mile wide. The smaller streams flowed into the rivers, which emptied eventually into a roughly hourglass-shaped lake in the centre. This was half a mile wide at the broadest parts and two miles long.

There were trees and farms and small parks and forests everywhere with villages here and there. The only structures over two storeys high were the barns. Each obviously residential structure was surrounded by a large yard and had a garden. Some of the buildings looked like schools. To each village was attached an open stadium where track and field meets, horse races, and games were held. One of the games was much like soccer and another was a form of basketball. There were also many public swimming pools, but no private house had any.

Through the binoculars given them by Hfathon, one of their captors, they could see much of what would otherwise have been blurred or unviewable. If there were tall buildings anywhere, they would have been able to detect them. The upward swell of the floor assured that.

Two-lane paved roads connected the towns and farms. They saw no trucks, though horse-drawn wagons laden with farm produce were plentiful.

Near the central lake was a long one-storey building into which people streamed in large numbers at 08:00. They left at noon and picnicked in parks or swam or boated in the lake. An hour later they re-entered; at 14:00 they swarmed out. Most went to houses within a range of a mile, but others bicycled or rode horses or even jogged to more distant dwellings.

Bronski thought that it might be the main administration building for the government.

'There's no telling how many levels there are under the ground.'

Opposite this, on the other side of the lake, was what had to be a university campus. Other buildings, from the number of people who entered them on the Sabbath, looked like places of worship.

All the structures were roofed. Orme wondered why they should be, since the entire hollow was probably air-conditioned. The fourth day, he found out why. Water rained from the ceiling of the dome for half an hour.

'So that's why the farms don't have irrigation systems.'

The captives had eaten their noon lunch, and then put the dirty dishes on trays into a wall-slot. Now they watched Martians driving up in two automobiles towards them. These disappeared below the porch, and presently the heads of those in the first vehicle appeared. There was a road leading up alongside the prison. But these people seemed to prefer walking to driving whenever possible.

So far, Orme and Bronski had no complaints about ill-treatment. They had been given thorough physical and medical examinations and had been interrogated, but they were well-housed, well-fed, and given plenty of privacy.

The six Martians paused while the shatterproof glass front of the room rose into a slot overhead. Orme knew that the transparent stuff was unbreakable because he had tested it with various chairs, his booted foot, and a heavy bronze vase.

Three of their captors were *Homo sapiens*, very tall, well-built, and wearing flowing robes. Two of these had long dark hair and full beards and were dark-skinned. The third had light skin, dark-blue eyes, and a golden-brown beard. All wore long curly sidelocks.

The other trio were humanoid, but a glance showed a Terrestrial that they came from another planet. They were

27

almost seven feet tall, no unusual height for Terrans in 2015 AD. This, their slimness, their long arms and legs, and their quickness would have qualified them for the best basketball team on Earth. They had five long-nailed fingers and toes and aside from their faces resembled humans closely. Their skins were a light bronze; their eyes, almost purplish; their hair was feathery. One was yellow; one, Titian; one, black. Both the female and the two males had hairless faces. Whether it was because they just lacked hair or because they shaved, the Earthmen did not yet know. Like their human companions, they sported long curling earlocks.

Their ears were much larger than any human's, and the convolutions were baroque, from a Terran's viewpoint. Their chins were huge, reminding Orme of photographs of people suffering from acromegaly. Their noses were very large and extremely aquiline, and the nostrils were edged in blue-black. Their lips would have been human if they had not been lined with a black-green pigmentation. Otherwise, they closely resembled *Homo sapiens*, even in the shape of their teeth.

All the newcomers wore robes, single-piece garments of a light thin material. Some were sleeveless, some had low collars, other were V-necked. The colours ranged from solid black, orange, and green to stripes of many colours. Most were ankle-length, but a few came to just below the knee. One male wore a cloak with clusters of four tassels at each corner. Their footwear was sandals or buskins, all open-toed. The female's robe was heavily brocaded with abstract designs, but she was not alone in sporting many jewelled rings, gold or silver bracelets, and earrings. The latter were secured by little screws.

All wore headpieces of different sizes and designs, one looking like a cowboy's ten-gallon hat and two like 18th-century tricorns, one of which flaunted a huge feather.

The female exuded a musky perfume, and her upper eyelids were coated with blue and her right nostril with a semicircle of yellow.

Hfathon, the chief of the non-humans, who were called Krsh, walked in first. Close behind him, as befitted the second in importance, came Ya'aqob Bar-Abbas, a human. He had a large aquiline nose, a bull neck, and extremely broad shoulders. He looked as if he was forty-five Terran years old. But if what he'd told Bronski was true, he was one hundred and thirty.

The other nonhumans were Hmmindron, a male, and Zhkeesh, a female. Yirmeyah Ben-Yokhanan and Sha'ul Ben-Hebhel were human.

Hfathon greeted the prisoners with a raised right arm, two fingers forming a V and a thumb extending at right angles to them. He smiled, exposing teeth blue from some sort of chewing gum. He spoke to Ya'aqob, who then said something in Greek to Bronski. Orme didn't understand more than a word of it. Bronski, the linguist, had discovered that neither Aramaic nor Koine Greek was the common speech, but scholars had preserved them and were quite fluent in both. Bronski could read Koine, or New Testament Greek, with ease, but he'd had little practice speaking it. However, if his interrogators spoke slowly, he could understand most of what they said.

There was a number of Krsh loan words used because the original Greek had no words for advanced scientific or philosophical concepts. These had had to be explained in Greek to him.

Orme was glad that at least there was one language available to both groups. Otherwise, it would take many weeks before they could communicate to any extent with their captors. Meanwhile, Danton and Shirazi were stuck up in the ship. If they didn't hear from their colleagues in three weeks, they'd be forced to return to Earth.

Or so he thought. For all he knew, the Martians had already sent up one of their own vessels, or ascended in the lander, and captured the two. Bronski had asked their captors if they had done so, but he had received nothing but a smile in answer.

As the questioning proceeded, Bronski interpreted some of the sentences for Orme.

During the first two days, they had been isolated from their interrogators by the transparent wall. But today the Martians had entered. This meant that the tests run on them had given them a clean bill of health. Physically, anyway. From what Bronski told him now, their captors were not so sure about their mental health. Or perhaps it would be better to say their theological state.

Ya'aqob said, 'Then on Earth *Iesous ho Christos* is worshipped as the son of the Merciful One? And he is also the Merciful One? Is this belief held by everybody or are there dissenters?'

Orme got the impression from the man's narrowed eyes that he did not like even to say the last sentences.

Avram Bronski said, 'As I have said, there are perhaps four billion or so Christians on Earth, but these are split into many groups, all holding many different views on the nature of *ho Christos*. The orthodox believe that *Iesous ho Christos* was conceived through the will of God by a virgin, Mariam. Moreover, Mariam was herself immaculately conceived. That is, her mother bore her free of sin. So, in a sense, her mother was the grandmother of God.'

The eyes of all six captors rolled, and they uttered a word which even Orme recognized was not Greek.

Bronski said, 'I should confer with Captain Orme on these matters. Though I've read much about Christianity, I am not a Christian. I am a Jew. The captain is a Christian of a sect called Baptists. He is a devout man and much more qualified than I to speak about the subtleties of his particular dogma.'

The Frenchman had been translating everything he said to Orme. 'That isn't right!' Orme said. 'You tell them that you're much more knowledgeable about comparative religion than I am. If you make any mistakes about the Baptists, I'll tell you so.'

Ya'aqob spoke machine-gun-fast Greek. Bronski asked

him to slow down. Ya'aqob repeated.

Bronski said, 'Captain, he asked me how I can call myself a Jew when I don't believe that *Iesous* is the Messiah. Anyway, he says, a Jew wouldn't be cleanshaven. He'd have a full beard. And sidelocks.'

Orme felt both confused and frustrated.

'You tell them we'll argue religious matters later. There are more important things to find out now. Hell, we don't even know where Hfathon and his kind came from! Or how the humans got here! And it's vital that we communicate with Danton and Shirazi!'

'That's right – for us,' Bronski said. 'But the religious issue, I'm afraid, is the most important one to them. I can't *make* them talk about what interests *us* most, you know.'

Bronski looked as troubled as Orme felt.

Orme threw up his hands. 'Who would have believed *this*?'

Hfathon said something.

Bronski translated, 'He wants to know what's wrong with the brown man?'

'Tell him I'm black, not brown.'

Hfathon rattled off something, and the others laughed.

Bronski said, 'He wants to know why a colour-blind person would be selected to lead a space expedition.'

'Tell him that "black" is a manner of speaking. If you've got kinky hair and everted lips and a dark brown skin, you're black. It's a . . . uh . . . semantic matter. Political. You can have straight hair and blue eyes and thin lips and still be black. Oh, what the hell!' he said, throwing up his hands. There they were, the first humans on Mars, or so they thought, and they were discussing religion and semantics.

'I don't think I'll interpret that,' Bronski said. 'We're confused enough without going into that sort of thing.'

Hfathon spoke again.

Bronski said, 'He says his skin is the same colour as yours, and he's definitely brown.'

Ya'aqob spoke sharply then, as if he realized the

interrogation was going astray. Bronski answered the question that followed.

'To explain why I consider myself a Jew would take even longer, and be as detailed as explaining why Orme is a black man. Can't we get down to more immediate issues? Won't you tell us something of yourselves? Once we understand how you came here and why you're still here when it seems, to me at least, that you could leave this planet, why, then we can get back to your line of questioning. We'll have a clearer idea why you are so interested in our theology. Rather, theologies, for there are many on Earth. Thousands, perhaps.'

The six Martians went into conference then, speaking the language which Hfathon had said was Krsh.

When they were through, Ya'aqob said, in Greek, 'You are probably right. Please pardon us for what must seem to you an excessive curiosity about certain matters. It is not excessive for us. Indeed, it is the only thing that really matters in our world. But if we're going to get any place we should proceed from the simple to the complex so that we may understand each other.

'But I do have a few questions which may seem irrelevant to you but which we'd like to have answered before we start our mutual education. For one thing, why, if the black man is a disciple of Christ, and therefore Jewish, is he not Jewish? Would a Gentile be circumcised?'

'It has long been the custom to circumcise male infants in the Western world,' Bronski said. 'Not because of religious reasons but for sanitation. Of course, the Muslim religion, which stems from the Jewish religion in part, also requires circumcision. Also, the ancient Egyptians, who held *our* fathers in bondage, circumcised.'

Ya'aqob looked blank, then said, 'Muslim? Well, you are right. One question only leads to a hundred others. But there is one more on this subject.'

He gestured at the blondish Sha'ul, who opened the box and removed a pile of rations from the lander. So the

Martians had entered the vessel. Danton and Shirazi must have seen this and so would all of Earth. He could imagine the consternation, the wonder, the frustration. Perhaps the two had tried to communicate with the invaders, but they would not have known, of course, that only New Testament Greek would be understood. Not that it would have done them any good. Neither could speak it.

Sha'ul held up a can of meat in his gloved hand. The top of it had been removed. Its casing was a thermoplastic hydrocarbon. It could be boiled in water to make a nutritious soup.

'What is this meat?' Sha'ul asked sternly.

'Ham,' Bronski said.

Looking disgusted, Sha'ul dropped the can on the table.

'At least you told the truth,' he said.

Bronski had guessed that the meat had been analysed. He had also anticipated the man's reaction.

After hearing the translation, Orme said, 'So what's the big deal?'

'The Martians are orthodox Jews,' Bronski replied.

4

Fifteen minutes before 'noon', five of the captors left. Sha'ul had departed immediately after ascertaining that the can contained unclean meat. Even though he had not directly touched the ham, he might have had to be ritually cleansed.

As they had done at 12:00 every day, the sirens began wailing. People poured out from the buildings and stood looking up at the burning globe. After three minutes, the sirens moaned off into silence. Another minute passed and then loudspeakers began a chant quickly joined in by the crowds. This was short, perhaps fifteen lines, after which the people dispersed, the office workers to their homes or to tables in parks where they ate, the residents to their houses.

Bronski shook his head. 'They look as if they're worshipping the sun. Its equivalent, I mean. But they can't be. No Jew would even think of worshipping an idol.'

'We'll find out in time,' Orme said. He sat down at the table and began cutting into the ham left by Sha'ul.

'They're watching you,' Bronski said. 'I think they left the ham to see if you'd eat it.'

Orme chewed vigorously. 'Man, that tastes good! I'm crazy about ham, bacon, sausages. Anything that comes from a pig, including the feet.'

'You mean hoofs.'

'We call it pig's feet.'

Bronski gestured irritation. 'I don't think you should have accepted it. It might make a difference in their attitude towards us.'

Orme looked surprised. 'Why? What do they care what *I* eat?'

'The ancient Hebrews wouldn't eat at the same table with a Gentile. My parents wouldn't either.'

Orme forked in another large piece. 'Something like in my grandparents' day, when whites wouldn't eat with blacks?'

'No, it's not the same thing at all. Gentiles ate ritually unclean food, tabu food. So, to keep from being unclean, the Hebrews refused to eat with Gentiles. They could become impure just by proximity.'

'But they did regard Gentiles as being inferior, didn't they? Gentiles were *not* the chosen people of God.'

'Not theoretically. All people were equal in the eyes of God. But practically, I suppose, the Hebrews couldn't keep from acquiring an attitude of moral superiority.'

A series of short whistles announced that lunch had been delivered. Bronski removed the two trays from the recess, put one on the table, and took the other to a chair.

Orme grinned at him. 'You aren't going to sit at the table with me?'

'I've been sitting with you at mealtime ever since the launch,' Bronski said. 'Even when you were eating the flesh of swine. Don't make light of this, Richard. It may seem a ridiculous matter to you, but to these people it is a very serious business. I'm not taking a chance of . . . uh . . . getting contaminated. One of us has to have some credibility. I mean, be looked at with some respect. They might not want to deal with you, so . . .'

'Just remember that I'm captain,' Orme said.

'To me you are. To them, well, I don't know. So far you're just a prisoner who offends them because of your diet preference.'

'Yeah, but you've offended them, startled them, anyway, because you aren't a disciple of *Iesous ho Christos*. Of Jesus Christ. How do you reconcile their Jewishness with their statement about Jesus?'

'I don't. I don't know what's going on here.'

Orme ate the bread (there was no butter), beans, peas, and

an apple. Bronski finished his mutton, lettuce, bread, and apple.

After a sip of the wine Bronski smacked his lips. 'Very good.'

The captain grinned again. 'Maybe we could get a monopoly on Martian wine. We could really clean up on Earth.'

He rose and went into an inner room. Shortly after the sound of flushing water reached Bronski, Orme reappeared.

'I've been watching them closely, but I never see them do anything or say anything to open the door.'

'A monitor must do it,' the Frenchman said. 'What would you do if you *could* get out?'

'Take off like a stripe-assed ape.'

'That'd be foolish. You wouldn't get more than a few steps.'

'Maybe. But I'd give it the old college try. Wouldn't you come along?'

'Not unless you ordered me to,' Bronski said. 'And I'd protest. Anyway, these people don't seem to have any sinister motives.'

'Not that you know of. But as long as we're being held in jail, we have a duty to try to escape.'

Bronski gestured impatiently.

'They have to quarantine us. We'd do the same if they had landed on Earth.'

'Yes, but you heard Hfathon say we had a clean bill of health. So why don't they let us out?'

'We can't learn the language if we're acting like tourists.'

'That's the best way,' Orme said. 'Talking to the people themselves. Anyway, they haven't even started giving us language lessons.'

Ten minutes later, he admitted that he'd been wrong, at least, in his guess about the Martians' intentions.

Immediately after entering, and making sure that the container of ham was disposed of, Hfathon sat down, holding a box with a large assortment of artifacts. He held up a fork with three very long tines. Articulating slowly, he said *'Shneshdit.'*

Bronski, the linguist, succeeded in reproducing the word after only two attempts. Orme had to try four times and only succeeded when Bronski told him that the *d* was pronounced with the tip of the tongue touching above the gum ridge and the *t* with the tip of the tongue against the roof of the mouth.

But they still didn't know if Hfathon was saying 'fork', 'a fork', 'the fork', or 'this is a fork'. Bronski asked Sha'ul to explain in Greek. He expected some difficulty because, as far as he knew, Koine Greek had no word for *fork*. That instrument had not been invented in the first century AD.

Ya'aqob protested that Bronski should be addressing his question to him, not to Sha'ul. He, Ya'aqob, was the chief human interrogator and was therefore the proper one to carry on this lesson.

Bronski smiled and said in English, 'Captain, whatever else the Martians are, they're jealous of their authority. They've got the same old *Homo sapiens* pecking order.'

'You can take the Terrestrial from Earth, but you can't take Earth away from the Terrestrial,' Orme said.

Ya'aqob asked Bronski what he had said. Bronski replied that he was merely translating for Orme. Ya'aqob said that he didn't think so. They were smiling, but there was nothing funny in anything they had said.

Bronski shrugged.

Hfathon spoke somewhat angrily in Greek. If these interruptions kept on, the lessons would be far behind schedule. From now on, if Bronski wanted to know the Greek equivalent, he could ask him about it. He was as fluent in that language as anybody else in the group.

Ya'aqob said, 'In that case, the rest of us might as well return to the university. However, this is a committee, not a military unit. Though you are the chairman, anybody has a right to speak up if it so pleases him.'

'Or her,' Zhkeesh, the female, said.

Ya'aqob smirked.

Bronski translated the exchange to Orme.

'They're academics, no doubt about that.'

'Well, what is it, a "fork", or what?' Orme said impatiently.

'*Shneshdit* just means "fork". It's a loan word in Greek, but it's pronounced slightly differently.'

'Don't tell me how it's pronounced in Greek,' Orme said. 'I just want to learn Krsh. For the time being, anyway.'

The lesson proceeded rather rapidly after that, though Bronski twice tried to ask when he and Orme would be released from their quarters. Hfathon said they would learn that in due time.

Both of the Marsnauts had excellent memories. In three hours they had mastered the names of twenty artifacts and also learned the names of parts of the human and Krsh bodies.

They had also picked up some short phrases. Of the four forks on the table, the fork nearest to them was *shnesh-am-dit*. A fork a little more distant was *shnesh-aim-dit*. A third fork even further away was *shnesh-tu-dit*. Two forks close to them was *shnesh-am-gr-dit*. And so on.

Orme had difficulty pronouncing '-gr-' without an intrusive vowel between the *g* and the *r*, especially since the *r* was pronounced with the tip of the tongue near the palate. He failed utterly to master two consonants produced deep in the throat that sounded like ripping sailcloth to him.

Bronski said, 'They have near-equivalents in Arabic. You'll get them eventually.'

'If I don't die of a sore throat first. Anyway, I can't tell the difference between them.'

'Your ear will become tuned.'

The session ended, leaving Orme sweating and tired. His only consolation was that Bronski also looked peaked.

Their tutors left them before supper, but an hour after the two had eaten they reappeared. Orme shut off the TV, which was showing a play of some kind. It looked to him as if it were the Martian version of a soap opera, but he couldn't be sure. However, during its course, he had recognized four phrases he'd learned earlier. But his attempts to reproduce them aloud had failed.

'Tell them I've had enough Berlitz lessons,' he said.

But they were in for another kind of gruelling session. This was conducted entirely in Greek except when Bronski interpreted for Orme. One question after another was fired at them about the history of Earth since about 50 AD. Occasionally Bronski's Greek failed him; he didn't know a word or a phrase. So many artifacts and social and psychological concepts had come into being since that time. Sometimes he would be able to explain by drawing a picture or a diagram on the electronic screen which Sha'ul had brought in.

Frequently, Hfathon would interrupt him. 'Let's drop that particular matter until later. It's too complicated and will only make us confused. Just give us the main movements in Earth's history.'

But when Bronski tried to do this, he had to go into details.

'So far you've taken us up to what you call the eleventh century AD. That corresponds, if I understand you correctly, to 4961 by the Hebrew reckoning. We'll try to get to the present by the end of tomorrow's session. Then we'll have to backtrack, start from the beginning again, so you can enlighten us on those things which require detail to be comprehended perfectly.'

After hearing the Frenchman's translation of this, Orme said, 'Tell him we're dying of curiosity about them. Ask him if we can't be told how and why they came to Mars. If not, why not?'

Hfathon said, 'We have our reasons for this method of procedure. You must bear with us. After all, you came here uninvited, so you can't expect to be treated as honoured guests. Still, we're enjoined to love the alien in our land as ourselves, because we were once aliens in Egypt. But to relieve your minds, you may know that we have no sinister intentions. Everything that is being done is done for the best. *Shalom*, my guests.'

Bronski said, 'But I've told you that our shipmates cannot stay in orbit for much more than three weeks. Then they'll have to return to Earth. This imprisonment is insufferable – from our viewpoint, anyway. Can't . . . ?'

He stopped. The six had walked out, and the transparent wall was sliding down behind them.

Orme poured out the last of the wine in a bottle which Sha'ul had given him. 'Damn it! I'm so frustrated I could bite nails! Or a Martian! What do you think they're up to, Avram?'

Bronski shrugged his shoulders. His lean aquiline face was set with doubt. 'I don't know. There's nothing we can do except go along with them at their own pace.'

'I'll tell you one thing. I think that all these questions about history are a bunch of bull. They pretend to know nothing of us since 50 AD. But they haven't been keeping their heads in their shells. At least, they shouldn't have. Look at how technologically advanced they are. What's kept them from building another spaceship and going to Earth? Or, if for some reason they haven't done that, though I don't know why they wouldn't, they could easily have been receiving radio waves all these years. It's only logical that they should. So wouldn't they know a lot more about us than they've been pretending to know?'

'It does seem likely,' Bronski said. 'But maybe they have a reason for not listening in.'

'Would Earth people under similar circumstances deliberately keep themselves in ignorance?'

'I don't know. After all, half of the Martians are descendants of Earth people.'

Orme was silent for a while as he walked back and forth, swinging his arms. He liked and needed hard exercise. Being imprisoned made him feel like a caged tiger. Pushups and kneebends were not adequate. He required exercise that was also fun: tennis, basketball, swimming. The ascetic Bronski, however, seemed quite able to sit or lie down for days without being bored as long as he had something to study.

'The way I get it,' Orme said suddenly, 'is that they're so interested in what happened after 50 AD, if they're not lying, that is, because they know what happened up to that time. Which means that they left Earth then and haven't been back. Or maybe they have been back to observe from a ship, but they don't know the meaning or the details of what they saw. They can get those only from us. So, to fool us into not knowing they do have a general knowledge of events, they get us to tell them the broad story. Then they can lead us into telling the details.'

'It's obvious that the humans are descended from people who were picked up by the Krsh in the first century AD,' Bronski said. 'Beyond that, all is speculation on our part. But if it makes you feel better to guess, go ahead.'

Orme said nothing. After a few minutes Bronski turned on the holographic TV. The show seemed to be a newscast. Orme was interested in it because there were scenes from other places than the cavern in which they were prisoners. He saw two outdoor events, one a festival of some sort and the other a stock-judging contest. Some glimpses of the hollows revealed that the entrances were not only different but that the lighting was provided by many small globes hanging from the ceiling. Another scene was in a large tunnel evidently connecting two of the hollows. A man had been killed by a horse. Though he couldn't understand the newscaster's speech, he had no trouble seeing what had happened.

'One picture is worth ten thousand words,' he muttered.

'What?' Bronski said.

Orme started to repeat himself, but he stopped almost at once.

'Hey, that's us!'

There they were being questioned by the six.

The images were snapped off abruptly; the announcer, a

41

somewhat red-faced, fleshy, old Krsh, said something.

Then another picture flashed on.

Both men leaped out of their chairs. There were Madeleine Danton and Nadir Shirazi getting out of the same kind of vehicle which had carried them from the outside tunnel to their prison. They had their helmets on, and their faces were not visible. But it had to be them.

Orme groaned, and said, 'So now they've got them! But how?'

5

Orme and Bronski had expected that their colleagues would be brought to their quarters. But on reflection they realized that Shirazi and Danton would have to be quarantined and so placed elsewhere. When their interrogators showed up in the morning, Bronski told them that he had seen the capture on TV.

'Of course,' Hfathon said.

Sha'ul opened a box and began bringing out new artifacts. Bronski got red in the face, and Orme growled.

Hfathon said, 'What troubles you?'

'Apparently you're just going to continue the lessons and not satisfy our curiosity,' Bronski said. 'Don't you have any feelings of empathy, of compassion? Aren't you human? You must know that we're bursting with eagerness to know what happened to our shipmates. Are they all right? How did you get them? What do you plan for them?'

Hfathon's long, lean face remained impassive.

'No, I'm not human, not strictly speaking. But I know what you mean. Yes, I appreciate your feelings. If I were in your situation, I'd burn with impatience. But this committee has been instructed by the Council to tell you nothing. I don't know why; it seems to be a security measure. The Council will tell us in its own good time why these restrictions have been placed.'

'For the love of God,' Bronski said. 'Can't you tell us anything at all?'

'We've been told to teach you our language as swiftly as possible. The Council apparently believes that time is vital. So, let us proceed.'

Upon having this translated, Orme bit his lower lip, and

said, 'Avram, you tell these hyenas that we're not co-operating with them until they tell us what's going on. Mum's the word until then.'

Bronski spoke Greek. The six looked grave, but only Hfathon replied.

'We have means to make you co-operate, but we are too humane to use them. Very well. Your comrades are unharmed and in good health. They're in quarters not unlike yours and not distant from here. The woman can't speak any language we know, but the man knows some Hebrew. It isn't quite the language used in our liturgies, but it's close enough for a limited communication. He's been told about you.'

'Ask him how those two were removed from the *Aries*,' Orme said.

Bronski reported that Hfathon said that the lander had been examined by some Krsh scientists. After determining its methods of operation, two of them had gone up to the ship. They'd been admitted and when the two Earth people had refused to leave, they'd been anaesthetized.

Orme said, shaking his head, 'Can you imagine the consternation on Earth when that scene was transmitted?'

Bronski spoke to Hfathon. 'Did it occur to you that this seizure might be regarded as a hostile act? Are you trying to start a war?'

Ya'aqob said, 'There is no need for war. What we've done has been for your good. It will all be explained in time to the satisfaction of your people. Now, let's get on with the lesson.'

The swift pace of the lesson allowed little time for thinking about anything else. Nevertheless, Orme couldn't help wondering now and then about everyone's reaction on Earth.' What were the governments of the North American Confederation saying about the forcible seizure of their citizens? What about the other nations which were members of the IASA and had contributed funds for this expedition?

Once Ya'aqob spoke sharply to him, saying that he must concentrate more. Orme glowered at him, then decided that he must not antagonize his captors. After that, he smiled often, though it was an effort, and even made some of them laugh when he deliberately made a pun in Krsh. Sha'ul especially seemed to enjoy it. Orme picked him as the person to cultivate, and, perhaps, use later on. The blondish man seemed more open and sympathetic than the others. If he could be talked into revealing more than he was supposed to, he might be the key to their escape.

Though it seemed impossible that he could get back to the lander, Orme had not given up the idea. If he was easily discouraged he would never have become the top astronaut of the NAC.

During the supper break, he turned on the TV. In the middle of a programme about medical research, the images faded out. There was Hfathon seated at a desk, the wall behind him decorated with bright abstract designs. He spoke in Greek for a minute. Bronski, smiling, said, 'They're going to let us talk to Madeleine and Nadir.'

Hfathon disappeared, and they saw their colleagues, each sitting in a chair and staring at them.

'Hey, you two!' Orme cried. 'Are you all right?'

For the next few seconds the four babbled at the same time. Orme called a halt to that.

'We don't know how long they're going to let us talk, so we better get the important stuff out of the way. Tell me, were the transmitters on when you were taken?'

Danton and Shirazi both started to talk. Orme whistled and said, 'You first, Nadir. You outrank Madeleine.'

'The IASA saw everything from the moment the Martians came out into the tunnel,' he said. 'At least, I think so. I know they were receiving up to the moment we let the two men in. It's possible that transmission was blanked out after that.'

'When you saw them get into the lander, what made you decide to admit them? Why didn't you take the *Aries* out of orbit and return to Earth?'

'It was a difficult decision to make. If we pulled out, we left

45

you two behind. We had no idea what kind of treatment you were getting, good or bad. But it seemed to us that if your captors were friendly, they'd have allowed you to tell us so. We made radio contact with the two Martians when they entered the lander, and they answered – in a totally foreign language. We had told the Centre what was going on, of course, and even with the transmission-lag, there was plenty of time for Carter to make a decision. He said there was no way to determine whether the people in the lander were hostile or not until they came aboard the *Aries*. And if they were friendly, and we repulsed them, then they might interpret that as hostility on our part. And we might be deserting you two, in effect.

'On the other hand, he didn't want to order us to stay and so possibly endanger us. In the end, he left the decision to us.'

'And so,' Madeleine said, 'he dodged his responsibility. He's a fine administrator, but he's essentially a politician.'

Shirazi smiled and said, 'If he'd ordered us to pull out, I don't know what I'd have done. I didn't want to go. For one thing, it would have meant leaving you in the lurch. It'd be another three years before another ship could have been sent. But even stronger was my curiosity. I could not endure not knowing what had happened to you and what all this was about.'

'And I,' Danton said, 'would have protested strongly if you had decided to return.'

'Did Carter say anything about sending a relief expedition?' Orme said.

'Yes. He swore that another ship would be coming along as swiftly as possible. Of course, he can't determine that. If the funds aren't available . . .'

'Do you think for one moment that all this hasn't put the public into a frenzy? They'll find the money, you can bet on that!'

Orme paused, then said, 'Okay. Now here's what's happened to us.'

46

There was a short silence after he had finished. Then Shirazi said, 'So these people are Jews? Including the Krsh?'

'Yes,' Bronski said.

'Yet they mentioned *Iesous ho Christos*, that is, Jesus Christ. And they claimed, by implication anyway, to be Christians?'

The Iranian-Scot was pale. *No wonder*, Orme thought. He's a Muslim. Maybe he's not orthodox enough to satisfy the more religious of his compatriots, but he·was brought up by zealous parents. And he is convinced that Mohammed was the last and the greatest of the prophets, even if he doesn't take literally everything in the Koran, the Moslem scriptures.

But if it was a shock for Shirazi, it had also been one for Orme, the only professed Christian of the four. And Bronski, though not an orthodox Jew, was also disturbed.

What about Danton, who had been raised in a devout Roman Catholic family, though she was now an atheist? She was sitting fairly relaxed, her legs out straight before her, her hands quiet on her lap. She was wearing a maroon robe given her by the captors, her slightly thick ankles and broad sandalled feet showing. Her garment hid the too-wide hips and the very narrow waistline but could not conceal the superbly large breasts. She had a rather striking face, broad, high-cheekboned, wide-mouthed, and big-eyed. Her nose was a little too long and curved, but it enhanced, rather than detracted from, her features. She'd had two husbands and was said to be a devil to get along with in her laboratory. But her brilliance in her field, biochemistry, and her overall psychological profile had made her one of the four top candidates for the crew. Certainly, during the training and the long flight, she had co-operated fully. She'd had no personality conflicts, and she was congenial enough, if you stayed away from the subject of religion. Then she clammed up, though it was obvious she would like to argue. And had the circumstances been different, she would have.

Perhaps she looked so . . . serene . . . because here, finally, would be proof that the founder of her natal religion was only

47

a man. It was obvious that the human beings here had been brought by the Krsh and picked up about 50 AD. It was also obvious that some of them had been acquainted with Jesus.

At least, it seemed to Orme that it was so. These people might have records, writings of eyewitnesses, perhaps even filmed interviews and testimonies from men and women who'd known Jesus intimately.

His heart was beating fast, and he was shaking a little.

Abruptly, Hfathon's image, smaller than the other two, and hanging above them, appeared in the set. He spoke to Bronski, and he disappeared.

The Frenchman said, 'We're being cut off. Good night, you two. Perhaps soon we'll be talking in person.'

The set went blank. Both were silent for a minute.

'I wonder,' Bronski said slowly, 'why the Martians permit the depiction of animal and human life on these sets yet bar it in their art? Theoretically, the Mosaic law should apply to images in TV, too. But then they may not be as orthodox as I'd supposed.'

Orme was somewhat irritated. 'Good God, Avram! Why worry about such a minor thing? We've got real troubles and big questions to consider, so who gives a hoot?'

Bronski shrugged. 'What else have we got to think about? There's nothing we can do except go along with our, uh, hosts. Anyway, points like that interest me.'

'Yeah? Me, too, when I've got time on my hands.'

Bronski looked around and smiled wryly. Orme burst into laughter.

'I see what you mean. What else do we have but time on our hands, heh? Well, let me ask you. Do orthodox Jews watch TV?'

'There's an ultraorthodox group in Israel, the Neturai Karta, who refuse to own or watch TV, or listen to radios, for that matter. They claim to be the only true Jews left in the world. They even refuse to recognize Israel as a state. But they're almost extinct, and the orthodox regard them with

48

horror – or perhaps pity. Yes, the orthodox do watch TV, though they turn it off on the Sabbath. But the Martian Jews could be the Terrestrial counterpart of the Neturai Karta, though I'd doubt it.'

Orme said, 'These people have been here for two thousand years. Surely, they've changed in that time? Even your superorthodox Jews don't stone women caught committing adultery or punch out a man's eye because he blinded someone?'

'I wouldn't expect it. The Mosaic laws were rigorously applied when the Hebrews were nomadic tribes, wild Bedouins, in many ways. The laws were barbarically harsh, but they were necessary to keep order and to preserve the faith. Savage as they seem to us, they were more humane than the laws of their contemporaries. After the Jews settled down in Palestine and became civilized, they gradually softened the letter of the law with the spirit of humanity and in accordance with the circumstances of the times and the environment. A century before Jesu's birth, stoning as a punishment for adultery had ceased.'

'But *John* says that when Jesus was in the temple some doctors of law and some Pharisees brought to him a woman caught in the act of adultery. They said that Moses had laid down the law that such women were to be stoned, and they asked him what he thought about it. They hoped to frame a charge against him. Now are you saying that story wasn't true?'

'The story may be true,' Bronski said, 'but its location could not have been Jerusalem. The incident probably took place in Galilee, where the natives were more conservative in religious matters – in some respects, anyway – and probably did stone adulterers, if they could do so without attracting the attention of the authorities. It *was* the law that any adulteress had to be brought to Jerusalem for judgement. There they would only have had to undergo the test of the bitter waters, and if they failed, they would have been punished – but

49

nothing like stoning or in fact any capital punishment whatsoever. They probably would have been divorced and returned in disgrace to their family.

'Anyway, the Martian Jews have had no alien interference or influence for two thousand years. So you can't expect them to have developed as their Earth counterparts did.'

'No alien influence?' Orme said. 'You unpuckering me, man? What about the Krsh? I'd say they're about as alien as you can get. They're not even human!'

'In a physiological sense, no. Otherwise, judging from our very brief acquaintanceship, I'd say they're very human.'

He sat up in the chair and then leaned towards Orme, his hands clasped.

'But here's what puzzles me about them. They were considerably more advanced technologically two thousand years ago than the people they picked up. In fact, they must have been more advanced than we are now. So, they were the superior species. To the humans, the Krsh must have seemed like gods. Angels, anyway. For the humans, the cultural shock would have been great. They would've been numbed.

'Any effect would have been one-way, from the Krsh to the humans. After all, what did the Terrestrials have to offer the Krsh? Now, we know that the Krsh language is the common speech of both Krsh and humans. Greek and Aramaic have been preserved, but only among scholars, and Hebrew is mainly a liturgical language. This is to be expected.'

He sat back but with his hands still gripping each other.

'We would also expect that the religion of the inferior peoples – don't grimace; I use "inferior" in the sense that the humans were technologically inferior and relatively deficient in knowledge – these inferiors would have been tremendously influenced by their superiors. Just as all primitive cultures either perished or were tremendously influenced and changed by the impact of the technologically advanced Westerners. Well, that's not exactly right, since the Eastern civilizations caused less advanced societies to run, die, or change. They were every bit as ruthless, exploitative, and uncomprehending as the Western . . .'

'I don't want a lecture,' Orme said.

'Sorry. What I started to say was that the humans should have been completely assimilated in culture. But they weren't. Why? Was it because the Krsh were dealing with orthodox Jews, who are peculiarly resistant, extremely stubborn, when it comes to their religion? It was an historical accident that the Krsh picked up people from this one group. Of course, I'm not saying that the Jews are the only group who've stubbornly clung to their religion. Take the Parsis, for instance, They . . .'

'You're doing it again, Avram. Look, I find all this interesting, but just now I'd like to stick to the essentials.'

'Very well. On the other hand, even if the Jews should refuse to convert to the Krsh religion, providing they had one, why would the Krsh, who're not even *Homo sapiens*, and were thousands of years ahead of the Jews in science and God knows what else . . . why should they take up Judaism?'

'Christianity.'

'That remains to be proved. These people are Jews who believe that Jesus is the Messiah. So your saying Christianity, in the sense you use it, isn't valid. At least, I don't think so. However, it's incredible that the Krsh should convert to a faith that, from their view-point, would have been no better than some Old Stone Age faith to us. Actually, there are many elements in the Judaism of that time which did derive directly from the Paleolithic. The use of flint knives in circumcision when iron was available, the dietary tabus, which have their corollary in other preliterate and ancient cultures, their . . .'

Orme shook his head. 'You should've been a rabbinical scholar.'

'My father was.'

'Well, how do you account for the Krsh converting?'

'That remains to be learned.'

A voice spoke from the TV. Orme turned to see Hfathon's

51

image in the box. He spoke to Avram, who looked astonished. The Frenchman replied rapidly – his Greek was improving – and Hfathon, looking grave, vanished.

Avram said, 'He asked me if Madeleine and Nadir were married. I said that Nadir had a wife, but she, Madeleine, had no spouse. He seemed upset at that, but he wouldn't tell me why.'

'Why would they care?'

Bronski twisted his lips to the right. 'I could speculate, but I don't want to.' He shook his head.

'No, it's unthinkable.'

6

The next day, Orme spoke immediately after their teachers entered.

'Why did you ask us if Shirazi and Danton were married?'

The six looked surprised. Their captive had spoken in Greek.

Hfathon replied in the same language, and Orme was lost. He had made Bronski teach him the phrase, but after that he had to depend on the Frenchman. However, he had wanted to fire the question himself to impress them with his concern.

The Krsh and Bronski exchanged some sentences. Then the latter said in English, 'They'd assumed Danton and Shirazi were married because they found them unchaperoned in the ship. But the first night in their quarters they were observed sleeping in separate rooms. It was assumed that the woman was menstruating and thus unclean. But the following night the two slept together, and there was no evidence that the woman had been bleeding.

'Women were sent in to examine her, and they found that she had had intercourse during the night. She was questioned through the man, but his Hebrew is so faulty that he didn't seem to understand. Or perhaps, Hfathon says, he was deliberately pretending not to understand.

'In any case, Hfathon called us up last night and questioned me about them. I told him the truth, but if I'd suspected what they were after I would have lied. Though it would have done no good in the end. They would have found out.'

Orme would have laughed if Bronski's expression had not told him that this was a serious situation.

'Madeleine and Nadir? But they've never shown any signs of sexual interest in each other! I don't believe it!'

53

Bronski made an impatient gesture.

'After all this time, don't you feel horny? And if you were imprisoned and scared and lonely, wouldn't you turn to a woman? Or, if you were a woman, to a man?'

Orme said, 'I might, but I'd never been unfaithful to my wife, my ex-wife, I mean, and believe me, I'd had plenty of chances. Still if this enforced celibacy went on long enough, I suppose . . .'

'Yes, and you're a devout Christian. Anyway, what you or I might do has nothing to do with it.'

'Yes, but Madeleine! She isn't a bad-looking woman, but she is so cool and detached!'

'The longer the volcano is quiet, the more the pressure builds up. The point is that the Mosaic law against adultery still holds.'

'Well, ask him!'

Bronski spoke, listened to Hfathon, then said, 'If Nadir is truly contrite, that is, repents, and he promises not to commit this sin again, and if his wife forgives him, then there will be no punishment.'

'Which would be what?'

'A sentence to hard labour for six months digging out a hollow in the rock. And perhaps a public shaming.'

'And Madeleine?'

'The same. As it is, the case is being considered by the judges now. There's a chance that neither will be sentenced, since this involves an unprecedented case. Until now, they've not had to deal with *goyim* criminals.'

'You tell them that they're acting mighty-god-awful arrogant! Their laws don't apply to us. Under our laws, those two have committed no crime!'

A minute later, Bronski said, 'He says that they can't permit anybody, even aliens, to break their laws. If a person comes here, he is under the jurisdiction of this land.

'He also says that Nadir has been taken to another prison so that the two won't be tempted to sin again. Nadir, by the way, is unclean until evening. Any man who has an emission of semen is unclean until evening comes.'

Orme threw his hands up.

'What next? Well, you tell him—'

'No,' Bronski said. 'I'll tell him nothing. We're completely in their power. We don't want to antagonize them.'

Hfathon rumbled something.

Bronski said, 'We're to start the lessons and cut out this nonsense.'

'Is *nonsense* his word or yours?'

'Cool down, Richard. There's nothing to be gained by losing your head.'

'I haven't lost it. But it is pretty hot.'

When the session was broken for the lunch-hour, Orme asked Bronski to ask Hfathon when the most recent case of adultery had been tried in court.

'He says it was two years ago.'

Orme grunted. 'And you say these people are human?'

Hfathon spoke to Bronski, and the six filed out.

'There won't be any more lesson today. They have other business, and Sabbath starts at evening. They won't be seeing us tomorrow, either.'

'Dawn' came but without the people streaming from the houses to work. Except for some farm animals in the distance, not a living being was to be seen.

'Everybody will be staying home to meditate and pray,' Bronski said. 'Later, however, they attend the synagogues. These have to be within a limited distance of the houses. It is forbidden to travel more than a certain distance from the residence on the Sabbath. And they must walk, not ride horses or vehicles.'

Orme turned on the set, but no images sprang forth.

'Looks like they can't watch TV either. Hmm. I wonder if they're watching us, though?'

'I don't know. If they're really strict, no.'

'You know,' Orme said slowly, 'if everything's shut down

on the Sabbath, that'd be the day to make a break for it.'

'First, you'd have to find out how to raise the wall.'

'I think it's done by an outside operator or automatic machinery. Have you noticed that just before the wall goes up, Ya'aqob puts his hand inside his robe? I think he's got an activator in an inside pocket.'

'How're you going to get it away from him?'

Orme didn't reply. He was imagining picking the man's pocket. If he could substitute something that felt like the activator so Ya'aqob wouldn't miss the real device . . . but the transfer would have to be made just after Ya'aqob had pressed its button. That would cut it close, and his attention, the attention of the others, too, would have to be diverted. If Bronski would co-operate to make a scene, it could be done.

However, if the device had to be activated to make the wall slide back down, then Ya'aqob would discover at once that he'd been slipped a fake. It seemed probable that this was the way it was done. Unless the wall slid down after a preset time without another wave-emission. No, that was too much to hope for. Though their captors usually walked out as soon as the wall rose high enough, there had been one time when they'd stood talking for at least ninety seconds.

Now, if he could determine that the other five also carried activators or that at least one other did, then he could make two dummies. But that involved picking two pockets. It also required that he cause the wall to come down at the same time that Ya'aqob pressed the button – or whatever he did.

How to make the counterfeits? He had no materials to carve one and no knife. Beside, they'd be watched on TV, which meant he'd have to escape the eyes of the monitors when he stole the devices, and he'd have to do the carving in the bedroom where, presumably, he wasn't being watched.

And even if he did succeed in this elaborate plan, he still wouldn't know where to go or what to do once he got free. He had no idea where the tunnels were that led to the lander.

Besides, their entrance would be guarded. These guys weren't stupid.

What about the Sabbath? Wouldn't the sentinels be home on that day? Maybe. Even if they were, there would be automatic alarm equipment. Considering the difficulties, he had to admit that Bronski was probably right. Escape seemed impossible. However, if they should be allowed out of their prison, they would, even if guarded, have a much better chance.

Bronski, who had been sitting wordless, his eyes rolling slowly, abruptly broke his silence.

'I've got it!'

'What?'

'I've been calculating. Today will also be the Sabbath in *Israel*. It could be just coincidence, but I don't think so.'

Bronski looked as pleased as Moses must have been when his spies brought word that Palestine, land of milk and honey, was ripe for the plucking.

'Interesting,' Orme said, 'but I wish you'd bring that great intellect to bear on getting out of here.'

'It'd be a nice exercise of the mind but practically unfeasible. Anyway, if you want the truth, Richard, I don't think I'd leave if I could. There's too much to learn.'

'What if I ordered you to do so?'

Bronski shrugged. 'You're the captain.'

He rose slowly and strolled to the window-wall.

'Here they come for the sun ceremony.'

After the ritual, or public prayer, or whatever it was, the crowds broke up into smaller masses, each of which went into a wide building on top of a low hill of stone, ascending by twelve broad steps cut into the stone.

'Synagogues,' Bronski said. 'The architecture is interesting. They have twelve sides, and the inner parts of the roof fold or slide in to expose the interior to the sunlight. The corners of the roof turn up. The carvings at the ends look like symbolic hands. They're not really representations, but they do suggest folded hands, praying hands.'

The rest of the day passed with Bronski stationed like a sentinel against the wall, except that he had pulled up a chair to sit in, commenting aloud. Orme occasionally went to the wall when Bronski pointed out something interesting, such as the children playing outdoors after the noon meal. But his thoughts were mainly on getting away. If they could seize one of those ground vehicles at night, they could speed to wherever the tunnel entrance was. There were cars all over the place. From what he could observe when the six drove off, they had no keys. Apparently, the Martians didn't worry about theft.

Their supper was especially large and varied, and they ate the roast beef, baked fish, beans, lettuce, onions, gravy, and fruit salads with gusto. What surprised them were the roasted ears of maize, Indian corn, still wrapped in their husks.

'Corn certainly wasn't included in the diet of the Old World ancients,' Bronski said. 'The Krsh must have picked up specimens of vegetable life from all over Earth before they left.'

'You can see fields of wheat and barley from here,' Orme said. 'But no maize. They must grow it in other caves.'

'Or in fields so far away we can't see them.'

The next day was Sunday or *yom shamash*, as it was called. Bronski had expected that it would be a normal workday. But as on the *shabbat*, no one went to work, except for the farmers, and they just fed the animals and fowl. There were three attendances at the synagogue, but the children played outdoors between the services. The greatest difference was the length of the noon outdoor ceremony. He'd timed the previous ones at ten minutes. Today's lasted twenty-four. During twelve of these, the crowd was silent while a cantor sang. The prisoners could hear and see everything clearly. The TV set was on. Bronski theorized that this was so that the sick and the very aged could watch it. The whole ritual was conducted in Hebrew.

'If I didn't know better, I'd swear they were worshipping the sun,' he said. 'I'll have to wait for an explanation. Still, the Essene sect had its hymn to the sun. Maybe this is something like that.'

Orme wondered why Hfathon hadn't told them they wouldn't be teaching on this day, too. But half an hour after the crowd broke up. Hfathon drove up with Zhkeesh.

When he entered, he greeted them with the usual '*Shalom aleikhum,*' and then said, 'My colleagues are home with their families. Our children are grown up and so are with their children. But tonight we are having a big family gathering, so we must leave early to be with the head of the family, my great-grandfather.'

'You are blessed indeed to have one,' Bronski said. 'I hope that he is in good health and of sound mind.'

'Not bad for a two hundred and forty year old man,' Hfathon said.

Bronski raised his eyebrows and so did Orme when the exchange was translated.

'Your medical science is far advanced over ours,' Bronski said. 'You're speaking in terms of Terrestrial years, not Martian, aren't you?'

'Of course.'

Orme, hearing this, said, 'If it'd been Martian years, he'd be about four hundred and eight years old. Wait'll the folks back home hear about this!'

Bronski considered briefly the implications of his statement. He shuddered.

'May I ask what age you are, Hfathon?'

'One hundred and sixty-nine.'

Orme whistled and said, 'He doesn't look much over fifty. Of course, he's Krsh, so it's hard to tell with him. They all look alike to me, anyway.'

Bronski said, 'Sha'ul seems to be about thirty. How old is he?'

'Eighty-two.'

Bronski said, 'This longevity is unnatural, isn't it? I mean, do you use chemicals or some sort of scientific preparations to slow your ageing?'

Hfathon said, 'Don't your people?'

Bronski thought about lying. But sooner or later the Martians would know the truth.

'No. We've been able to slow down ageing in laboratory animals to some extent, but nothing like what you have accomplished. So far, we've nothing for human beings.'

Hfathon and Zhkeesh sucked in their breaths.

'You still die like the beasts? As you did two thousand years ago?'

Bronski said nothing. The two Krsh must realize what the news would do to Terrestrials. Once they found out, they'd clamour for the treatment or elixir or whatever it was. If, that is, the Earth governments released the news. Though the world birth rate had declined since the Sixties, overpopulation was a terrible problem.

Hfathon said, 'Let's start the lesson. But first, please take these.'

He withdrew two large green pills from the inner pocket of his robe.

'Swallow these. They won't harm you. They're memory aids. You'll be able to learn quicker and to retain the knowledge one hundred per cent. We'll double the speed of progress.'

Bronski held up the square pill between thumb and forefinger.

'Why weren't these given to us when we started?'

'You were. In minute amounts in your food and wine and water. Each day the dosage was increased. You've built up an immunity to the side effects, some of which are unpleasant.'

Bronski explained to Orme what the pills were for.

Orme said, 'The quicker we speak the language, the sooner we get out of this prison.'

They swallowed the pills with a water chaser.

Orme stood blinking for a moment, then said, 'I don't feel a thing.'

'What did you expect? Lightning? A sudden increase of IQ?'

'I don't feel any smarter.'

But the pills worked. They mastered sixty new vocabulary items, didn't forget any, and grasped much more of the Krsh syntax than they'd been able to do in previous sessions. Moreover Orme had much less trouble in reproducing the sounds.

'Will these pills – what do you call them?'

'*Gbredut.*'

'. . . *gbredut* . . . help a person of low intelligence?'

'Not as much as one of higher intelligence.'

'Man,' Orme said, 'these will be of great value on Earth. Now, if I could get a monopoly on these . . .'

'Can't you think of anything else but how to get rich?' Bronski said.

'I think of lots of other things, but there's no reason why I should pass up an opportunity like this.'

Hfathon sharply recalled them to their task, but Orme couldn't keep from imagining how much money he could make if he could get a franchise on Earth. Of course, this pill – he'd name it the 'wogglebug' pill after the giant insect of Oz who gave his students instant-learning pills so they could spend all their time playing – would be of immense benefit. He wouldn't charge high prices for it – he wouldn't have to.

But what if the Martians just gave the *gbredut* to Earth? Or would they even permit Earth to have it? After all, its possession gave the Martians an edge.

But if they were as ethical as they claimed to be, they wouldn't withhold this boon any more than they would deny the longevity treatment. Or would they?

After the lesson was finished, which Hfathon said had gone well, and the two Krsh had left, Orme spoke to Bronski.

'Do you think we could get away with not swallowing the

pills tomorrow? We could palm them. The only thing is, we'd have to fool them into thinking we'd learned everything. That'll be a strain, but we might pull it off.'

Bronski stared at him.

'You want to keep some so they can be analysed when we get back to Earth?'

'That's the idea.'

'And so you can become a plutocrat?'

'What's wrong with that? Somebody'll be doing it. Why not me? I won't be hurting anybody.'

'Why don't you just ask them for a sample? Or for the formula? They might give it to you.'

'And if they refuse? Then they'll know I'm up to something and they'll watch me like a cat watches a mousehole.'

That night they were permitted to talk to Shirazi and Danton. They verified that they were in separate prisons. Neither one seemed embarrassed at being caught in bed together, though they didn't like the consequences.

Nadir said, 'If I understood my interrogator, a man named Iyyobh, we have a choice. We can go into a work company, and then when we're free we'll wear a label for a year proclaiming us adulterers. That's a better deal than we'd have received under the old Mosaic life. We'd have been stoned to death. The other choice is marriage.'

'You already have a wife!'

'Yes, but I told them, and it's the truth, that I am a Muslim. I had to explain what that was, but they regarded me as some sort of heretical Jew. Anyway, I said that a Muslim could have more than one wife. That was the law of the land.

'Iyyobh said that monogamy was the custom here, though in the beginning, when the population was low, polygamy was permitted. If I understand him correctly, the Krsh can determine the sex of an unborn child, so they produce three girls to one boy. That way, a man could have three wives and produce many more offspring.'

'What about cloning?'

'I don't know. I'd guess their religion would tabu it. Or it would result in too much genetic similarity. Anyway, they have decided that Madeleine and I can either marry or suffer punishment.'

'I wouldn't take a second making up my mind,' Orme said.

Madeleine said, 'Neither did we. We're not in love, but we're very compatible in bed, and we won't have to suffer from sexual tension. The only thing is, my contraceptive will be absorbed in six months. Nadir didn't get any insertion, so he'll be fertile. We'll have to quit having conventional sex after six months. I'm not taking any chance of getting pregnant.' She said this matter-of-factly.

Orme said, 'You're lucky. Bronski and I only have each other, and he looks prettier every day.'

Bronski looked indignant. Orme laughed.

Madeleine said, 'You talk rather lewdly for a devout Baptist.'

'Talk doesn't hurt anything. In fact, it helps relieve the tension. Anyway, that's between my God and me. How're the lessons going?'

Nadir said they were progressing as well as could be expected. Orme said that they could expect to go faster in a few days, and he told them about the 'wogglebug' pills. They were interested in these, but the news about the prolonged longevity of the Martians amazed them.

'If they refuse to give the Earth the formula, there'll be a war,' the Iranian said.

'Probably,' Orme said. 'But I'm not sure they will tell Earth about it. One of the reasons they're so hot about our learning their language is that they want to find out just what kind of people we are. I think they might decide to stay completely isolated when they do. Isn't that right, Avram?'

'We don't really have enough data to go on.'

Another week passed. Nadir returned to Madeleine's quarters after they were married. Their marriage hadn't been performed by a rabbi since they were considered pagans. But

Nadir told them that under the law of the land, all he had to do was to announce publicly that he and the woman were married in the eyes of God. This was not true. Since the Martians didn't know any better, they couldn't object. Everybody was happy about the marriage, although Nadir was worried about what might happen when he returned to Scotland.

'Bigamy is illegal there.'

'Don't bother about it,' Bronski said. 'You won't be married under Scots law. But you'll give the lawyers there something to argue about. Is a marriage on Mars legal?'

'Besides,' Orme said, 'you may never get back to Earth.'

That was a sobering thought.

On the thirtieth day of imprisonment, without previous announcement, the four were released. Hfathon, smiling, informed them that their freedom had its limits.

'You'll be given quarters near the government building. Your house will be across the street from the Shirazis'. But when you go any place, at first, anyway, you will be accompanied by two guides.'

Orme said, 'We thank you. But may we communicate with Earth now?'

'In due time. We believe it best that you learn more about us so that you may report accurately to your government. We don't want any misunderstandings. Also, we must get more data about your people. Peoples, I should say, since you are highly heterogenous. Also, you will start teaching us some of your more important languages.'

'But it's vital that Earth understand that we are not prisoners here.'

'But you *are* prisoners.'

And then Hfathon said a strange thing.

'We must be cautious when we deal with the Sons of Darkness.'

Orme bristled. 'What do you mean by that?'

'It will be made clear to you. Meanwhile, let's go to your

new home.'

On the way, while riding in a car. Orme said, 'In an early conversation, you said something about Jesus Christ. Will you tell us about Him? Are you worshippers of Him or are you really Jews?'

'We are Jews who know that Jesus is the Messiah. No, we don't worship Jesus. He is a man, and there is only One we worship. But Jesus is with us.'

Hfathon pointed at the bright globe hanging below the roof of the cavern.

'He lives *there*.'

7

Sometimes, Hfathon came alone after breakfast to talk to them. Other times, Sha'ul or Ya'aqob came alone. Occasionally, they were accompanied by people from different branches of the government or professors of science, the arts, or humanities. Before entering, they asked permission, apparently to give the Earthmen the impression that the house was their home and so put them more at ease.

In the afternoons the Terrestrials were free to stroll or ride where they wished, within limits. Now and then Hfathon or Sha'ul would drive them through the tunnels to other caverns. There were forty of these, and a new one was being carved out to make room for the expanding population. The four went once to watch the excavations. Here giant lasers were disintegrating hard granite and basalt as easily as an acetylene torch burned paper.

'You have the same type of laser equipment, of course,' Hfathon said.

Orme nodded.

'When you do communicate with your people, you must tell them that if they send a ship here, it must not be equipped with such burners. Or with fission or neutron bombs. In fact, with any tools for waging war. We would regard that as a hostile move.'

Hfathon smiled as if as to weaken the sting.

'We've now set up detection equipment and weapons on the surface. It's a purely defensive measure. But I can assure you that no armed enemy vessel or missiles would get within 50,000 miles of here before being destroyed.'

Orme asked how the Martians could board a ship in space to check for weapons. After all, they had no spacecraft.

'*Had* is correct.'

The Krsh wouldn't say any more about that, but Orme supposed that the wrecked ship had been repaired. However, if this was so, then the surveyor satellites would have reported this to Earth. Or had the wreck been left untouched while another ship, or ships, was built underground? And why, since the Martians could have built space vessels any time in the last fifteen hundred years, had they waited until now?

He didn't ask Hfathon about this, but he did inquire about why the magnetometer instruments on the Terrestrial satellites had not detected the many immense hollows under the surface.

'We have means to give false readings,' Hfathon replied.

On the way back they stopped at a restaurant. As always, the four from Earth were given a table to themselves.

'It makes you feel unclean,' Orme said in a low voice.

'Which, ritually speaking, we are,' Bronski said. 'But what's the difference? We get the same food as they do, and it's good. We also get a chance to talk among ourselves without being monitored.'

Orme said, 'I'm not so sure of that. How do we know we're not being bugged?'

Madeleine said, 'But we use English. They don't know that language.'

'So *they* say,' Orme said. 'How do we know they don't? Because they say so? Maybe that's so we'll talk freely, and they can find out if we're planning anything.'

'Have you found out where the tunnels are that lead to outside?' Shirazi said.

'No, and it wouldn't do any good if I did,' Orme said. 'Now that they've got their ship in readiness, they could overtake us easily even if we did get aboard the *Aries*.'

'You're sure of that?' Bronski said.

'Their ship has to be a hell of a lot faster than ours.'

'Perhaps,' the woman said, 'they just told us that so we would abandon any plans to escape.'

67

'It wouldn't make any difference. Their lasers could easily burn us out of the sky. If, that is, they have set them up outside. Maybe they're lying about that. But should I – we – take the chance that they are?'

When they re-entered their 'home' cavern, Orme pointed up at the globe.

'He's supposed to appear from there in a month. Do you think they mean *symbolically* or are they putting us on?'

Bronski said, 'They'll tell us *which* when they think the time's right. Or perhaps they'll wait until the event and let us see for ourselves.'

They passed a marketplace in which several hundred people were trading or buying cattle, sheep, goats, horses, chickens, ducks, pheasants, turkeys, parrots, and many small birds striped orange, black, and green which sang like no other birds they had ever heard. These were descended from pets the Krsh had brought from their native planet, Thrrillkrwillutaut. Orme had told Hfathon how beautiful he thought they were, and the next day the Krsh had given him two. They didn't need a cage since they were housebroken.

There were also agricultural goods, art objects, and many household items. All were paid for, when not bartered, in thick plastic money of various sizes, shapes, and colours. The crowd was noisy but good-humoured. Everybody seemed to be happy.

From what Orme had seen, this society was far more congenial and free of crime and vice than any on Earth. If what Hfathon said was true, the last case of theft had been ten years ago, the last murder, six years ago. What other population of a million could boast of that?

'Sounds great,' Orme said. 'How do you know so much about this?'

'I've talked to our teachers and to the people in the street, both human and Krsh.'

'They may be feeding you a line of bull. Maybe, though, they are sincere. But you know how reality fails to match the ideal, though people will tell you only about the ideal.'

Bronski said, 'I've a feeling they're telling the truth, not just as they see it, but as it is. Anyway, there's an intense family relationship here, a beneficial one. Though I suppose there are disadvantages, just as there are in everything. But the advantages far outweigh the drawbacks.

'Here, the former Hebrew word for *cousin* has been borrowed by Krsh to mean *citizen*. Everybody's related. You should see the geneaological tables, which have been kept faithfully since the day they landed. These include gene charts, by the way.

'But I'm getting off the subject. There are no orphanages here; an orphan is adopted by his closest relative in most cases. Of course, there are very few orphans, since most people live out their full life span. Anyway, members of a family and the aunts and uncles and nieces and nephews are all very intimate, and they keep a close watch on each other, but mainly to make sure that everybody is loved.'

'Great!' Orme said. 'But what do they mean by love? You know how meaningless the word is on Earth. It's interpreted in a hundred ways and perverted in a thousand.'

Bronski shrugged and said, 'They're human beings, and you know what they are. But then there's the influence of the Krsh – whatever that is.'

Bronski believed that the Martians had a near-Utopia because of the unique religious-social-political system.

'Its roots are their religion, and so is the stalk and the flowers. But it's not a rigid system. It's open-ended, ready for any beneficial evolutionary change.'

'What's their definition of beneficial?'

'Let's wait and see. Sha'ul told me that the time may come when we'll be invited to live in a Martian home for a while so we can soak up the atmosphere of their way of life.'

'Will we be allowed to eat at the same table with them?'

'I think so. It'll be soon. If we couldn't, we would feel like strangers, outsiders, and so could never really know their society. We still won't be citizens, since we haven't converted. But I think they expect – or hope – we will.'

Orme said, 'If we did that, we'd become Martians. And we'd be traitors to Earth!'

'The Martians have a saying: "The only traitor is he who betrays the truth".'

Bronski proceeded to tell them something about the governmental system.

'Each neighbourhood is self-governing on matters involving its own concerns. These make up a township, and they send their representatives to the township council. Each county has its judge, who heads the council, and the counties send representatives to the cavern council. This is headed by a judge, the final authority for the cavern. The buck stops with him, though he does have limitations on his power.

'The judges are more than just judicial authorities. They are also governors. They're like the judges in the pre-monarchical period of the Hebrews. You've read the Old Testament, you know what they are.

'The central government is headed by a council of representatives from each cavern, and a judge is the head of that council. At the moment a Krsh, Zhmrezhkot ben-Rautha, is the supreme judge. He . . .'

'Just a minute,' Madeleine Danton said. 'Are all the councillors and judges male?'

'About five-sixths are.'

Danton looked indignant.

Bronski smiled. 'It's not as bad as it seems, Madeleine. Aside from the top government administrators, the proportion of women in the lower levels of government and in the professions is much higher. Almost half of these are women. But these are all older people. A woman is required to spend her child-bearing years at home. This is about from age twenty-seven to forty-seven. Remember that the longevity treatment means a longer period of childhood and youth.

'When the children are grown up, a woman can go into any

field she wishes. If she opts for taking care of children because she likes to, she can teach or be a live-in auxiliary mother. These people place great value on their children. There hasn't been a case of child abuse, physical or mental, for three hundred years.'

Danton's face had been getting redder. Now she exploded.

'But what about the women who don't want to be mothers? Those who don't have the proper temperament or the inclination? What about lesbians – including those who'd like to be mothers but prefer adoption or artificial insemination?'

'The Krsh eliminated the biological basis of lesbianism in the second generation here. After the first, there were no more.'

Danton sputtered but managed to get control of herself.

'Why, that's ridiculous! In the first place, it's a violation of civil rights!'

'Is it? Anyway, remember that this society isn't Earth's. But they can offer Earth the solution to the problem of homosexuality.'

'Nonsense! What about those whose homosexuality is determined by family environment? Where the father is weak or absent and the mother domineering? What about that, heh?'

'The *psychicist* whom I talked to says that the family environment doesn't determine homosexuality. Many men have weak fathers and strong mothers on Earth, you know, but are not homosexual. He said that only those with a genetic tendency to homosexuality are influenced by the weak father-dominant mother syndrome. But if those genes are altered, then there's no tendency, no matter what the familial situation is.'

'You're talking about male homosexuality! What about lesbians?'

'The same applies. Look, Madeleine, I'm not defending the Martians, though I do admire the results of their attitudes. Yehudhah ben-Yonathan, he's a Krsh, by the way,

71

said that sometimes a child does exhibit incipient homo-sexuality drive. But he or she is a mutation.

'Diabetes was eliminated in the genes, but still a very rare diabetic child occurs. Even with a mile of rock above the cavern, radiation affects the cells. When homosexual be-haviour or diabetes is detected, the child is treated. The gene complex is altered.'

'They're creating robots!'

'You mean a person should be given a choice as to whether or not he wants diabetes?'

'The Earth could benefit from their genetic engineering,' Orme said. 'They're way ahead of us.'

'Are you thinking about cornering the market on that, too?' Bronski said.

'There's no harm in making a profit if you're benefiting people. However, the Martians must practise birth control; yet it's strictly forbidden by the Mosaic laws.'

'If they didn't practise it, they couldn't hollow out caverns fast enough to keep up with the population growth. On the other hand, the women never have abortions.'

'What if,' Danton said, 'a woman doesn't want to quit having babies?'

'After she's had three, she's through. But she can be a substitute mother; and she can help take care of other women's children.'

'They're totalitarians!' Danton said.

'In some respects, I suppose. But they're the only genuine theocracy in the solar system – if what they say is true.'

'You mean, governed by priests?'

'No. They don't have priests, though descendants of Aaron abound. They don't have a temple. For them, the only temple is the one in Jerusalem. By the way, Yehudhah was very excited when I told him the Romans had destroyed that temple in 70 AD. The Martians didn't know that, of course.

'Then he said, "It will make no difference. We will rebuild

72

it." He paled a little, and he looked as if he'd said something he shouldn't have.'

'Aha!' Orme said. 'So they *do* have plans for Earth!'

Shirazi said, 'So, if they don't have priests, how can they be theocrats?'

'Well, it seems to me that they're ruled by Him.'

'Him? Who's him?' Orme cried.

'Who's He, you mean.' Bronski pointed a finger at the burning globe.

Orme felt as if his skin was evaporating, as if his nerves were suddenly exposed to the flaming air.

'You can't mean . . . Jesus?'

'According to what Yehudhah said, Jesus does arbitrate the most difficult judicial cases and occasionally interferes in the executive process. He is, in effect, if not in name, The Big Judge.'

Cold slipped up Orme's spine and over his neck and scalp. The globe looked like an immense fiery eye. Was it gazing at him?

'Perhaps,' Bronski said, 'theocracy is not the exact definition. After all, he is said to be the Son of Man, which means he is just a human being. He is not supposed to be the son of God, except by adoption, nor God. Still, in effect . . .'

Orme told himself that he was reacting overemotionally. The Martians had to be conning him. Nevertheless, when he said his prayers at bedtime, kneeling on the floor, he realized that he was facing in the direction of the globe. He got up quickly, his face warm, as if he'd been caught in a very embarrassing – indeed, sinful – act.

The next day he was summoned with his colleagues to Hfathon's office in the Tleth'sha, the main university. Waiting for them were the other five interrogators and teachers, Ya'aqob, Zhkeesh, Sha'ul, Yirmeyah, and Hmmindron. The Earth people sat down and were offered water or fruit punch and wafers with strips of dried fish. Orme wondered how they'd go for bagels, cream cheese, and lox, a

73

combination these Jews had never heard of. If he could get a patent on that, he might clean up. But would they give a monopoly on such a thing to anyone, let alone a Gentile? Anyway, what good would Martian money be on Earth? Still, maybe the time would come.

After Hfathon had inquired about everybody's health – as if anybody ever got sick here – he said, 'We've called you here to tell you some of our history. We have audiovisual aids in this office to complement the verbal delivery. Though you've progressed very well in learning our language, I may use some words or constructions you don't know. If so, please feel free to ask about them. Otherwise, I would like silence until the lecture is ended.'

Aside from the anticipated questions, no one spoke while Hfathon talked. For the first fifteen minutes he sped through the evolution of life on Thrrillkrwillutaut, the planet of the Krsh. (Orme noticed that he never said what star it orbited.) Life there had developed much like that on Earth; the Krsh had evolved from an apelike creature.

'Similar planets produce similar life forms,' Hfathon said. 'At least, those we found have done so. Though I must admit that we encountered only two others like yours and ours. One was still in the Paleolithic. The other, well, I'll get to that.'

Prehistory and history had progressed through the various stone ages, the bronze, iron, and plastic-electronic-atomic ages. As on Terra, there had been different races. Representatives of all these had been on the starship which had set out for interstellar exploration. But while on Mars miscegenation had made the Krsh a homogeneous people.

Orme was entranced when he saw the holograms of the Krsh civilization. Even then, two thousand years ago, no, more, since who knew how long the voyage had lasted before the ship came to Earth, these people had a science and technology that made Earth's seem primitive.

Then why hadn't Krsh science developed even more? It didn't seem any more advanced than when they had left their home. In fact, in many respects it had regressed. Most of the Martians used horses for riding and ploughing. Cattle and horse manure were the chief fertilizers.

Hfathon's exposition of the building of the starship and the launching made Orme forget his questions. The vessel was truly colossal, much larger than the exposed portion had suggested. Whatever its form of propulsion – Hfathon omitted that – it must have been incredibly powerful. It hadn't been constructed in orbit; it had lifted directly from the planet's surface.

There were fascinating holograms of life aboard the ship, though activity there was limited. The voyagers took turns manning the vessel or lying in suspended animation.

'It took forty years, travelling at one-quarter of the speed of light, to reach the first system,' Hfathon said.

There were flashes of holograms of a world which resembled that of Earth circa 20,000 BC. The beings were humanoid but had pointed ears, catlike eyes, and teeth which clearly indicated their purely carnivorous origin.

'On this world evolution took a slightly different path. The Divine Presence guided a primitive form of feline towards sapiency.'

The second voyage was to a star which, like Earth's, the Krsh's, and the third planet, was a G-type.

'This trip lasted fifty-five years of objective time,' Hfathon said.

Here the Krsh found two inhabited planets, the third and fourth out from the luminary.

The fourth planet had recently been deluged with vibration bombs (Hfathon didn't define these), but there were survivors, tiny groups wandering the land, trying to find food and at the same time escape the conquerors.

'Apparently it was the beings from the third planet who had won,' Hfathon said. 'We don't know what they called themselves, but we do have photographs of them.'

A screen showed a squat, heavily boned, heavily muscled

creature dressed in what looked like chainmail. In its broad-fingered hand it held a silvery helmet with a serrated crest. A close-up of the fingers, however, showed that it lacked nails.

The head was much like an Earthman's, but the creature could never have passed for one. Instead of hair it had short thick bristles reminding Orme of a porcupine's quills, though they could have been much more pliable. The skull was larger in proportion to the body than that of a normal Terrestrial's. The ears had somewhat different convolutions, and the tips were split into two long fleshy parts. The chin was very massive. The lips extended almost to the lower jawbone. Its mouth was open, revealing quite human teeth. The nose was very short and broad but the bridge bore a round hump from which a few quills projected.

The eyebrows were thick, their hairs, or quills, corkscrewy. The upper and lower eyelids moved when it blinked, one going up, the other down. The lower was blue-black, the higher, the same colour as the facial skin and the hands, reddish-brown. The eyes were a solid russet.

'Other specimens show different skin, eye, and hair colours,' Hfathon said. 'But all their hearts are black. Or perhaps I should say, to be charitable, that the heart of its government is evil. There may be good people on that world. Whatever the case, we were attacked without warning, though we had come in peace.'

Fortunately for the Krsh, they were equipped for self-defence. And their weapons were superior, though not overwhelmingly so.

Orme noted that Hfathon did not specify the nature of the weapons.

The two ships that tried to destroy the Krsh were themselves destroyed. Still, the Krsh made an attempt to communicate with the aliens, but it was ignored, and another attacker was annihilated. Forced to abort their exploration, the Krsh departed for the next star on their schedule: Earth's sun.

'But the Sons of Darkness pursued us, though we were not aware of that until some time after we'd reached Earth. There we placed the ship into orbit. After observing that we could easily handle any armed attack from the primitive peoples of Earth, we sent down a survey ship. Many specimens of plant and animal life were picked up and frozen to be taken back to Thrrillkrwillutaut.

'Obtaining samples of the sentient life presented a problem. We were forbidden to abduct any, since that would violate our ethical standards. But we did as we had on the first planet we visited. We flew around until we observed beings in dangerous situations, including illness. We rescued them hoping that their gratitude would be so great that they would willingly co-operate in our study of them. Afterwards, they would be released near the place where they were picked up.'

8

Hfathon paused to drink fruit juice.

'Of course, we hoped that some of those would be curious enough to wish to return with us. We had had no luck on the Paleolithic planet. Our "guests" were too tribal; they would have died if removed from their own people too long. So, after studying them, we returned them.

'But here were civilized people, though mightily uncivilized from our point of view. Out of the two hundred we got, fifty were so hysterical with fear that we quickly put them back where we'd found them. Most of those left were from the Mediterranean lands or from a land through which ran a great river called Sindhu, or they were from the far east. The latter were brown people with epicanthic folds. A few were from a city in the middle of a continent across an ocean west of the largest continent. Or east.'

Here Hfathon interrupted his lecture to ask the four if they had names for these.

'The land of the Sindhu river would be India,' Orme said. 'The far east people would be Chinese or other Mongolians. The land that connects the two continents would be Central America and the people from there would, I suppose, be Mayans. By the great continent I think you mean three continents, Europe, Africa, and Asia.'

'We thought it was one continent,' Hfathon said. 'It looks like one land mass from the photos I've seen.'

'They may be connected, but they're three separate continents,' Orme said. 'Though, actually, Europe isn't. It's considered to be a separate land mass because of historic and racial reasons. But that big land mass to the west of Eurasia is also two continents, North and South America. The narrow portion where you got the Mayans or whatever they were is Central America. It connects the two.'

'I don't want to get into geographical disputes,' Hfathon said. 'Most of those we brought back to the mother ship were sick with disease. We cured them and then learned their languages before we gave them the choice of going back or staying with the ship.

'One of the persons was from the continent you call Africa, in an area not too far from Khem, or Aegyptos in Greek; he was a Hebrew named Mattathias or Matthias for short. He was the disciple of the Messiah, the one chosen by lot to succeed Yehudhah. In Greek, *Ioudas Iskariotes*, the apostle who betrayed the Messiah.'

'You're talking about Matthias and Judas Iscariot!' Orme said in English, incredulous.

The Krsh ignored his outburst. He pressed a small device in his hand, and inside the huge set on the wall appeared a small bearded man talking to two Krsh in a small room.

'What language is he speaking?' Orme whispered to Bronski.

'I think it's Aramaic.'

'That is Matthias,' Hfathon said.

He paused. 'He was the thirteenth apostle, and he knew Jesus well before he was crucified. He walked and talked and ate with him here.'

Orme wanted to ask him to explain just what he meant by his last remark – 'ate with him here' – but Hfathon was talking about the sudden appearance of the Sons of Darkness.

'Our detectors picked them up as they came from behind the planet you call Jupiter. We had three choices, hide, fight, or run. We could have concealed the ship beneath the surface of an ocean, or we could have escaped from the system readily, since we could outrun them. But we did not know what they would do to Earth. From what we'd seen, they were ruthless and savage. They had a high degree of technological

79

civilization, but that does not mean an equally high ethical standard.

'What if they would destroy Earth as they had the fourth planet in their system? Or perhaps they might enslave the Earthmen. Since we were the ones responsible for their being here, we had a duty to protect Earth. Our policy was to interfere as little as possible in the development of another species, though it might hurt us not to rectify the evil things done there.'

He paused again.

'At least, that was our policy then.'

Orme sat up straight. What did that enigmatic statement mean?

'So we decided to fight.'

Orme said, 'Pardon me, Hfathon, but I just can't restrain myself. You said, "Our policy then." What . . . ?'

'That will be explained later.'

'Okay. But what I also want to know is how you could identify the ships of the "Sons of Darkness", as you call them. Was it their configuration or what?'

'They were shaped like those which had attacked us before. We didn't know, rather, our ancestors, the crew, didn't know how they had managed to follow us. A spaceship doesn't leave spoor. At least, we didn't think so, though perhaps those Sons of Darkness were more advanced than we thought.

'Also, they had to have had starships when we visited their system, though we hadn't observed any. Anyway . . .'

The Krsh ship, with the Terrestrial 'guests' still aboard, met the enemy 100,000 miles beyond Mars. The battle was brief and furious. Pieces of the attackers floated towards the sun. But the Krsh had been hard hit. With only one engine operating, it made for Mars and crash-landed. Fortunately, the impact was not serious to the crew and passengers. But the vessel could not be repaired, and the smaller survey ship was ruined.

The Marsnauts watched pictures taken of the flight and the

wrecking, and of the measures taken for survival. With the equipment at hand, the Krsh hollowed out of the hard rock a temporary base. From the minerals they made oxygen and food. And as the years went by, they expanded, eventually ending up with the great underground complex.

Orme found this account interesting, but he was more eager to get back to the story of Matthias. He felt awed. The apostle had actually been with these people. And, as Hfathon's holograms showed, he was buried in the rock here within a short drive. The camera had swooped over the cemetery, showing first the gravestones of the early inhabitants. They were inscribed with letters in Hebrew, Greek, Latin, Krsh, ideograms in Chinese, and several in what he supposed were Mayan hieroglyphs.

As the camera moved towards the later graves, all the lettering became Hebrew. The stones were of the same size since the law required that. According to the Hebrews, all persons were equal in death, holy and sinful, rich and poor, young and old, men, women, and children.

Bronski translated the inscription.

'*Mattathias bar-Hamath*. The years in the Hebrew chronology correspond to 2 AD and 149 AD respectively.'

Near the apostle's stone were ten others which Hfathon pointed out.

'These were Matthias's companions, his disciples rather, who were stricken with a disease when we picked them up. They were Libyan Jews whom he had convinced that Jesus was indeed the Messiah. It was Matthias who, with his ten, converted all his pagan human companions. But we Krsh were not yet shown the light. Most of us were agnostics or atheists, though there were some who clung to the religions of their ancestors. We did not interfere when he brought all our humans under the law of Moses, even though, in our ignorance, we could see nothing but senseless brutality in some of their laws.'

Orme could contain himself no longer. Rising to his feet, he shouted, 'And what made you change your hearts?'

'The Messiah himself appeared to us. And he did that which convinced us forever.'

9

Philemon Zhbeshg Mosheh ben-Yonathan was a young man of thirty-five. He was a bit of a dandy with his violet-dyed sidelocks, his large silver cart-wheel earrings, and his rainbow-striped robe. His elderly relatives thought his apparel scandalous. His ornamented buskins and scarlet toenails caused them to reproach him openly. He listened meekly and silently, but when he had heard them out he went on dressed as before. Like so many young people, twenty-two to fifty, he dressed as he pleased, to be fashionable.

Unlike his contemporaries, however, he was not given to excessive drinking, that is, drinking more than three glasses of wine in a day. Because he was an athlete, he permitted himself only one glass of wine during supper.

Orme, who'd won three Olympic gold medals (100 and 200 metre sprints and the long jump) went down to the central gymnasium to work out. He was, of course, eager to see what kind of athletes the Martians were. He expected that 2000 years of life on a planet with a gravity much lighter than Earth's would result in weaker muscles. But he was wrong. The natives ran and jumped and wrestled as if they'd been born on Earth.

Orme was attracted to Philemon by his friendly cheery manner and intrigued by the fact that he was the champion sprinter. He struck up a conversation, limited by his deficiencies in Krsh, and the sixth day after meeting him challenged him. To his surprise and chagrin, Orme was bested by several metres in each event.

'Well, I'm not in top condition,' he said between gasping

breaths. 'I need about five months of working out. Besides, I'm not accustomed to running here. Every stride I take is five metres long. Also, I'm past my prime, though I think you'd have beaten me anyway. Thirty-five is very old for a sprinter. For an Earthman, that is. And I'm not used to running with bare feet, either.'

He paused to grin and said, 'Maybe I can think of some more excuses.'

It was then that Philemon told him that he was the same age as he.

'Yes, but I haven't got the age-delaying treatment. Physiologically, you're only about nineteen, I'd bet.'

'Haven't you asked for the treatment?'

Orme was taken aback. 'Why, I just took it for granted I'd be denied it. After all, I am an alien.'

'Ask Hfathon for it. It wouldn't hurt.'

Orme talked to his crewmates that evening, and they decided to petition Hfathon in the morning.

Bronski asked Orme many questions about the gymnasium. Finally, Orme said, 'You seem very interested in sports now. I always thought you were indifferent to them.'

'I'm curious because the ancient Jews hated the gymnasium and they weren't wild about sports. They associated games with the pagan Greeks and Romans. But time changes attitudes. After all, the modern Israelis are very athletic-minded. The orthodox Jews in Israel are in the minority.'

In the morning, the moment their teachers arrived and greetings were exchanged, Orme made his request.

Hfathon was silent for a minute, his hands making a church steeple.

Finally, he said, 'Yes, I knew you'd ask for that. We had a conference last night about it. Not that it lasted long. We decided that we cannot, at this time, give it to you.'

Hfathon looked as if that was the end of the matter. But Orme said, 'Why not?'

84

'Why should we?'

'It would be the humane thing to do.'

'Ah, would it? We still don't know much about your people. How do we know that its overall effect would not be evil?'

Madeleine said, '*Evil*? You mean that it could result in physical trauma because our metabolism might be different from yours? Or do you mean that it might have a destructive effect on our society?'

'In any event,' Nadir said, 'how could giving it to just us be evil for the citizens of Earth?'

'To answer your second question first, Madeleine. It could disrupt society on Earth in a social sense. It would be evil. I notice that you have avoided or disparaged such terms as evil and sin. Don't you believe these exist?'

Hfathon was skilled at switching from a subject he didn't want to talk about.

'I prefer to use scientific terms,' Madeleine said.

'There is more than one kind of science. And there is a knowledge outside of science. But we won't argue about this now. To answer your question, Nadir. If you were given the treatment and then went to Earth, your scientists could analyse its chemical components from your blood. Although, from what I know of the state of your science, I'd say that treatment already could be known. Of course, it would not be as efficient as ours. But for some reason it has not been revealed to the public, perhaps for reasons similar to those which make us deny it to you. At this time, anyway.'

Orme knew by now that it was no use arguing or pleading with the Martians. He said, 'Very well. But you can understand why we want it, can't you?'

Hfathon smiled. 'Yes. By the way, the quick-learning pills will be discontinued. The blood samples we took yesterday show that you are near the danger point from the side effects.'

85

'What side effects?' Madeleine said. 'I haven't noticed anything.'

'Nor would you until they occurred. Which would be about three days from now. You may suffer some slight withdrawal effects, a feeling that people are in the next room when they aren't, and other paranoiac symptoms. You see, from what you've told me of your people, many would not take the pills as prescribed. Foolish people and criminals would abuse them.'

She said, angrily, 'I suppose no one here would abuse them?'

'No.'

She did not reply, but it was evident that she was fuming. Orme also felt resentful, as if he'd been unjustly reprimanded for something. But he had to admit that the Krsh was right.

At the gymnasium that afternoon, he tried subtly to get information from Philemon about the tunnels leading to the surface. Philemon, however, did not fall into any of Orme's verbal traps. He didn't seem to be aware of what Orme was doing; it was just that he tended to veer away from where Orme was steering him. He wanted to discuss athletics on Earth. The Canadian wondered if he was not as innocent as he seemed. How, for instance, had Hfathon known that Orme was going to bring up the longevity treatment? Was Philemon being pumped in the evening about what Orme said to him in the afternoon?

Or was the Martian wired for sound transmission? The Krsh had once told the Earthmen that they would not be unaccompanied when they went free. Orme had expected that a guide would be assigned to him. But this had not been done. After the first week, he was able to go wherever he wished without a companion. And the other three had reported that they were also free.

Somehow, they were being monitored from afar. Or had the Martians decided to get their information from those to

86

whom they talked? As for visual checking, that could be done by hidden cameras in the ceiling of the cave. When they went into a house, the TV there, though it seemed blank, could be operating as a camera. Or the Martians could have implanted a tracker-audiomonitor in the flesh of their captives.

Orme sometimes wondered if he wasn't suffering from the side effects of the wogglebug pills. Was he becoming paranoid?

One day, at about 13:00 hours, Orme got tired of trying to read a textbook on differential photonic-drive mechanisms. He set the book on the floor so it could make its way back to the proper niche in the library file. He strolled over to the language department and looked through the catalogue of popular literature, which listed many books of poetry, one-half of which were religious. He decided that even if he were more fluent, he would have trouble understanding the poetry because of its compression of ideas, obscurity of reference, and tendency to puns. Krsh poetry used quantity in its metre instead of accent, much like ancient Greek and Latin poetry, and it depended heavily on alliteration and parallelism. The latter, a professor had explained, had been borrowed from Hebrew poetry.

He decided that he would return home and there continue his reading of *The Testament of Matthias*. But while walking home, he changed his mind. Why not borrow a car and drive around? If the authorities objected to this, they'd let him know soon enough.

There were no attendants at the municipal parking lot. A dozen of the topless vehicles were arranged in two neat rows on the stone. He got into one, pressed a button to start it, and the electrical motor was ready. There were no keys since individuals did not own cars. All were either the property of a community or of the central government. When a person wanted one he just got into it and drove off. There were very few trucks since the farmers used horse-drawn wagons, and supplies were shipped in pneumatic-driven capsules in underground tunnels.

The streets and highways were a thick rubbery material that gave a nice ride and was easy on the pedestrians' feet. The car rolled out on the street in manual drive. He could have given his destination verbally to the vehicle's computer and sat back while it got there by itself by the quickest route. Very few people used this automatic system, though, since they enjoyed driving.

Proceeding at twenty miles an hour – the car's limit was thirty-five – Orme steered down the street and on to a main highway. This took him in great curve around the main part of the city and out into the country. There were no stop signs, lights, or road signs. There weren't even street signs. It was assumed that a citizen would know his own community. If he was a stranger, he could find out where somebody lived by asking another citizen or consulting a computer. There was also no postal system. People used their TV sets to commmunicate or to transmit printed papers.

Orme had found out that the cavern in which he lived was the first one to be made. By consulting a government informational facility through his TV, he had been shown a map of the tunnels and caverns. No doubt his call had been monitored, but nobody had said anything about it nor had any information been refused. He had not asked for the location of the entrance to the tunnels that led to the surface. He'd try to figure that out himself.

After fifteen minutes of pleasant travel, no dust, very few other cars to worry about, no blasting of horns, he turned off to a road that would lead him to the highway that ran along the perimeter of the cavern. Here he had to slow down to ten mph because the road went through a small town. The largest building here was a dome about twenty feet high with a diameter of three hundred feet. This was the top of an underground station which received grain brought in by farmers.

Orme slowed even more to drive around some small children playing a game like lacrosse. They stopped to stare at the black man. He grinned back at them, evoking smiles from a few. Then a woman carrying a large leather bag ran up to him and asked him to stop. He did so, wondering what she wanted.

'Are you going to Yishub?' she said.

'I don't know. Where's that?'

'About six miles straight down this road. I have business there, and all the cars are taken. I'd walk, but that'd make me late.'

'I'm going that way. Get in.'

She threw the bag into the back seat and got in beside him.

'I'm Gulthilo Ribhqah bat-Yishaq. I know who you are, of course. Richard Orme, the Earthman.'

She was good-looking, several inches taller than he, busty, slim-ankled, with curly yellow hair and dark blue eyes. He wasn't surprised at her Gothic name, meaning Little Golden One, since some of the Terrestrials brought here had been picked up in Northern Europe. That accounted for such names as Fauho, Rautha, Swiglja, and Haurnja.

Nor was he surprised to encounter a blonde. Though most of the human Martians were dark-skinned Mediterranean types, there were some with blue and green eyes and red or yellow hair. They did not get these naturally, however. Some of their ancestors may have been blonds, but the genes for light pigmentation had been wiped out during the twenty generations of inbreeding. However, occasionally parents wanted a lighter colouring for their children for the sake of variety, so the bio-engineers accommodated them with genetic tampering. Thus, Gulthilo resembled her remote namesake ancestress.

He started driving again, and said, 'What do you do?'

'I teach flute-playing at farms and some of the towns. Usually, if I can't get a car, I ride my bicycle. But mine broke down this morning, and everybody was using theirs, so I couldn't borrow one. Fortunately, you came along. I'm very pleased, since this may be the only chance I'll get to talk to one of you.'

Her story sounded reasonable, except that it seemed odd that no bicycles were available. Perhaps some unusual activity had required them. However, she could have been planted here. Maybe the authorities hoped he would let his guard down if he thought his meeting her was accidental.

I'm not really paranoid, he told himself. My suspicions are based on reality. Perhaps, though, I'm doing her an injustice.

'Where are you going?' she said with that open curiosity that distinguished these people. Like children, they did not fear strangers, not even those from another planet.

'I'm just riding around to enjoy the scenery and see something different. I got tired of the university. I wanted to relax.'

'Are you married?'

Though he was getting used to the Martian frankness, he was startled by this. He said, 'I was, but my wife divorced me.'

'There was a programme on you Earth people the other day. Did you get to see it? No. Well, the commentator said that there are many divorces there. You can get one for any reason or no reason at all. That seems strange. Here only unbelief, adultery, cruelty, or a high incompatibility are grounds for divorce. Infertility used to be grounds, but no one is sterile now. And everyone believes in the Messiah of course. Though that doesn't stop some few evil people from secretly opposing him.'

So even here there were dissenters.

'When my wife married me she knew that I only wanted to be an astronaut . . . a space-voyager. But after I had a near-accident, she wouldn't give up trying to make me quit and get a safe job. So we parted.'

'Are you engaged?'

He smiled. Then he said, 'Are you married or spoken for?'

'No, my husband was two hundred and forty years old when I married him. He died shortly after our youngest child entered the university two years ago. I have a dozen suitors, but I haven't made up my mind yet. Besides, I am rather enjoying my freedom from marital responsibilities. You might say I'm on a vacation.'

Orme wondered how it felt to know your father was two hundred years old when you were born. If you were a Martian, you probably wouldn't think anything at all about it.

Orme was excited by this woman. Though the robe was pinned to the neck and it was ankle-length, its thinness showed her lush figure and long legs. Her face was sensuous: full lips, a slightly curving but delicate nose, dark thick eyebrows, soft skin. And a bright light in her blue eyes. He sighed. She could never be his, even temporarily.

Finally, as they passed a farmhouse, he said, 'Two years is a long time without a man. Or don't you think so?'

He looked at her when he said that, and she blushed.

He thought, 'Oh, oh! I've gone too far.' But blushing! He didn't remember seeing a female blush since he was a child.

She said, 'How long have you been without a woman? Six months? Isn't that a long time?'

'It hardly seems forever,' he said and laughed.

She was silent for a moment. Then she said, 'Pull over under that tree.'

He looked at her but said nothing. When he'd stopped the car, he observed that the tree and the field of tall *sheshunit*, a sunflower-type plant, kept them from being seen by anyone except a passerby on the road. And there hadn't been one in the last five minutes.

She moved over close to him. Her thigh was touching his.

'Now,' she said smiling, 'don't get me wrong. But I do want this.'

Her arms came around his neck, and her lips were pressed against his. Then her tongue slipped in and moved against his.

This can't be happening, he thought. But it was.

She allowed him to feel her breast, but when he tried to unpin the robe, she drew away. Both were panting.

'I just wanted to find out how it feels to kiss an Earthman,' she said.

She reached out a hand and ran it over his hair.

'Also, I was curious about that. It feels so strange. But good.'

'Maybe it'll give you luck,' he said. 'In the old days, white people would rub a black's wool. They did it for good luck.'

'That's strange.'

'Well, now you've kissed an Earthman, how did it feel?'

'Very exciting. Almost too much so. But then I haven't kissed anyone but my relatives for two years. I'm getting very passionate. And I have been reprimanded for being too bold. But I'm not a bad woman. I just couldn't help myself.'

'I've never kissed a Martian before,' he said.

He paused.

'We could go into the field.'

She blushed again, but she smiled a moment after.

'If we did that, we'd have to get married.'

'I won't tell anybody.'

'But I'd know. Anyway, I'm not in love with you. I'm sorry. I shouldn't have done that. Only . . .'

'Don't apologize. It was wonderful while it lasted. But I hope you don't tease other men like that. You might get raped.'

'Only an evil man would do that. And he'd get sent to She'ol.'

'Where's that?'

She shuddered.

'I don't want to talk about that. Please, let's drive on.'

92

'As you wish.'

After a minute, he said. 'This is easily the most moral society in the solar system. Or the strictest, anyway. Yet basic human nature must be the same everywhere. How many of your brides are pregnant before the ceremony?'

She laughed. 'Oh, it's been estimated that about one-fourth are. But no woman is ever shamed. She is never rejected by the man responsible. He wouldn't dare.'

'I would think that that'd make for a lot of unhappy marriages.'

'No. Why should it?'

He didn't think he had the answer to that. He'd have to know even more about these people's attitudes before he could argue about this. Terrestrial conditions were obviously not always, or not often, like those here.

She pointed to the sun.

'He wouldn't like it.'

'Ah, he! But why should fear of him make for happiness?'

'We love him,' she said. 'We would adore him if he would permit it. But he keeps warning us that he is not the Merciful One.'

Orme decided to change the subject. All this talk, though informative, was irrelevant to his purpose. Since she was so frank, why shouldn't he be? And perhaps surprise might work.

He said, 'By the way, where is the entrance to the tunnels that lead to the spaceship?'

'Over there.'

She pointed past him at the blue wall of the cavern. He followed the invisible extension of her finger, but he could not see anything significant.

'If you'll drive to the road that parallels this one five miles from here, and then go straight towards the wall, you'll come to the road that winds up the side. Then you'll come to a shelf of rock on which will be a small building striped blue and red.

Behind it is the entrance.'

How easy it had been. Perhaps too easy.

'Is it a guardhouse?'

'No. Why should there be guards?'

Was she putting him on? Or did she really believe that the Earthmen would no more think of escape than a fat steer in a lush meadow? Did the authorities believe that?

'If you get lost, you can ask directions at the village of Gamaliel. Slow down, please. That's Wang Ben-Hebhel's farm. I teach his son and daughter.'

Orme turned on to the cement-paved horseshoe-shaped driveway and stopped in front of the house. Like most of the residences it was of wood and seven-sided. (The number seven had great symbolic meaning in this culture.) It was a storey and a half tall, and the wood composing it would be, he knew, very hard (of Krsh origin) and very thin. The boards were vertical, and there were big windows everywhere. The pagoda-like roof was red; a light-blue verandah surrounded the house. The eaves were very broad because of the Jewish tradition that, if a man fell off the roof, no blood should touch the house itself.

A big animal that looked like a black wolf, but whose ancestors had come from Krsh, rose from the verandah floor and chirrupped loudly. A moment later two youngsters, about ten and thirteen, ran out. A slim dark woman, a beauty, followed them a few seconds later.

All three looked surprised on seeing Orme. When Gulthilo introduced him – as if they didn't know who he was – they smiled broadly and seemed genuinely delighted. Gulthilo thanked him for the ride, at the same time giving him an enigmatic look. Apparently, he was dismissed. But before he could turn away for the car, she said, 'Wait a minute,' and she rattled off Krsh to the woman, Ester.

Gulthilo said, 'Are you hungry?'

'I did skip lunch, but . . .'

'You're invited to eat with us. Please accept.'

'With you?'

'Yes. Ester told me she just heard over the TV that the Council has decided that you Terrans may eat at our tables. You aren't able to eat unfit food now since your provisions ran out, and there's no harm in eating with us. Of course, this applies only to ordinary meals. Feast days and holy days are out for you. And you must observe the rules.'

'It's nice not to be treated like a pariah,' Orme said.

He thanked her and followed them through a wide doorway on the sides of which were mezuzahs, little boxes containing holy writings. The only residences on Mars that did not have them were the two in which the Earth people lived. The first room was tall and airy. The wall boards were painted alternately in pale white and pale blue. No wallpaper. From the storey-and-a-half-high ceiling hung three large chandeliers of cut quartz, each bearing six huge electric lights. The only wall decorations were two big, very thin TV sets and a gigantic spear on brackets. Every household had at least one such weapon. It had been an ancient Krsh custom for the father to give his son this ceremonial spear when he got married. The humans had adopted this custom about the time the sixth cave was hollowed out.

The floor was polished mahogany with bright patterned throw rugs here and there. The furniture consisted of a very large table in the centre, five sofas, some small sidetables, a lectern, and a huge desk. The latter had at each corner a tall round post on which were carved six-pointed stars and floral designs.

The room led directly into a square central court. Every room had access to the court, a most charming place. Polished granite slabs formed its floor. In the centre was a large seven-sided pool from the centre of which there were openings in the floor from which grew twenty-foot-high trees with wide-spreading branches. Yellow and scarlet canarylike birds sang or twittered in the branches or pecked at purple, apple-sized, pear-shaped fruit.

In one corner a lion-coloured cat the same size as its Terrestrial counterpart watched her three kittens play. Its great ears and facial markings and large green eyes were lynxish.

Ester led the way along the edge of the court to the other end of the square. Here they entered a hallway, where he was shown a large bathroom. After closing the door, he relieved himself and washed his face and hands. The bathtub was large enough to hold three people comfortably and was cut out of a single block of glossy black basalt.

He joined the others, who had also washed, and they led him into a gigantic kitchen with a fireplace big enough to roast a calf. It didn't look as if it was used much, however. One wall contained racks of knives, saws, cleavers, and table utensils. Another held dishes, pots, and kettles. A big chopping block stood by the sink. In one corner was a large electric range with a microwave oven above it. There were also a dishwasher, two towering refrigerators, and, in the centre of the room, a table large enough to seat twenty or so. It was set, however, for six.

Ester bustled around putting dishes of food and bowls of fruit on the table. The little girl helped her, but the boy stood staring at Orme until his mother sent him down into the cellar, the trapdoor to which was at one corner. He came out a minute later with two large bottles of wine. At the same time the head of the household Wang Elkanah Ben-Hebhel, entered. Gulthilo introduced Orme. They bowed to each other, the farmer frankly curious about this fabulous creature, the black Terrestrial. His stare would have been rude on Earth, but here it was only good manners.

Ben-Hebhel had just come in from the fields, where he had been inspecting the barley. He had, however, hastened to wash and to doff his working robe and put on a clean white robe. His hat, which looked like a cowboy's sombrero, was also white. Over his shoulders he wore a silvery prayer shawl, a tallith. The boy ran out of the room and returned with prayer shawls for the rest of the family and for Orme.

Gulthilo said, 'You aren't of our faith – as yet – but the Council has also decreed that you may pray with us. If you wish. However, the woman, Danton, can't share in the prayers as long as she remains an atheist.'

'I'll be happy to pray with you,' Orme said.

Here, however, the blessing and the thanksgiving came after the meal was eaten.

They began eating the delicious vegetable soup, the tasty black bread, the salad, and the cheese. On Mars lunch was a light meal. Since there was no meat on the table, they did not have to be careful to keep it separate from the dairy products.

Orme had to answer a lot of questions, though mostly from the children. With the help of Gulthilo, he answered them as best as he could.

Once, Orme quoted the New Testament.

'The Sabbath was made for man, not man for the Sabbath.'

Wang said, 'So, you know that statement of the Messiah. Then you have read *The Testament of Matthias*?'

Orme explained that Earth had testaments from other disciples of Yeshua'. These had been collected to make a book which was the sequel to what Terrans called the Old Testament, the holy book of the ancient Jews and of the modern ones, and also one of the holy books of the Christians.

Gulthilo said, 'Yes, we heard about that. Two weeks from now the first of a series of programmes will be given which will tell us about the history of the followers of the Messiah since Matthias the prophet left Earth.'

Bronski had been the chief informant for those preparing the series, though Orme had contributed as much as he could. But he had been more chagrined than pleased because of his ignorance of his own religion. The scholarly Jew had known far more about it than he.

'To get back to *The Testament of Matthias*,' Wang said. 'You didn't say whether or not you'd read it.'

'I'm about a quarter of the way through it,' Orme said. 'It's hard going for me because I'm not fluent in Krsh yet. On the other hand it is in simple language. I can't read the original at all, which is in Greek.'

'And do these New Testament writers, as you call them, agree with Matthias?'

Orme smiled. 'Well, in many places, yes. But in many others, no. He says nothing of the virgin birth, for instance, or the Holy Trinity, or Jesus's genealogy, or . . . many things.'

Bronski, who had by now read *Matthias* four times, had told Orme that all of the New Testament books were written long after Jesus had been crucified. And many, especially Mark, Matthew, Luke and John, showed evidence of tampering.

Orme had denied this, but Bronski, whose Biblical scholarship was profound, had cited him chapter and verse of the Book and the many commentaries on it.

'Matthew, Mark, Luke and John never heard of the virgin birth. Paul never mentions it, and you can bet that if he had, he'd have made a long comment on it. The references in the first four gospels are obviously later interpolations, pious frauds. And it's evident from the first four gospels that Jesus was a Jew who thought of himself as the Messiah of the Jews, the saviour of them *only*.

'The extension of the faith to the Gentiles was chiefly the work of Paul and Barnabas. Most Jews rejected Jesus as their Messiah, and so certain accommodations of the Mosaic Law were made for the pagans. Such as, for example, giving up circumcision and the dietary tabus. Also, the belief in virgin birth was common among the pagans; their myths and legends had hundreds of accounts of them.'

'Why hadn't I heard about all this?' Orme had said.

'Because, like most Christians, you didn't bother to read what was available. Of course, many have, but they've rejected scholars' findings. They ignore them. They believe blindly. Or if they do accept them, they rationalize them and become watered-down liberal Christians. On the other hand, the fundamentalists believe everything in the Bible in a literal sense. That is, there was an Adam and an Eve and a garden of Eden and the snake did tempt Eve to eat the fruit of the knowledge of good and evil, and the snake was cursed and lost its limbs and had to crawl on its belly forever after. Haw, haw!'

Orme had got angry and had finally quit arguing with Bronski.

He couldn't deny that Matthias knew nothing about Jesus's resurrection, though he had heard rumours of it. And he, the thirteenth apostle, had known intimately all those closely connected to Jesus, and none had claimed to have seen the risen Jesus.

'So,' Bronski said, 'the accounts of this in the four Gospels are fabrications attached to them. Mark, Luke, Matthew, and John give contradictory stories, and the Christian apologists have written many books attempting to explain these discrepancies. None are convincing. They're splendid examples of the power of the human mind to rationalize, and that's all!

'The only conclusion to draw from this is that Jesus is a few mouldering bones in some stone tomb or merely dust. But then there is undeniable proof that Jesus did suddenly appear on Mars shortly after the digging into Mars had started. He wasn't on the Krsh ship when it left Earth, at least his presence aboard had gone undetected, and then presto! There he was! And Matthias, who'd known him well, recognized him. It was then that Jesus said that he had died on the cross and been buried in a tomb. But, unlike the accounts in the Gospels, some of his disciples had taken the body away and reburied it. They were accused of doing that by their enemies, you know.

'However, this Jesus said that his spirit had been taken to heaven, and then he was sent back to the material world by God, but not to Earth. God had informed Jesus that he had been mistaken – Jesus, not God, of course – about the nature and the time of the Last Days. He was sent in a new body, which looked just like his old one, to Mars to rule over his people there and to prepare them for their rule in establishing Zion on Earth. What do you think of that?'

Numbed, Orme could only reply that he had nothing at this time to say. Except that it sounded very fishy to him.

'The fish was the symbol of the early Christians,' Bronski said. Orme didn't ask him what he meant by that.

Meantime, he was reading Matthias's testament as fast as his ability permitted him. So far he had only got to the section where Matthias and his companions were sick with the plague in Libya and praying that The Divine Presence would deliver them from evil as He had the Chosen People in the time of Moses.

The rest of the meal was occupied with Wang's jokes. He seemed to be a great story teller, and Orme could easily have spent the day there trading stories with him. However, none of Wang's tales were 'dirty'; that was forbidden.

Finally, Wang said he had to get back to his chores, and Gulthilo had to start the lessons. Orme thanked them for the meal and got into the car while the others stood on the porch saying goodbye and inviting him to come again.

Before he could drive away, the blonde ran down from the porch. She leaned across the seat and touched his wrist.

'Maybe we really shouldn't see each other again,' she said. 'But I would like it if we did. If you come this way again, ask for me in the village of Nod. Or you can call me through the TV.'

'I'd like that very much. But I don't know. The authorities

might interfere. And what would your family do if they thought I was courting you?'

'We'll worry about that when it's time to do so,' she said.

She withdrew her hand, leaving a warm tingling spot on his wrist. 'It's up to you. I've been too bold as it is.'

He drove away without looking back. It had been a pleasant experience, one which had done much, even if only temporarily, to alleviate his loneliness. Except when he was with Philemon and his fellow athletes, he'd felt that he was truly an alien. What was it? 'A stranger in a strange land.'

The hospitality and the genuine friendliness of the family, and the attraction Gulthilo felt for him, had made him feel warm and somewhat secure. But, he warned himself, this was illusory. There was danger in seeing the blonde, and the Ben-Hebhels had shown to their guest a welcome that their Law probably required.

No, that wasn't fair. Their reception of him had not been the polite formality that was demanded if correct behaviour was to be observed. They'd seemed genuinely interested in him. Of course, that could be because he was a curiosity, something they could talk about to their friends, a conversation piece.

As long as he had no evidence, he told himself, he was being paranoid again. Why take them at their face value until he had proof it was false?

Wang had given him a bottle of wine. He drank from it now and then so that when he reached the wall he was half-drunk. He realized that he was stupid to be in this condition. He had to have all his wits when he was trying to locate the tunnel entrances. It was then that he knew that he was drinking because he did not really believe that he was going to get away with his effort. They – the enemy – were too indifferent. They didn't care if he took a car and drove around doing what he wanted to do and eventually found the entrance. They knew where he was; they could stop him any time they wished.

By the time he'd finished the bottle, instead of feeling audacious and exhilarated, he was in a funk. He was a fool to think he could boldly drive up to the escape route and go through it. No intelligent people – and the Martians were intelligent even if they did have some weird religious convictions – would leave the way to the surface unguarded.

Or perhaps they had done so because, once he reached the surface, he'd find that the lander wasn't operable. Or that it had been removed.

Nevertheless, he drove up the winding road to the dome, which he had seen from the ground level. What the hell. He might as well go through with it.

Before him was a metal door, two doors, in fact, set into the wall of the cavern. On his right was the hemisphere, shining in the decreased light of late afternoon. There was no one around. They felt so secure they hadn't even posted guards.

He stopped the car and punched the *off* button. For a minute he sat listening, his gaze moving around to take in everything it could. He turned around once and looked behind him. No one was coming up the road after him. The only near vehicle in sight was a large horse-drawn wagon a half-mile away, piled with something shaggy. Probably a farmer taking a load of plants to some destination.

It was very quiet here. A slight breeze moved over his face; the normal air-conditioning in this immense hollow. The sun's rays sparkled here and there, rays glancing off white houses and storage domes, off a brook or creek, and once an intense flash as if from a mirror. A red deer trotted out from the edge of a thick wood near the wall, looked around, and disappeared back into the trees.

It was all very quiet and pastoral. Yet it was a time-bomb ticking away; it could explode on Earth. Perhaps. What did the Martians plan?

Orme got out of the car and walked over to the dome. Its great windows were open, and the door stood ajar. No sound came from it. But when he looked through a window, he saw a male Krsh sitting at a desk writing with a pen.

The Krsh looked up as if he had heard Orme, though he had made no sound.

'Come in, Richard,' Hfathon said. 'I've been waiting for you.'

10

His heart beating hard, Orme entered. He took the chair indicated by the Krsh. Hfathon leaned back and smiled at him across the desk. Orme thought he looked smug.

Hfathon gestured at an instrument-control console against the wall.

'There is the means to open the tunnel door. You probably would have figured out how to operate it. And then what? You'd have triggered alarms in the central government building and within the tunnel complex itself. There are men stationed at all times in the complex. Even if they weren't there, you couldn't open more than one door within without a coded sonic device nor without the co-operation of two human monitors in the government building.'

Orme shrugged. 'I had to try.'

'Of course. Very commendable. It was your duty to make an attempt. But I am surprised, and disappointed, that your colleagues lack your courage and determination.'

'They think escape is impossible. So I didn't enlist them. Anyway, they're so fascinated with their studies that I don't think they really want to leave. Even if it is their duty to get back to Earth if they can.'

'However,' Hfathon said, 'from another viewpoint your duty should not be to your nation if that duty means preferring evil over good. There is Someone higher than nations or a whole world. You should have thought about that. If you had, you would have seen that the Sons of Light are to be preferred to the Sons of Darkness. You would have cast your allegiance to them. That is, you would have if you could see that most of Earth's inhabitants are of the Sons of Darkness. So . . .'

'Why would I think that?' Orme blazed.

Hfathon said, calmly, 'It is obvious. You and your fellows have told us much about conditions on Earth. It is plain that injustice, misery, poverty, murder, every conceivable kind of crime, and, above all, hatred and hatefulness abound there. You have the means for making Earth as near a paradise as is possible, but you pervert these means.'

He paused, then said, 'I'm assuming, of course, that what you tell us is the truth. I can't see that you'd paint such a bad picture deliberately. Now, be truthful, isn't it far superior here to anything you know on Earth?'

'Yes,' Orme said. 'I admit that what I've seen so far is incomparably better. But then you have a small society here, and you're not subjected to the many influences existing on Earth. I mean, you're homogenous. Here you don't have many races, many nations, languages, and differing ideologies and religions. Nor do you have the thousand clashing traditions and the many hostilities of classes, races, and political systems. These were wiped out when you formed a single political-religious-economic entity. You took one tradition and developed it without interference from others. You did that a long time ago, and you also had a superior science and technology enabling you to give your people the benefits we Terrestrials lacked then.'

'True,' Hfathon said. 'So . . . we might give you those benefits you lack now. But not just as gifts which you will inevitably pervert.'

'I'd like a drink of water.'

Hfathon rose, saying, 'Allow me to get it for you. I am your host . . . though I didn't invite you here.'

He went into the next room and came back holding a tall glass.

'Here. This is much better for you than the wine you drank so immoderately today.'

Orme drank, and said, 'Thanks. Okay, so I got loaded. The pressure has been heavy. And getting free for just a little while made me want to celebrate.'

'You were never free in that you were away from observation, or had any chance to escape. Just as you've never been free in any sense. The only genuinely free man is one who has rid himself of evil. The half-free man is one who is battling to do that.'

'Spare me the platitudes.'

'Perhaps you are right. It is example, not words, that work best. By the fruit of the tree shall you judge it. Let's go back now. I'll drive.'

Orme followed him, wondering how the Krsh had got here. There were no other cars in view. Either he'd been driven here or there was an underground system for travel besides that for shipping.

As the car started down the road, he said, 'I suppose you saw everything?'

'No,' Hfathon said, looking sideways at him and smiling. 'We didn't see you while you were in that house. Nor did we observe you while you were parked under the tree with the woman, Gulthilo bat-Yishaq. By the way, what were you two doing?'

'That's our business,' Orme said.

'No doubt, if both of you have the consciences to handle it.'

'We didn't do anything wrong,' Orme said angrily.

'Perhaps not from your viewpoint. But this is a trivial matter – so far. Let's drop it. Now, Richard, I know that you and your companions have been disturbed because we wouldn't let you communicate with Earth.'

'Disturbed? Outraged!'

'Understandably so. But, you see, we didn't want you to send any report until you could make a complete one. You have to comprehend us thoroughly, know us to the bone, before you can describe us. That takes time. If you were to tell about us now, you'd only give half-truths, incorrect impressions. We want Earth to understand exactly who and what we are.

'In fact, at this stage, any messages you sent would probably be disbelieved. But twelve days from now, when you report, you can verify that all is true. Not just by your words alone, however.'

Orme said, slowly, 'All of what is true?'

'What you'll see in seven days. You'll have no doubts about it. And, I hope, neither will your people on Earth. Still, they might need more . . . Well, let's not think about that.'

Hfathon's expression bordered on the ecstatic. After a while he began humming a song which Orme had heard before in the streets and, once, from Philemon.

'I'm glad you're happy,' Orme said. 'I'm just bewildered and mystified.'

'That will change,' Hfathon said, and he laughed.

'For the better, I hope,' Orme said sullenly.

'You life depends on that.'

Orme didn't ask him what he meant. He was tired of all this dodging of questions which his captors seemed to enjoy so.

Shortly before entering the central section, Hfathon's wrist chronometer buzzed. He spoke into it, then held it to his ear. He frowned, said a few low words and turned to Orme.

'Cancer of the liver has just been detected in Madeleine Danton.'

Orme felt shock, and for a moment he could say nothing.

'The examinations that began two days ago have just revealed it,' the Krsh said.

'But she was given a clean bill of health before we took off! And believe me, we all got a very complete going over.'

Hfathon shrugged. 'It may have been too small for your instruments to detect. Or it may have started afterwards. In any event, she is at the chief hospital now. She was rushed there the moment the physicians found the cancer.'

'Poor Madeleine,' Orme said. Then, 'Who would have thought that cancer would be something we'd encounter on Mars?'

'It's nothing to worry about,' the Krsh said. 'No one ever dies from it now.'

At Orme's insistence, Hfathon drove to the hospital, a small one-storey building near the main administration building. However, its smallness was only a surface appearance. It had ten storeys below the ground; Danton was on the sixth. Orme noted, as he passed the windows, that the personnel and patients would have no sense of being buried. On each window was a scene of rural beauty; trees, birds, deer grazing in the meadows, children playing in the distance. The pseudo-scenes looked real.

He found Shirazi and Bronski in a waiting room. They rose as he entered, but they did not have long faces. Indeed, Shirazi was smiling.

'I just heard,' Orme said. 'How's Madeleine?'

'Madeleine's fine,' Nadir said. 'She'll be leaving in a few minutes. The treatment is short but tiring, so she's resting.'

'You mean it's all over? Diagnosis and cure, all done? How?'

Nadir said, 'I find it hard to believe, too. But the doctors have assured me that she is completely well. Moreover, the cancer won't recur.'

Bronski said, 'I was told about her at the university. They thought I should know, but they might just as well have waited until it was over.'

'You're not disturbed because you were interrupted, are you?' Orme said.

'Of course not. What bothers me is that they probably called all of us in to impress us. They wanted to show us how superior their medical science is. And to give us one more item to report to Earth.'

'Wait a minute,' Orme said. 'You've been told, too? I mean that we'll be allowed to communicate with home in twelve days?'

'Yes. Trrwangon – she's my mentor – told me just before I got word about Madeleine.'

Hfathon said, 'The Council decided that it might ease your anxiety if you knew you had only a short wait. Also, you may start preparing your report now. The first part, that is. The second part will be prepared after the eighth day from now. Both parts will be transmitted together.'

'That's great,' Orme said. 'At least, I think it is. Frankly, I think you're up to something we might not like.'

Hfathon smiled.

Nadir Shirazi said, 'It does seem inhumane, if you'll pardon me for saying so, that these wonderful cures should be withheld from Earth. If they were to be transmitted at once, it could mean saving the lives of millions. And it would alleviate much suffering, too.'

'I doubt it,' Hfathon said. 'From what you've told us, even if we gave your scientists that data at this moment, it would be several years before your governments would allow our drugs to be used. First, the data would have to be studied. Then experimental tests on animals would be made. Then the legislators would have to decide whether or not the drugs could be given. Of course, they would eventually do so because of popular demand. But the total process would require anywhere from four to six years. Am I correct?'

'I am afraid so,' Orme said.

'Yet, when, or perhaps I should say *if*, the formulae and the two thousand years of data were given, and the data proved conclusively that the cure rate was 100 per cent, your governments would still require an independent study of their own, right?'

'Right.'

'So what's the rush?'

'We were just thinking about all the people who could be saved,' Shirazi said.

'Not to mention,' Orme said, 'the longevity treatment. The longer the delay in getting it to Earth, the more people will die of the diseases of old age.'

'True. But that can't be helped. If we do give you the age-delaying formulae, we'll do so only under certain strict conditions. The socialist countries will have to treat everybody, no exceptions, at government expense. There will be no such thing as selling it for a profit and so making it available only if the purchaser has the money. The communist countries will have to do the same. They won't be allowed to withhold the treatment from political prisoners.

'Moreover, to ensure that this is done, we will set up administrative units in every country. They'll be organized in such a manner that the governments will not be able to interfere in any way.'

Orme looked at Bronski and Shirazi. Each knew what the other was thinking. It was possible, but not probable, that their own countries would allow this. They would resist, but once the people knew that the treatment would be available, the people would bring irresistible pressure to bear. Even so, the governments would attempt to have some sort of control.

As for the communist nations, they would not permit aliens to move in in the large numbers required for administration. They would suspect that they were spies, and they'd fear the dissemination of anticommunist ideas along with the treatment.

But could they withstand the demands of their citizens once they discovered that extended longevity was being denied them? Wouldn't that lead to riots, even revolution?

Either way, there would be a tremendous disruption. Things would never be the same in any country, no matter what its ideology.

The Martians had a terrible weapon. They could blow Earth apart, in a sense, without firing a shot. In fact, they would wage war under the disguise of conferring a great benefit. Longevity was only one weapon. The elimination of disease was another. But Orme felt that these were feeble compared to something else the Martians had not yet revealed completely. He would, he suspected, soon know all about it.

As a Christian, he should be looking forward to the seventh day from now with ecstasy. But he was shaking with fear – fear which was an anticipation of horror.

11

Hfathon had told them that they could put together a 'programme' lasting four hours. It would be up to them to say and show what they wished. They wouldn't be censored unless their statements were misrepresentations, or outright lies. In these cases, their 'hosts', as Hfathon referred to the Martians, would enlighten them so they could speak truly. But nothing would be excised.

It wasn't as easy as the four had thought it would be. It was difficult making a balanced 'show' because each of the four wanted to present his own speciality as much as possible. After a day-long discussion, they agreed, though reluctantly, that each should cut down his own portion of the programme.

'What's vitally important now is the Martians themselves,' Orme said. 'Their history, including the origins of the Krsh. How they managed to survive and the present state of their society. That is what will really interest our people. The exact details of their sciences can come later. Anyway, if you get down to it, we don't have the information on the really important scientific and technological stuff. And this is obviously just a prelude, a summary of what's happened to us. And how much of that can we get into four hours? We'll have to compress it so much, just skim the surface, that even that'll be bewildering to the folks at home. They'll be so numbed by the first ten minutes they won't comprehend the next two hundred and thirty.'

'Besides,' Madeleine Danton said, 'we really don't know yet how much of what we're preparing now will be shown. We have to save time for whatever happens six days from now.'

She seemed healthy enough, but she was obviously not sleeping well. The suddenness of the discovery of cancer and

112

its equally swift and unexpected treatment had shaken her. Orme suspected, however, that this was not the major factor in her insomnia. The coming event, the appearance of the Messiah, was disturbing her deeply. She just could not believe what the Martians had told her of him. Yet, in light of her experiences here, she could not believe the Martians were lying.

It was strange, Orme thought, that he was as struck with anxiety as she. She was an atheist and so could be expected to be in an emotional turmoil, especially when you considered the devout upbringing she'd had. The conditioned reflexes established in childhood were eating upwards through the dark layers. The religious upbringing hadn't been dissolved; such things never were.

But he . . . he had been born and raised in a fundamentalist Baptist family. To them, everything in the Bible was taken as literally true.

Orme tried to recall everything he knew about Jesus as told in the Bible. Jesus Christ had been born of a virgin, and had died on the cross, atoning for people's sins and assuring them salvation, resurrection and immortality in heaven, if they believed that he was God's son and also God, and if they followed the golden rule, believed certain dogmas and were spiritually 'born again'.

All this Orme had believed, despite certain early convictions and doubts, until he was in high school. From then on the overwhelming evidence for evolution, the billions-year-old age of Earth, and many other things had led him to fall from fundamentalism, but not from grace.

Though he did not believe that the Old Testament was to be taken literally, he did think that the events in the New Testament had happened as portrayed. His parents were horrified at his new attitude. They thought he would go to Hell if he didn't revert to the truth. Though sorrowful because of this, he continued to adhere to his somewhat more liberal Christianity. No longer did he believe that he would go to a hell of fire and brimstone and eternal physical torture if he lacked faith in the utter literalness of the Old Testament. He might go to hell, but it would be a spiritual one, the horrible knowledge that he would be forever cut off from God.

Also, he did things that he knew were wrong. Occasionally, he got drunk, and he lay with girls before he got married. But once he'd taken a wife, he was faithful to her, though it wasn't easy. The divorce had been shattering. Hadn't Christ said that the only excuse for divorce was infidelity? But he lived in a society in which divorce was almost as easy as marriage. In any event, he had not wished for the divorce, but it had been useless to fight against it in the courts.

So, here he was, a man who prayed to God and His son every night and sometimes in the day, who hoped some day to see His son face to face.

If the Martians were to be believed, he soon would be face to face with the living Jesus. Why, then, this quivering unease, thudding heart, sickness in the stomach, and desire to run? Was it because he would have to decide whether or not this was the true Christ? That was a judgment that he did not think he was competent to make, though the Bible certainly gave the clues to help separate the true from the false.

But here were the Martians, saying that Jesus dwelt with them, though he stayed most of the time in the globe that replaced the sun for them. They said they had undeniable proof of their assertions. Yet from what Matthias said, who had known Jesus in Palestine and on Mars, he was only a man, though in a sense more than that since he was the Messiah.

Matthias had been one of the Purishim, the 'separatists', of the Pharisees. Jesus had cursed the Pharisees and the rival party, the Sadducees. But the maledictions against the Pharisees had been only applied to the hypocrites among them. Unlike their rivals the Sadducees, they believed in the resurrection and the angels, which Jesus also believed in. And though they were stricter than he, still they admitted that the

114

laws of Moses were subject to evolution. They wouldn't blindly follow them if they disagreed with reason or conscience.

When the Pharisees rebuked Jesus for breaking the Sabbath or for sitting down to eat with tax-collectors and other sinners, and for not washing his hands before taking a meal he had replied, 'The sabbath was made for man, not man for the sabbath.'

This was a principle that, in theory at least, the Pharisees could have agreed with. Their reply to Jesus was not recorded in the New Testament, but Matthias said that in time many of his interrogators came to agree with him on this point.

The Pharisees were also deeply concerned about salvation. Not just the salvation of the Jews, but the salvation of all humanity. Eventually, they believed, all Gentiles would accept the Law and have but one God, though the Law would be that of Moses and God would be Yahweh. The nation of Israel would be foremost of all, an elder and wiser brother. Also, the Pharisees, unlike the other sects, believed in vigorous proselytizing and converting the pagans to Judaism.

Jesus, though not a Pharisee, did agree with many of their tenets and practices. For a time, he had been an Essene, according to Matthias, but he had found the community around Qumran too strict, lacking in the humanity of those who truly loved the sons of Adam and Eve. So he had departed.

Orme, unable to read Matthias's book swiftly enough to finish it before the coming great event, had insisted that Bronski read it aloud to him. The Frenchman had done so, though he stopped now and then to explain difficult passages.

When the end was reached, Orme had shaken his head. And he'd said, 'I'm more confused than ever. Matthias was a disciple and an apostle, and he knew Jesus intimately, accompanied him throughout Palestine. He should be giving the straight stuff, since his account hasn't been tampered with. He says nothing of the virgin birth and he doesn't know the doctrine that Christ's death was an atonement for the sins of mankind and therefore their route to salvation. He says nothing of the miracles which the Biblical writers say he performed. Apparently, he didn't see them, though he was with Jesus much of the time. He does say that he heard stories about the miracles after Jesus had died. But he discounts them, since he knew they weren't true.

'His account of the trial before Pilate differs considerably from that in the Gospels. And he was there. He says Pilate didn't wash his hands of the whole affair . . .'

'That,' Bronski said, 'was a reconstruction by later writers who wanted to fix the blame entirely on the Jews. That is, those Jews who refused to accept him as the Messiah and as the parthenogenetic offspring of God and Mary.'

'Yeah, I know. No miracles while Jesus was on Earth. But after they are forced to land on Mars and to dig in, then Jesus appears and Matthias instantly recognizes him. And *then* Jesus performs some miracles. *Then* . . .'

'That,' Bronski said, 'explains why the Krsh were converted to Judaism.'

'They wouldn't have accepted them without rigorously produced scientific evidence,' Orme said. 'So what am I to think?' -

'Wait and see what happens.'

'You seem to be ready, whatever happens,' Shirazi said. His tone was slightly scornful.

Three weeks before, Bronski had quit shaving, and he had started to grow sidelocks. Instead of going to bed when Orme did, he would sit up in the living room reading the Pentateuch in Hebrew, a direct descendant of the copy which Matthias had brought with him from Earth. Orme had asked him why he was doing all this.

'This isn't Palestine, and I haven't returned to the ways of my forefathers. Not yet. Nor am I anything but an agnostic. But . . . well . . . I have had this strange feeling that I've returned home after a long, painful voyage. Home! On Mars!

There's no explaining it now. Maybe I never will be able to. Still . . . here I am, like Ruth standing in the alien corn, and the corn doesn't look so alien.'

'Be sure it's not corny,' Orme said.

'Yes. Perhaps it is pride, an unwillingness to admit that I've been wrong, to destroy my self-image utterly, that keeps me from making the final step. Anyway, even if I went to the synagogue, I wouldn't be admitted. I'd have to acknowledge that Yeshua' is indeed the Messiah. I don't know about that . . . yet.'

Shirazi had observed all this, but until now he had said nothing to Bronski. He was as much in a quandry as the others. Perhaps more so. He was a Muslim, though not particularly devout. Like his three companions, he'd been shocked to discover that Mars was a Jewish domain. After all, if they'd guessed who might be its inhabitants, they would never have included this possibility in the list. He might have been expected to be uneasy in a place where he was the only Muslim among a million Jews. But these people had never heard of his religion until he had arrived. Besides, Shirazi was a well-educated, urbane man who seldom failed to meld smoothly into any society in which he found himself. In his native land, though, he had got into trouble because of his protests against its censorship policy and its police methods.

Moreover, in some respects the Martian ways paralleled those of his country. The men were circumcised; the women were expected to choose motherhood as their first career; there were certain strict dietary prohibitions. There were certain allotted periods for public prayer, and the Sabbath was well observed.

Also, here Jesus was regarded as a prophet, though the attitude differed from that of the Muslims. These held Jesus in high esteem, but they ranked him as second to Mohammed, whereas here Jesus was the last and the greatest of a line starting with Abraham. The prophet of Islam, Mohammed, was a total nonentity.

Despite the differences, there were enough similarities to make the Iranian feel somewhat at home. And here there was no tension between Muslim and Jew because the Jew still occupied Palestine.

But when it became obvious to Shirazi that Bronski was thinking about 'relapsing', as he put it, into orthodox Judaism he became sarcastic. He'd even hinted that Bronski was an opportunist.

'Besides,' he'd once said during a heated but restrained exchange with the Frenchman, 'you won't really be a Jew. You'll be a Christian.'

'Not so,' Bronski had replied. 'A Christian is one who believes that Jesus is the virgin-begotten child of God and Mary and that he was sent to atone for the sins of the world, to be the scapegoat of ancient Hebrew custom. The Martians regard Jesus as their Messiah, and that is all. Anyway, you Muslims, if you believe Mohammed, must believe in Jesus's virgin birth. It is stated in the Koran that He was indeed born of the virgin Mary. Though Mohammed did say that Jesus was not really crucified. He said that it was a phantom, a ghostly similitude of Jesus, that was nailed to the cross and appeared to die.'

Surprisingly, Shirazi had laughed, and some of the tension had evaporated.

'In the first place, I've met many Christians who disbelieve the virgin-birth story. They think it's a myth, that Jesus was conceived just as you and I were. He was only a man, though the greatest. And there are many Muslims who take certain stories in the Koran in a symbolic or pedagogic sense. I'm one of them.

'So, when you speak of a person as a Muslim or Christian, you must define what sort of Muslim or Christian he is. However, this is getting us nowhere. If I've said anything to offend you, I'm sorry. But I cannot understand why a highly intelligent, highly educated man can be tempted to regress to a primitive state of religion.'

Bronski had thrown his hands up in the air and walked out.

As he went through the door, he had shouted, 'I'm not tempted! There is no temptation! Because this isn't a primitive religion!'

Now, when Shirazi said that Bronski seemed to be ready for any contingency, he was hinting again that Bronski was using protective coloration. So far, he had not said that possibly Bronski was a traitor to Earth.

'What you don't seem to understand,' Bronski said, 'is that religion is a choice, not of the intellect, but of the spirit. By spirit I mean the irrational being of a person. But I am not using "irrational" in a disparaging sense. The irrational is that part of a man that yearns for immortality despite the evidence of his intellect that says there is none. It also yearns for the Creator, his Father, for whom there *is* much evidence of existence. It acknowledges a Power behind all powers. It is as much a person as his brain, and without it a human being is not truly human. He may be humane, but he is not thoroughly human. That is because . . .'

Orme said, 'Look. This has gone far enough. You two can continue this some other time. Right now we have to get this show together. We don't have much time left.'

Madeleine said, 'I think you've having a nervous break-down, Avram.'

'That's enough of that!' Orme said. 'We're all under a hell of a strain. And I'm not sure that Earth won't think we're crazy when they see this. But we have to tell them what is. So, let's get to work.'

Since the viewers on Earth knew what had happened up to the moment that the tunnel door had shut on Orme and Bronski, it was decided to take it from there. The Martians had photographed the two being carried unconscious to their prison. They also had holograms of everything significant that had taken place since – Orme suspected they had recordings of much of the insignificant, too – so the four could pick what they wished to show.

They took turns narrating the segments, in many of which they were active participants. Or perhaps not so active, since they were being conducted on tours or being taught by the Martians. By the time they were finished, they had what they considered a good overall picture of Martian life and of their experiences since they'd been here.

Of course, Earth would have a thousand questions. These wouldn't be answered, but what could you do in four hours? Besides, many of the questions would have answers which they did not yet know.

'But we should know some of them tomorrow,' Orme said.

'Yes, but they'll generate even more questions, which we won't be able to answer,' Bronski said.

They went to bed late that night, tired out but unable to get to sleep. All had the feeling that the morning would bring the most important day of their life.

Finally, Orme fell aleep, Bronski having subsided into a gentle snoring. But he awoke an hour later. Someone, he felt, had been standing by his bedside.

12

'Tomorrow's the Day,' Orme said.

The four Terrestrials were sitting in the living room of the Shirazis. After supper, they had dropped the cassette – actually a cube about an inch across – into the receptacle on the side of the TV set. They had watched, for the fourth time, the programme they'd put together. As the Martians had promised, little of it was censored. The last half hour had been made by their hosts, and this was composed in the main of films of Jesus's activities when he 'visited'. There were also some scenes of Earth life taken by the Krsh about 50 AD, of the space fight with the Sons of Darkness, and of the digging into Mars after the Krsh's vessel had crashlanded.

The programme ended with Hfathon speaking briefly in Greek except for his final word.

'This is all true. We will communicate with you again in a few days. *Shalom.*'

Orme could imagine the shock, the consternation, the bewilderment, the frustration on Earth. Of course, there would be many who would deny the validity of the programme. They would denounce it as a hoax perpetrated by the Martians, by their own government, or by some other government. However, those in authority would have to accept that, whatever the content of the transmission, it had originated from Mars. Also, the programme had been repeated enough times to ensure that both hemispheres of Earth received it.

'Yes, tomorrow,' Bronski said gloomily.

Madeleine Danton laughed, though not merrily.

'You're afraid that you're going to have to believe in Christ, aren't you? You, the agnostic, will see and touch and hear, and therefore have to believe! I say, nonsense! It's a charade put on by the Martians for some sinister purposes of their own!'

'You're a scientist,' Bronski said, 'but you're not thinking like one. I believe that, even if the evidence becomes overwhelming, 100 per cent authenticated, you'd still reject it. You'd allow your emotional, irrational attitude to control you.'

'And you,' she said, 'aren't even waiting until the evidence is in. You're ready to believe!'

He shook his head. 'No, I'm not. But all that's happened so far . . . well . . . you must admit it's been totally unexpected, it's fantastic, and yet it's happened. Do you doubt for one minute that Matthias did exist, and that Matthias knew Jesus very well indeed? Or that a person called Jesus does dwell in that sun?'

Madeleine said, 'I admit nothing. How can I? I haven't had a chance to examine the evidence in a scientific manner.'

'How can you?' Nadir Shirazi said. He threw his hands up. 'This is something to which science can't be applied.'

'Oh, yes it can!' Madeleine said, and at this moment Orme interrupted.

'It's useless to argue about what might happen. Why don't we shelve speculation now, since it's just going to make everybody angry. I'm going out out to watch the celebration. Anyone want to join me?'

Bronski and Shirazi said they'd like to. Madeleine refused, saying she was tired. Evidently she wanted the Iranian to stay, too, but she would not say so. He just looked at her and shrugged. Orme wondered how long they'd be able to stay together. Though he hadn't witnessed any arguments, he had noticed a coolness between them lately, one interspersed with restrained disagreements.

'I'll be back early,' Nadir said.

This time, she shrugged.

He laughed, and he followed the other two out.

Once outside the well-insulated house, they could hear the

music and the shouting and laughter several blocks away. They walked to the big square of the village, lit by hundreds of torches, where many acquaintances grabbed them and offered them wine and food. Orme drank several glasses and then joined in the dancing. This was very active, involving much whirling and kicking and hopping. It reminded him more of Russian peasant dancing than Israeli, and the music was, literally, unearthly, since it was derived from that of the Krsh.

After an hour he was worn out, though the lesser gravity should have permitted him to continue longer. Perhaps it was all the wine he drank, since many of the dances also required the participants to leap around without spilling the wine, and at certain pauses everybody downed their drinks and then people ran and refilled them. Or perhaps it was the nervous strain he'd been under. He hadn't been sleeping well lately. Nightmares, visions of the Last Judgement, of mysterious faceless figures pointing their fingers accusingly at him, of groping through a fog and suddenly finding himself on the edge of an abyss, had filled his nights. And more than once he'd been awakened by the feeling that someone had been standing by his his bed.

Panting, he'd walked away. 'I've had it! I'm going home!'

The others decided to retire, too. But as they made their way through the noisy throng, he felt a hand on his shoulder. He turned and looked into Gulthilo's blue eyes.

'What're you doing here?' he said. Then, 'I'm sorry to speak so abruptly. But you startled me. You're so far from your village.'

She smiled and moved closer to him so he could hear her above the din.

'I'm being bold and brash again. I came here just to be with you.'

'What'll your family say?'

'They don't own me. Would you like to dance with me?'

Orme looked at his colleagues, who were standing a few feet away.

'You guys go on!' he shouted. 'Avram, don't wait up for me!'

Bronski, frowning, walked up to him.

'Richard, don't get into any trouble. You know the moral code. They . . .'

'I can take care of myself,' he said. 'You go on. I'll be all right.'

Bronski, still looking grave, walked off, said something to Shirazi, and they left, though not without some backward glances.

'I'm too pooped out to dance,' he said to the woman. 'Maybe we could just sit down and talk.'

Gulthilo took his hand and led him through the crowd. When they were out of the square, she stopped, gracefully sat down on to the grass of a front yard under a tree, and said, 'Sit with me.'

He did so, but he looked worriedly around him. There were at least a dozen couples sitting or lying nearby in the shadows. From what he could see of one, he imagined that their marriage would have to be announced soon.

She kissed him on his cheek and he almost jumped.

'Don't be so nervous, Richard,' she whispered. 'I'm not going to seduce you.' She laughed softly. 'Not that I would mind if you seduced me.'

'Don't talk that way,' he said. 'I'm very vulnerable. It wouldn't take much, you know. But *here*, well, you're supposed to be in love when you, ah, lie with a woman. I think you're very beautiful, very attractive, but . . . I'm not in love with you.'

She didn't draw away from him.

'Thanks for being frank. How could you be in love with me when we've only been together once for a short time? But,' she paused, drew in her breath sharply, and said, 'I think I'm in love with you.'

The sweat pouring down his face was not just from dancing. Nor was the shaking entirely caused by over-exertion. He put his arm around her shoulders but dropped it after a few seconds.

'I don't think we should be so close. I need cooling off, not heating up.'

She laughed again.

'But if we mated, you'd be doing it because of passion, for lust, right?'

'Well, I don't really know. What the hell kind of conversation is this? It's unbelievable. Are you drunk?'

'No, I've only had four glasses of wine in the past two hours. And those were in my village. I just left the festivities there, without a word, and I drove here. It wasn't just on impulse. I'd been thinking about you all day, but I had to work up my courage to the point where I could do what I wanted to do.'

He started to get up, but she pulled him down.

'Don't be a coward, my brave spaceman.'

'It's not cowardice, it's, uh, just good plain common sense, discretion. And I'm afraid I'm losing them fast. Listen, Gulthilo, this is crazy! If we were on Earth, I wouldn't hesitate a second, since we'd both know exactly where we stand. But we're on Mars, and this society is different from mine. Mine has been very permissive, but even there attitudes are changing, and things are not going to be so loose. But that's not the point. Even if you were willing to take the chance, uh, to do it just for the sake of passion . . . what am I saying? I'm talking like somebody in a Victorian novel! You know what I mean.'

Gulthilo stood up. Though it was dark, there was enough light for him to see that she was still smiling. If she was hurt, she wasn't showing it.

'You're wrong to believe that I wouldn't lie with you unless you were in love with me.' She paused. 'I think.'

He didn't like looking up at her, so he stood up. But he still had to bend his head back. She was so tall.

'Little black man whom I love so much, I'm going back to my village now. I may or may not see you again, though I think I will. I'd like it very much if you came to see me instead of my seeking you out. But if you do, then I'll know that you know you're in love with me.'

'You mean, I'll be asking you to marry me?' he said, hoarsely.

'Of course. You're vibrating like a plucked harp string. You're shaken, aren't you?'

She reached out and enfolded him in her arms and kissed him on the mouth. For a moment, feeling the large soft breasts crushed against him, those large soft lips against his, he almost weakened. But she released him and he stood back, her hand on his shoulder. She had a very strong grip.

'*Shalom*, Richard. Though I imagine you don't feel so peaceful just now.'

Laughing softly, she swayed away.

Orme expelled a long hard breath. What a woman! A lioness! And what a state she'd left him in! His groin ached; he was quivering.

On the way home he began to feel cooler, and his thoughts stopped seething. Perhaps, and he cursed his eternal suspicion, she was working for the Martian government. It had appointed her to seduce him so that he'd marry her. And if he did that, then he might abandon his Terrestrial ties, become a Martian.

Or perhaps she was supposed to seduce him and then, if he refused to make her an honest woman, as the old phrase went, he could be imprisoned as a criminal. Or perhaps . . .

To hell with those speculations. If she was a seductress, she certainly was not a conventional one. She could have had him if she'd really tried.

Near his house he passed a drunken half-disrobed couple under a bush. One more marriage in the making.

Bronski was sitting in the front room watching the

festivities on the TV. He looked up as Orme entered but said nothing.

'You can quit worrying,' Orme said. 'Here I am, and the virtue of the native women is untouched. At least, the one you saw with me is as chaste as she ever was.'

'It would have been a damn fool thing to do,' Bronski said. 'Who was she?'

'The woman with the Gothic name. I told you about her.'

The Frenchman stood up. 'I'm going to bed. I was really concerned about you. You could have got into terrible trouble.'

'Not to mention the moral reflection on you and the others,' Orme said. 'No, there wouldn't have been any terrible trouble. All I'd have had to do was marry her. And she's certainly willing.'

'You mean . . . ?'

'Yes. She proposed.'

'And . . . ?'

'I turned her down, though I didn't really put it into words. I mean, I told her I didn't love her.'

'And if you did love her?'

'I don't know. If I marry her I have to convert to Judaism. Or the Martian brand of Christianity or whatever it is. You know that. Once I do that, I become a Martian. My loyalties to Earth are dissolved. At least, they're supposed to. Could I do that? I mean, turn Martian? It sounds too much like a turncoat.'

'Not at all,' Bronski said. He was smiling, caught up in a problem that probably seemed to him rabbinical.

Bronski said, 'For one thing, your loyalties are not to Earth, as you put it. They're to your nation, Canada, primarily. Secondarily, to the North American Confederation. You have no loyalty whatsoever to the communist nations. You're thinking of Earth as a monolithic entity as opposed to the monolithic entity of Mars. Mars is one, but Earth is not. You

127

need to reorganize your thinking, not to mention your emotions.'

'What's the difference between the two?'

Bronski frowned, then smiled.

'In most people, there's none. Well, you ponder on it. I'm going to bed.'

He started towards the bedroom, then stopped.

'Say, you know when you said that you showed perception.'

'What?'

'About the difference between thinking and emotion. Or I should say, to quote you, "What's the difference?" Very good.'

Orme said, 'Wait a minute. I only said . . . I don't know what I was saying.'

'The basic part of you did. Good night, Richard. You should get to bed too. Tomorrow . . . that may be the most important day of our lives. You should be rested. You'll need all your strength, physical, mental, emotional. If there's any difference in them.'

Orme said goodnight, but he paced back and forth for at least two hours. His thoughts alternated between Gulthilo and that man who was said to live inside the Martian sun. Both offered, or seemed to offer, a new life. Yet, at this moment, both were unacceptable. And, if they became acceptable, they would present him with new problems. But any new life, however better than the old, introduced new problems.

Did he really believe in the validity of either? She might be an agent to tempt him into becoming a Martian. As for the man called Jesus, he could be a hoax. Or, if not that, something other than what the Martians claimed he was.

Whatever he was, he wasn't what Orme had expected him to be. Orme believed, or thought he'd believed, that Jesus was the only begotten son of God, and that his purpose had been determined always, from before the beginning of time. He

128

had sacrificed himself so that all the world might be saved, might live forever in blessedness, in the ecstasy of seeing God face to face. One day, a day that had been promised for more than two thousand years, the Last Judgement would come with uttermost terror and absolute joy. And those who had rejected God would go to hell. Hell would be the realization that God was forever denied to the damned.

But here was Jesus, not on Earth but on Mars. And he was only a man who had thought of himself, when on Earth, as the Messiah, a Jew come to restore the holy kingdom of the Jews. Very little that had been written about him in the New Testament was true.

Orme should have been shattered by this revelation. The shock had been great but not as great as it should have been. Why? Because his belief had not really been as deep and firmly fixed as he had thought. He'd paid more than lip service to his religion, but it hadn't been rooted in his heart. He hadn't really been convinced. Not down there where the genuine, the living, convictions lived and looked up through the deep at the pseudo-convictions, the half-dead, swimming in what they thought was the light. The real light was in the darkness.

He went outside. It was quiet now. Everybody had gone home; the houses were dark. Possibly there were policemen patrolling the streets, but he saw no one. Anyway, though he knew they existed, he had never seen a policeman. According to what he'd been told, they didn't wear uniforms, and there were very few of them. That told him a lot about this society, the only one of its kind in the solar system. Where was there a better place to live? Nowhere.

He walked out into the silent street and looked up at the globe hanging below the apex of the cavern. It shone now with a candlepower equal to that of Earth's full moon. It even had the same markings, the man in the moon if you were a Westerner, the hare if you were a Japanese.

Up there, inside the glowing sphere, a man did live – if you could believe the Martians. There was no reason not to but he just could not accept the reality.

He stood for a moment, his neck bent back. And then he lifted up both hands and shouted, 'You up there! Do you have the answers to my questions?'

There was, of course no reply.

13

The sky was a great light show.

Orme, looking out of the window, saw that the blue had become spectra. Horizontal bands of bright and flashing purples, blues, oranges, red, greens, yellows, whites, and blacks were spread around the dome. Here and there, gold, indigo, scarlet, and silver stars were born, expanded, and exploded. Variously-shaped clouds of different colours and hues sprang from scattered points, swelled, raced writhing across the sky, and the starbursts momentarily met, coalesced, glowed, pulsed then faded away.

'Hey, Avram, come look at this!'

Bronski joined him, and his eyes grew large.

'It makes me shiver.'

'I wonder how they do that?' Orme said. 'The whole dome must be set with electronic devices.'

'No, I don't think so. You forget how far ahead of us they are. I'll wager that they use some principle unknown to us. Anyway, that's a small item to consider today. Forget you are an engineer, Richard. At least for today.'

The people were coming out of their houses. They were dressed in their best, both sexes clad in long silky robes of many colours, wearing flowers in their hair. They were laughing and skipping, many hand in hand. Orme opened the door and stepped outside. Now he could hear music from a distance, many bands playing: drums beating, trumpets blaring, flutes and fifes shrilling, harps twanging, cymbals crashing.

Abruptly a voice spoke from behind them. Orme turned to see Bronski gesturing for him to come back in. He did so and found the holograph image of a smiling Hfathon before the set.

'We expect you at the square in an hour,' he said. 'You'd better start out at once. It won't be easy to get through the crowds.'

Orme looked at his wristwatch.

'Yes, we know. Couldn't you send someone to drive us there?'

'The only one who rides today is the Messiah,' the Krsh said. 'Last night everybody drove or walked in and set up camp or stayed with relatives or friends. Perhaps I should have told you you'd be expected to walk. Please hurry. May he smile upon you. *Shalom.*'

His image blinked out.

Orme looked at Bronski, shrugged his shoulders, and said, 'You'd think they'd give us special treatment. After all, we are their guests. And part of this is for our benefit.'

The Frenchman looked at the gloriously pulsating sky.

'You still suspect that this is a hoax?'

'Now, I didn't say that!' Orme said. 'It's just that I have to keep a tight rein on my emotions.'

'You're not the only one,' Bronski said. 'Well, we'd better get going.'

They went out of the house again. Orme thought of how nice it was that he didn't have to lock the door. Then he thought, that was an irrelevant thought. Or was it? I've been trying all this morning to think of irrelevant things. To get my mind away from . . . Him. But it's like trying not to think about a hippopotamus.

They went out into the street, which was by then empty of Martians. Shirazi, looking pale and grim, stepped out of the house directly opposite theirs. Orme met him in the middle of the street.

'Where's Madeleine?'

'She says she's not going. She doesn't feel well.'

'Did she tell Hfathon that?'

Nadir shook his head. 'No. She didn't say a word to him.'

Orme grimaced. 'That's a hell of a note. Is she really sick?'

Shirazi nodded. 'Yes, but I don't believe it's from any physical cause. She's emotionally upset. She keeps saying that this is all a trick, a big con. So why should she go? I told her she had to because it would insult the Martians if she didn't.'

Orme got angry, but he told himself that perhaps he felt so furious because he was experiencing the same emotions as she. It was fear that was making her sick, the fear that this might be true.

But why should he, a Christian, be so terrified? Shouldn't he be as joyous as the Martians?

'This is nonsense,' he said loudly. 'Let's get her . . . if we have to drag her there!'

He led the others into the house. He had expected that at least she'd have the TV set on so she could see the events. But it was off, and she was lying in her bed. When she saw him storm in, she sat up.

'You might at least have the decency to knock!'

'You knew we were coming. Come on, Madeleine, get up and get going. Quit acting like a child!'

That brought her to her feet. Eyes wide, face distorted, she spewed French at him. Then she stopped, passed her hand over her face, shook, and said, in English, 'You got me mad to make me get out of bed, didn't you?'

He nodded. 'You have to go, Madeleine, unless you're really sick. In which case, I'll get a doctor.'

He didn't add that the doctor would be able to determine if she really were ill; she couldn't fake it.

'I don't know what's the matter with me,' she said. 'But I can make it. It's just that . . .'

'That you're like me,' he said. 'You're afraid it might be true.'

133

'What? But you . . . ?'

'Let's talk about it some other time.'

They went out into the street and walked down along it until they came to the edge of the crowd. Neither said a word and the two men spoke in low voices to each other infrequently. When they reached the square, they drowned in a seastorm of noise. Everybody was talking, and what seemed like a hundred bands were blasting away. As for the numbers here, Orme thought there had to be a million people at least. They were squeezed shoulder to shoulder, breast to back, forming a colossal ring around a broad high stone platform in the centre of the square. Orme had never seen it before. The reason for that was that its top had been flush with the pavement. It was rising slowly now out of the ground. On its top stood about fifty men and women.

Shirazi yelled, 'How can we get through? It's hopeless!'

'Hfathon must have known this!' Orme yelled. 'What's he up to? He should have made arrangements to get us here early!'

He jumped as someone touched his shoulder. Turning, he saw a Krsh dressed in a green robe with a crimson slash angling across its chest.

Behind him was a long silvery boat. At least, it looked like a rowboat, though there were no oarlocks or oars.

The Krsh turned and walked away, gesturing at Orme to follow him. Orme got the others' attention, and led them to the craft. The Krsh reached into his robe and pulled out a small metallic cylinder. Holding one end against his lips, he spoke. His voice blared out.

'Please get into the *shrrt*.'

The four looked at each other, shrugged, and climbed in, where they sat down on low high-backed seats. The Krsh sat down at the chair in the bow and pulled out from under the bow covering a small box with levers. He turned and spoke through the bullhorn.

'Hang on. It'll just take a minute.'

He did something to the levers. Gently, the boat lifted off the ground straight up, paused when it was twenty feet above the ground, turned towards the platform, and slowly accelerated towards it. There was no noise from any propulsive unit, though it could have been drowned by the roar of the mob. Nor was there any feeling by the passengers that power was being applied.

When the boat was above the platform it lowered gently, landed, and the Krsh indicated that they should get out. A moment later it rose and, going faster this time, shot out beyond the crowd. There it landed, and the Krsh got out.

Hfathon said, 'You could have got here by asking the people to step aside. They would've made a path for you. But you were behind schedule, so I ordered a *shrrt*.'

His expression indicated that they had failed some sort of test. Probably the IQ, Orme thought. He did not mention Madeleine's reluctance. The Krsh, however, must have known that there was something wrong with her. Her skin was almost grey, and her eyes moved from side to side as if she expected something to come at her. Possibly, though, he didn't look any better. Was he pale beneath his dark pigment, and did his face look strained?

Neither Bronski nor Shirazi looked at ease.

The platform was still moving upwards slowly, but when it was about thirty-five feet above the ground, it stopped. Minutes passed. He looked up near the globe, shading his eyes. It was burning as brightly as ever.

A Krsh stepped out of the closely packed throng in the centre of the shaft. His robe was branded with alternating white and blue, over his real beard he wore a false one, long, curling, and red, and in his right hand was the shaft of a shepherd's crook of some dark blue wood.

'Rabbi Manasseh ben-Makhir,' Hfathon said in Orme's ear.

135

The rabbi lifted the staff. The roar and the music faded to a complete silence except for a number of crying babies. A woman at the edge of the crowd below the platform uncovered and stuck her nipple in her baby's mouth, and then it fell silent. Orme, seeing the magnificent breast, felt a surge in his groin. A moment later, he felt shame. Here he was waiting for the Messiah to appear, due in a few minutes, and he was sexually excited.

'Lord, forgive me,' he murmured.

But he thought, how could I help it? It's been a long time, and I'm no saint.

The rabbi began chanting, and on the third phrase the crowd joined in. The words were in Hebrew, which Orme did not understand but he chanted with them, filling in with nonsense words for a while, then switching to the Lord's Prayer in English.

Hfathon nudged him then and said, 'It's not necessary for you to join in with them. Better to be silent than say the wrong words.'

Orme felt his face burning.

The rabbi lifted his staff again. Silence once more, except for the screaming of babies. This time, though, there seemed to be fewer. Orme didn't look down; he didn't want to be distracted by bare breasts. Nevertheless, he thought, he can read my mind, and he'll know. But a second later he thought that that was surely nonsense. After all, according to what he'd been told, the Messiah was only a man – though adopted by God – and was not a telepath. And then he thought, anyway, I don't know that he is what they say he is. Maybe Danton is right.

A moment later, he murmured, 'Oh, Lord, help me get rid of my doubts. Make me believe the truth.'

Ah, so there it was! But was that just the child in him speaking, the child who had believed everything his father and mother had told him? The child that never dies?

He became aware that while he'd been lost in his thought the rabbi was leading the crowd in another chant, this one in Krsh. That he could understand, or much of it anyway, and he joined in. But the third chant was in Hebrew, and he kept silent, aware of Hfathon's stern gaze.

The rabbi lifted his staff; the million voices, except for the infants', fell away like a dying surf. Slowly, the glowing pulsating lights died out to be replaced by the solid blue. But, immediately, the sun began to get dark, and at this a long drawn-out cry of awe arose. Swiftly, the blue sky became dull, then black. The sphere glowed redly, then became invisible as night filled the cavern. Orme could not even see Hfathon or Danton next to him. There was only a total darkness around him and inside him, and the only sound was the singing in his ears, the blood moving through its channels. Even the babies were quiet now, though he would have expected them and the younger children to cry out.

How long did this last? He couldn't say. It seemed like many minutes. Suddenly, there was a thump, and he jumped. It was the butt of the rabbi's staff striking the stone, and then his voice lifted up, and the crowd chanted again.

He had not ceased to look up, so he saw the first blackish-red glow of the sun returning to life. Gradually, it became brighter, and then its glow stayed at a level which enabled him to see the others near him and the inner circle of the crowd. But it was a ghostly light, and the people looked like phantoms.

Again, the people sang, and at the end of it the sun became somewhat brighter. Once more, there was an exclamation of awe from the people. Now he could see a black dot against the orange globe. It moved down towards him, becoming larger.

The sun brightened some more, though not so much that he could not look into it for a second or two at intervals. The object descending was now near enough to be seen as a tiny man.

He moaned, and he gripped Danton's hand. It was cold and wet.

Behind him, someone farted loudly.

Orme giggled; he couldn't help it. He expected the culprit to be reprimanded, but the others on the platform broke into a loud laugh. He looked around and saw Ya'aqob grinning but red with shame. The rabbi, who did not find this amusing, though he must have known that the laughter was release from tension, thumped his staff on the stone and shouted for silence.

Orme looked upwards again.

Danton said, 'Your teeth are chattering, Richard.'

He ground his teeth together, became aware that he was shaking as if he had a fever, and he said, 'You don't look so great yourself, Madeleine.'

Neither did Shirazi seem well composed. His skin was pale, and he was biting his lip. Bronski's lips were open, his teeth clamped together, his hands raised half-clenched to the level of his chest.

A man clad in a sky-blue robe floated downward. His feet were bare. His long hair trailed behind him, hair that seemed to be dark-red. His arms hung down at his sides, and his head was thrown back.

The rabbi cried, '*Ya Yeshua' ha-Meshiakh*!' and the mob roared out the same greeting.

'Oh, Jesus the Messiah!'

The man who alighted on the platform amidst the screams and yells and sobbing of a million people was about five feet eleven inches tall. His hair was Titian and so was his beard. The face was that of a handsome Levantine. It did not, however have the features impressed upon the famous shroud of Turin. His arms were muscular but not massive. His hands were large, but the long fingers made them seem less broad.

The eyes were black, liquid, and luminous. The lips were,

Orme thought, a little too thick for a Caucasian's, but then who was he to criticize? The cheekbones were high; the cheeks, somewhat sunken; the nose, long and slightly aquiline; the chin, strong and well-rounded and deeply clefted. His skin was a beautiful golden-brown.

He stood there for a moment, looking at the people upon the platform. Then he turned and raised his right hand and spoke in a rich baritone, a voice with great authority.

'May The Spirit of Holiness continue to smile upon you, my children. He has been well-pleased with you, and the Day of the Return is near.'

The crowd cheered for many minutes. Finally, he raised his hand for silence, and he got it at once, except for the babies, who were crying again.

'The Return is close, but there is much work to be done before then. Tomorrow, your leaders will tell you what the details are; you know the outline of the plan. Thus, I will not, as I have in the past, spend this day with you.'

The crowd groaned.

He smiled, and said, 'But I will not be going back to my home as soon as I have been accustomed to. This time I will be with you for two weeks.'

A million cheered.

Hfathon bellowed in Orme's ears. 'You four are especially honoured! He must be staying because of you!'

Orme scarcely heard him. He was getting numb, though not so much that he was not aware of his trembling. He felt an intense painful urge to urinate. The figure of Jesus was wavering as if he were seeing it through heat waves.

Jesus lifted his hand. Again, as if a switch had been pulled, the noise of the mob was turned off.

'Go now, my children, to the synagogue and worship your Father and afterwards enjoy yourself with feasting and laughter and love and all the good things that your Father has blessed you with. *Shalom.*'

Jesus turned then and walked towards the four. Orme sank to his knees and kissed the hand held out to him.

'Forgive me, Lord,' he said. 'I doubted; I've done bad things. I . . .'

Everything whirled. The next he was aware, he was on his back looking up at the bearded face.

'What happened?'

'You fainted,' Hfathon said. 'So did Madeleine.'

14

The four Terrestrials were in the front room of the Shirazis' house.

'It was all emotional,' Orme said. 'A matter of conditioned reflexes; my childhood beliefs took over. I'm okay now. Cool, real cool. I can look at him objectively.'

He added, grinning faintly, 'As long as he isn't around.'

Madeleine had said very little since she had left the platform and, supported by Nadir, had walked home. Orme supposed that she was ashamed and humiliated. No wonder. She'd been a staunch atheist since she was eighteen. She openly scorned those who believed that God could exist and she laughed at those who claimed that Jesus was His Son. It was true that the Martians had made no claim about virgin birth. In fact, they denied it. Nevertheless, the sight of a man floating down from the sun, a man whom the Martians not only believed had lived over two thousand years but who could prove it, and this man's close resemblance to the portraits hanging in her parents' home and to those in churches and art galleries, all this had stormed through her. And the long-buried but never-dead beliefs had taken over.

Or was it that she had suddenly doubted that she had been right? And her self-image as a scientifically minded sceptic, a thoroughly rational person, had been destroyed? One of the worst things that could happen to a human being was to have the self-image brutally crumbled and swept away in a very short time. There were no defences against that except insanity or suicide – unless the ravaged person was very strong.

She was strong, or at least he had always thought so until now. At this moment she looked as if she were partially recovered from a long illness.

Avram Bronski broke the long silence that had followed Orme's words.

'I was almost overcome, too,' he said. 'So don't you feel so bad about it, Richard. It was a tremendous experience. However, as you say, we have to remain cool. After all, there are explanations for his being able to float through the air without any visible means of support. *Visible* is the key word. Who knows what device he had under his robe? That aircraft that took us to the platform didn't have any visible means of propulsion either. So why couldn't he?'

This was reasonable. Yet no one really thought this was the right explanation. The man called Jesus radiated a power that made it very difficult not to believe that he was what the Martians claimed he was. It wasn't his words, since these were not extraordinary. Nor was it his features or bearing, which, though handsome and strong and imposing, were equalled or exceeded by many men they'd known. It was a force, a charisma (a word which meant little now because it had been used too much and too inappropriately), an invisible lightning leaping from him. The Krsh and the humans here strongly desired to see him, touch him, be with him, so they could receive this flow of power. But the four Marsnauts were afraid of him and dreaded seeing him again. At the same time, they were attracted by the human magnetic field he radiated. But they had to be with him in the near future. There was no easy way of avoiding it.

Perhaps it was not that they feared him: they feared themselves.

His force was not restricted to contact with the flesh. Later that morning when they turned on the TV, they saw him coming out of the main government building, and the effect of the holograph image was almost as great as that on the platform. Danton got up in the middle of the programme and turned it off. No one objected.

'I don't know,' Madeleine said, shaking her head.

142

'Don't know what?' Nadir said.

'I just don't know.' Without excusing herself she went into the bedroom. The Iranian started to get up to go after her but changed his mind. Sitting back down, he said, 'I'm worried about her. I can't get her to talk about what's troubling her.'

'You know what it is,' Orme said. Shirazi didn't reply. What was the use?

At that moment the TV came alive, and Hfathon's two-foot high image was standing before them.

'*Shalom*' he said. 'I'm inviting you to come at once to the university so you can start work on the next transmission to Earth. After that is sent, you'll be allowed to talk with your people from time to time.'

If he'd expected joy at this news, he was disappointed. The three looked gloomy and for a moment didn't speak.

Then Orme said, 'We'll be right over, Hfathon. Three of us will be, anyway. I don't know about Madeleine.'

The Krsh's feathery eyebrows rose. 'She doesn't have to if she doesn't want to. But you'll have to explain to your colleagues on Earth why she's absent. Otherwise, they might have some sinister interpretations.'

Orme knocked on the bedroom door, since Shirazi showed no signs of going after her. Surprisingly, she said she'd be out in a minute. Orme returned grinning to the front room.

'Maybe we're overly concerned about her. She sounds okay to me. After all, she's about as psychologically stable as a person can get. If she wasn't, she wouldn't be here.'

Bronski smiled lopsidedly. 'Everybody has a breaking point, and the breaking can be caused by things that don't show up on a psych profile.'

'That's right,' Orme said. 'Be a pessimist.'

Madeleine was not actually vivacious, but she did talk when spoken to. But when they entered Hfathon's office, she gasped, and she looked as if she would like to run away. Orme didn't blame her; he was startled, too. Sitting at the Krsh's desk was the Messiah.

He rose and said pleasantly. '*Shalom*, my friends. I'm here to help you prepare your programme. I can expedite matters considerably.'

Orme reached down inside himself and dragged up his courage. Why should he feel like a naughty child who'd been caught doing something very bad by a stern powerful elder? He was a man and a damn good one, and it was ridiculous to let this man buffalo him. Jesus hadn't threatened him. He seemed very friendly, quite ready to treat others as almost-equals. So why shouldn't he relax?

That was easier thought than done. Nevertheless, he advanced to Jesus, his hand out, and he managed a weak smile.

'*Shalom*, Rabbi.'

Jesus looked down at the hand and then inquiringly at Hfathon.

The Krsh said, 'Rabbi, on Earth it's the custom to shake hands when greeting.' He spoke to Orme. 'But here you kiss the Messiah's hand.'

Orme felt a little better. The Messiah was not all-knowing.

Jesus said, 'They are our guests. There is no harm in honouring a harmless custom.'

Jesus extended his hand. The Marsnaut took it and felt a powerful grip and a slight tingle. He had the impression that this man could have pulped his hand if he wished to. But perhaps he was letting his imagination stampede.

Jesus then shook hands with the others. Madeleine must have summoned up her nerve; she gave him a quick strong shake and looked directly into the large, dark, deerlike eyes.

'Good woman!' Orme thought. 'She's as tough as any of us.'

Nevertheless, she looked a little pale and so did Shirazi and Bronski.

'With your permission,' Jesus said in a tone that showed he expected unreserved consent, 'I am going to do something that I seldom do. The people like it when I do these things even though I've told them that they're too much like cheap pseudomagical tricks. And I've told them that *they* should be able to duplicate them and could if they had enough belief in their own powers. From what Hfathon and his colleagues tell me of this book you call the New Testament, I was reported to have performed these so-called miracles while I was on Earth. I didn't, but I could have, though I didn't know it then.

'Even the Son of Man is not perfect, as I once said in Palestine. Only The Divine Presence is perfect, only He is good. But I am His adopted son, and therefore I can do some things which other mortals won't do. At least, not at this time.'

He went to a table and poured out wine into five glasses.

'First, we'll have a drink. Come join me, my friends.'

Orme took the glass from him. He thought of his parents, who steadfastly refused to drink any alcoholic beverage whatsoever, even though they believed that Jesus had turned the water into wine at the marriage in Cana. If they could see Jesus now, they'd have a psychic haemorrhage.

They drank the wine and then followed the Messiah through many rooms and into an enormous auditorium. Waiting for them were TV crews, many of the university staff, and a large number of government officials. There were also a few of the more favoured students and, no doubt, some relatives of the higher-ups in the administration. Here, as on Earth, nepotism wasn't unknown. It was just more restrained.

Jesus went ahead to talk to the TV directors and producers, each of whom had to kiss his hand first. Orme enjoyed that. They were so respectful and humble. His experiences with TV executives on Earth had soured him, they were so authoritative. Especially the civil-service TV officials. Not that they wouldn't in turn, kiss the asses of the high-echelon executives and the politicians.

He wandered around for a few minutes. The cameras were intriguing, cigarette-package-sized machines that the camera-people held one hand while looking through a telescope adjustable lens attached to the top of the camera. Some wore headbands to which were fixed cameras fitting over one eye. They looked through a hole in the camera and could zoom in or away by regulating a small wheel on the side of the camera. There were no attached wires or cables.

At one end of the room were crews which monitored the transmissions from the cameras, edited them, mixed shots, and did other strange things that so mystified the layman.

Near these was a rostrum on which a band sat. Orme, looking them over, was startled to see Gulthilo. She was practising bars on her flute.

He went up to her at once.

'Gulthilo!'

She stopped playing and smiled down at him.

'Richard Orme! How is your health?'

The Martians still said this after two thousand years, though scarcely anyone got sick.

'I'm fine, though a little bit shaken. He—' he gestured at the Messiah – 'isn't easy to get used to.'

Gulthilo looked adoringly at Jesus.

'You will never get used to him.'

Then she looked at him and smiled. He felt as if he were melting. She was so beautiful.

'Have you been thinking about the other night?'

'It's never been out of my mind, day or night.'

That was a lie, but he *had* thought much about her.

'And the result?'

'A lot of erections,' he said, wondering if the moral code of these people permitted such frank talk.

She lost her smile, but it quickly returned.

'Is that all?'

'No, not at all. Look, Gulthilo. I think I'm in love with you. But do I really know you? Do you really know me? We come from such different cultures. Could we get along without friction? I mean, there's always a certain amount of that between two married people even when they're from the same culture. There's the basic friction that results from individual differences and that from the difference between sexes. But in this situation . . . it's not just that you're Jewish. You're a Martian Jew, and what a world of difference that means! If it weren't for that . . . well . . .'

'But,' she said, 'you'd become Jewish. We couldn't marry if you didn't, and I wouldn't marry you if you didn't.'

There was a silence between them, though elsewhere it was certainly noisy. The musicians were blowing, scraping, tootling, tinkling, beating. Further away there were shouts from the TV crews, and laughter at something, perhaps what Jesus had said, since it came from a crowd around him.

'I'm not going to argue or plead with you,' she said. 'But I don't see how you could hesitate. I mean, converting. You're an intelligent man. If you weren't, I wouldn't even consider becoming your wife, no matter how physically attractive you are. But I know that we could be a very loving couple, for sixty or seventy years anyway, maybe more. I sent in our physicochemicopsychic recordings to the centre, and it reported that we are a well-matched couple. And your genes are quite acceptable, though there's a hereditary tendency to diabetes, and liver cancer would have started at about the age of fifty-five. But that's been rectified. We would have beautiful intelligent children, and we'd be quite happy. Not that there wouldn't be periods of conflict and unhappiness. These are not unconquerable, however.'

Martian life seemed for him to be a series of stunning revelations. He was unable to say anything for at least a minute. Then he exploded.

'Jesus Christ!'

Gulthilo looked puzzled. He realized he'd spoken in English.

'I mean,' he said in his slow Krsh, 'you went ahead and submitted my genetic chart or whatever they're called here without *asking* me?'

'Why should I ask?'

'Well, I'm the other partner. Shouldn't you have asked me? And what if the charts had shown a bad mismatch? Do you people go entirely by those? Aren't you allowed to make up your own minds to marry regardless of what the charts say?'

'Oh, yes. We're allowed. A few do ignore the charts. After all, there's passion, you know. You should know. But over two thousand years, the charts have proved to be 98.1 per cent correct in predicting good marriages. I didn't say ecstatic marriages. There are no such things except perhaps in the first year. Good solid marriages with a steady abiding love. But then, from what you've told me, the majority of people on Earth don't have the character for such marriages.'

'Maybe I exaggerated somewhat,' he said. 'Okay. What about the 1.9 per cent?'

'They don't have children. Somehow, they're sterile.'

'I thought your scientists could make anybody fertile?'

'Theoretically, they can. But in these cases, they can't.'

She hesitated, then pointed swiftly beyond him and dropped the hand.

'It's never been said, not publicly. But it's generally acknowledged that he's responsible for the sterility.'

Orme turned to look. 'Who? Oh, you mean *him*?'

Gulthilo nodded.

Orme looked incredulous. 'Come on now! Do you know what you're saying? He can prevent conception by just . . . what . . . ? Thinking? Telecontraconception?'

'I don't know how he does it. But he does. At least, we think so. How else explain it?'

'Quite possibly your scientists are responsible. Or I should say, your government.'

'Oh, no!' she said. 'No, that would be against the law.'

'And so *he* commits illegal acts?'

'He is the higher law.'

Orme sighed. She was naive if she thought that the chiefs of state wouldn't do anything underhanded. Or was she? After all, she knew her world better than he did. And would the government dare do anything criminal? All its members were deeply aware of the two eyes that looked down upon them from the sun and, theoretically anyway, saw everything.

'We're getting away from my question,' she said.

Orme was saved from answering. A Krsh came to him and told him that he should sit with the others in the privileged section. He was to keep silent until it was his turn to speak.

Orme touched the blonde's foot and followed the Krsh to a corner of the chamber. He sat down by Bronski and Shirazi, who looked as if they'd like to talk but didn't dare.

A few minutes later the orchestra began playing a soft slow music. Hfathon, bathed in bright light, stood in the middle of the huge room. A dozen cameramen stood at various places, looking through the eyepieces of the cases in their hands. Orme, glancing upward, saw that there were two cameramen on balconies high up on the wall. A director gave the signal; the music faded into a wail terminated by a clash of cymbals that made Orme jump.

Hfathon, smiling, began talking in Greek.

15

About eleven minutes from now, Orme thought, the satellite relay stations above Earth would be receiving this. And in stations all over the planet there would be scholars, specialists in New Testament Greek, who'd be translating as quickly as they could into their native languages. There would be some words that would puzzle them, since the known vocabulary was limited. These would have to be figured out later.

Hfathon and ten others had been learning English from their 'guests', but the lessons has been not more than an hour long and not every day. It would be a few months more before the students could speak fluently and they'd be restricted in vocabulary. Hfathon and three others, however, had a perfect standard Toronto pronunciation and would be understood by an English speaker anywhere.

Orme had suggested that he do all the talking. This would eliminate the need for interpreters. But he'd been turned down without an explanation for the rejection.

He believed that the Martians insisted upon using Koine because it helped to establish their authenticity. Terrestrials could not doubt that the Martians did know New Testament Greek and better than the Earthly scholars. This was one more item of evidence that their story was true. The Terrestrials might have rationalized that the language had been learned from Bronski. However, he was fluent only in reading it. Besides, it was too much even for the profoundly suspicious to believe that the Martians would go to the great trouble of learning Koine just to add one more layer to an already thick hoax.

Hfathon suddenly ceased talking. The orchestra played a few bars of a piece that reminded him of the opening of the overture to Beethoven's Seventh Symphony. Yeshua' ha-Meshiakh, Jesus the Christ – or a reasonable facsimile thereof, Orme thought – walked slowly to the centre of the room. Hfathon, facing him, walked backward into the shadows.

Jesus held up his hand; the music stopped. He began speaking in Greek in the deep voice that sent thrills up Orme's spine and chilled his scalp.

Orme looked around, saw no one was watching him – though hidden cameras might be focused on him – and whispered in Bronski's ear.

'What's he saying?'

Bronski turned his head and put his mouth close to Orme's ear. At the same time, he tried to watch the speaker with one eye.

'He's saying that he doesn't like to do it, but he believes that it's necessary to demonstrate his powers. He realizes that such things can be faked, but he's done the same things under rigorous laboratory conditions. The films of these will be transmitted later. Of course, it's entirely possible that his people could be lying about the results. So, at some time later, we four will observe another demonstration and so satisfy ourselves, and Earth, that his powers are indeed what they seem to be.'

'Yes, but they'll say we were coerced to affirm them.'

'That's just what he's saying now. Oh, oh!'

'What? What?'

'He said that if this isn't enough, he will convince everybody when *he comes* to Earth!'

The audience said, 'Ya Yeshua!' in a low deep voice.

Orme started to say something, but a hard object poked him in the back. He turned around and saw a giant Krsh standing behind the seats. In his hand was a long wooden pole, the end of which he had thrust against Orme. The Krsh shook his head and held a finger against his lips. Orme turned away feeling as if he'd been reprimanded by an usher in church.

The figure in the blue robe in the centre of the room lifted his arms above his head. Then he levitated to about ten feet above the floor, turned slowly, his arms held out from his sides now, until he completed three circles. The orchestra began playing a wild music in a minor key.

'Just like a magic show,' Orme muttered. But this, he was convinced, was no trick.

What was the effect of Jesus's announcement that he would be coming to Earth? Consternation, of course. Especially among the statesmen and the religious. This was the most upsetting news that had ever come to Earth, and its implications were more than religious. They would reverberate throughout every field: political, religious, scientific, economic, psychological, you name it.

How many countries would allow their citizens to see this? Surely not the communist nations. The communist upper-echelon government officials would be viewing this. But they would not relay this to the populace. But word of this couldn't be kept from the masses forever and there would soon be smuggled cassettes circulating despite the most intense efforts to suppress them.

For that matter, what would the governments of the socialist democracies do? Were they transmitting this to the people? Or were they agonizing now about what to do? Many groups would be possessed with utter fury if this was broadcast. The fundamentalist Christians, the Roman and Eastern Orthodox Catholics, possibly the orthodox and reformed Jews, the Moslems, though the latter were not a potent political force in North America, and who knew how many other off-beat cults? The reaction of the more liberal churches wasn't predictable. But everybody, including the liberals, would share one speculation. What if this was Jesus, and they had been wrong?

As for the Hindus, they would attempt to assimilate this Martian Jesus in their religion, as they had taken in just about every new god. No, they couldn't, because this Jesus denied that he was a god. Besides, he would reject the totality of the Hindu religion.

As for the agnostics and atheists, they'd be just as upset, and they'd be equally denunciatory.

This was a political fission-bomb placed in the laps of Earth world leaders. What were they going to do with it? They couldn't ignore it. The politicos would be sweating, their stomachs would be souring, and the lines to the executive toilets would be increasing by the minute.

Orme abandoned these speculations as Jesus gently landed on the floor. He said something, smiled, and then turned towards the seats and pointed directly at Orme. At least, he seemed to be doing so.

'He's going to . . .' Bronski said in a low but excited voice.

Richard Orme didn't hear the rest. Suddenly, he was floating up and off the seat and moving out over the floor towards the man whose finger had been pointed at him.

Orme didn't struggle. After all, he was used to freefall. He felt numb, but not so much that he hoped that he didn't look scared or ridiculous. The least that Jesus might have done was to warn him.

'Do not be frightened!' Jesus shouted in Krsh. 'You will not be harmed!'

He said something in Greek, probably, Orme thought, a translation of what he'd just said. Orme didn't have time to consider this trivial item. He shot upward then, until his head was almost touching the ceiling. To one side and below, the cameramen in the balcony had their cases centred on him. He tried to smile, but he went into a somersault then, and, still spinning, though not so swiftly he got dizzy, he descended.

Seven feet from the floor, the whirling stopped, and he hovered.

'My apologies to you, Richard Orme,' Jesus said. 'But it is necessary that I do this, since you are the captain of the Earthmen, and your word should have great authority.'

He crooked his finger, and Orme landed gently upon his

two feet. Suddenly, weight was restored. He stood there, blinking and smiling now. It was a foolish smile, though.

'Now,' the man in the blue robe said, 'I would be pleased if you would tell your people, in English, of course, that there was no trickery involved.'

The large deerlike eyes seemed to twinkle. But Orme felt that the light was reflected from steel. And, though stars twinkled, their light came from a fire that could destroy a man in a microsecond.

Orme started to speak, realized he was panting, waited until he'd got his breath, and spoke.

'What Jesus says is true. There were no wires attached to me, no propulsive devices . . . nothing. And this was a complete surprise to me. I don't know how he did it, but . . .'

He should not have used the name of Jesus. That would indicate that he believed this man to be what he claimed.

Well, didn't he?

'Thank you,' Jesus said.

Orme turned and started to walk towards the seats. He stopped. He was trembling too much to continue; his legs felt as if they would give way. And then he was lifted up and propelled towards the chair, was halted just above it, turned, and lowered gently onto it.

The crowd boomed, 'Ya Yeshua' ha-Meshiakh!'

Jesus held up his hand. There was silence. Presently a Krsh and a man came into the lights. They pulled on ropes to which a wheeled cage was attached. Inside it was a huge ram. Behind the cage was a Krsh carrying in one hand a short slender spear with a bulb on its butt and in the other a large axe.

The ram bleated and thrust its horns against the bars in front of the cage. Whatever fate awaited it, it was not afraid. It was ready to fight.

The men halted near Jesus, bowed to him, and one opened the door of the cage. For a minute the ram stood motionless but not silent, then it charged out of its prison, making straight for the man in the blue robe. The crowd gasped, and some called out. Jesus paid them no attention. He fixed his gaze and the point of a finger upon the ram, and it stopped, quivering.

The Krsh, a male much more massively muscled than most of his fellows, stepped forward. Standing to one side of the animal, he lifted the axe. Light reflected from the steel of the head.

Jesus said something, and the Krsh brought the axe down. Its edge sheered through the woolly skin, the heavy muscles of the neck, the bones, and the skin. The head fell off; blood spurted out, soaking the lower part of the blue robe and the bare feet beneath.

Orme felt as if he would vomit. Bronski and Danton said something strangled. Shirazi exclaimed in Persian. The crowd, however, remained silent.

Bronski whispered, 'That's not the proper, kosher method of killing an animal. But I suppose it's not going to be eaten, so it makes no difference.'

Jesus walked through the blood, stopped, picked up the ram's head and held it high. The blood ran down his hands and arms. Then he got down on his knees, affixed the head to the ram's body, and stood up. He raised his eyes upward; his mouth moved silently. He knelt down again, ran his fingers over the severed portion, and stood up. He backed away.

The ram rose groggily to its feet. Its head did not fall off.

Jesus pointed a finger, and the beast trotted off into the cage. The door was closed, and the cage and the two haulers and the axeman went into the shadows.

'Ya Yeshua' ha-Meshiakh!'

The shout was a mixture of awe and triumph.

Bronski clutched Orme's arm. 'For God's sake, the blood is evaporating!'

It was true. The red liquid was boiling away. Within twenty seconds, the floor, the robe, and the man were as clean as before the butchery.

Jesus lifted his hands and uttered something in Hebrew, probably a benediction. Then he walked away, and Orme saw no more of him that day.

Though Bronski was as shaken as his companion, he still retained his rabbinical curiosity.

'I wonder,' he murmured, 'if he has to be ritually cleaned now that he's been drenched with blood? Or if, being the Messiah, anything he does is kosher? Or, perhaps, since the blood was evaporated and he's physically clean, there was no uncleanliness? Or what?'

16

At 'sunset' in the cavern, an observer on the central administration tower would have seen no light except for the two Gentile houses and the pale globe hanging below the roof of the hollow.

And then, suddenly, tiny lights would appear in the front windows of every house as if God had said, 'Let there be light.' These were the lamps which the men of the house lit, lamps of burning oil made from the fat of 'clean' animals. By their flames the evening prayers were said, the families standing by the window while the father recited the litany to the Creator.

Afterwards, the lamps were extinguished and the electric lights were turned on, and the families sat down to a good and generous meal and cheer flowed like the wine.

The supper that evening in the Shirazis' house, where all four Terrans were eating, was lively though not cheery.

'The sheep could have been a robot,' Madeleine Danton was saying. She put down her fork by the plate, on which her food grew cold. 'In fact, it must have been. That's the only reasonable explanation, and I'm not going to listen to anything unreasonable.'

'You're unreasonable,' her husband said. 'Could we make such a lifelike robot?'

'Not quite. But then these people are far ahead of us in technology.'

'Perhaps you think that Jesus is a robot. Or that all the Martians are.'

'You needn't be so sarcastic, Nadir. Nor do I care for your implication that I'm paranoiac.'

'I don't think that,' Shirazi said. 'What I do think is that you are not taking a scientific attitude. You're too stubborn. Not only about this but about other things, too.'

He was still angry because Madeleine refused to cook their meals. She claimed that that was no more her responsibility than his. Anyway, she didn't know how to cook.

'And you a biochemist,' Nadir had said disgustedly.

That remark hadn't lessened the tension between them.

'Well, I'm not a robot,' Orme said. 'And I know that no mechanical or electrical devices were used to levitate me. If these people have antigravity, they didn't attach any anti-gravity machines to me.'

Danton picked up her fork again, looked at the roast beef, boiled potatoes, and asparagus, and put the fork down.

'Perhaps they have some sort of tractor beam.'

Orme laughed and said, 'Surely I'd have felt it.'

Bronski said, 'How about the evaporating blood?'

'A chemical compound or mixture of some sort,' she said.

'But,' Orme said, 'surely you could feel the aliveness of that animal?'

'I felt nothing.'

'You don't feel *anything*,' Nadir said. 'I've noticed that lately.'

'Let's keep this conversation on an impersonal level,' she said, coldly.

Nadir rose abruptly, and, scowling, strode out of the house. Undoubtedly, he would have liked to bang the door behind him, but a hydraulic device prevented him.

Danton said, 'I don't know what to do with him. We could get along fine if only it wasn't for this . . . Jesus thing.'

Orme and Bronski were silent. What was troubling the Iranian was also troubling them. But Nadir's resistance was even greater because he was a Moslem. Bronski, after all, had been raised as an orthodox Jew. To rejoin the faith was easier for him. Orme was a Christian, and, though he would become a Jew, he would also, in a sense, still be a Christian, though not what most Terrestrials would define as such. Not as yet, anyway, he thought sombrely.

Nadir Shirazi, like his two male colleagues, was over-whelmed by the evidence that the man known as Jesus Christ was more than just a man. In his religion, Jesus was a great prophet, the greatest until Mohammed had appeared. No devout Moslem spoke disparagingly of Jesus. It was the idolatrous attitude of Christians towards Jesus that the Moslem objected to. He was not the son of God by divine intercourse and also God, and there was no Holy Trinity. But here was a man who seemed to be Jesus, and he disclaimed godhead and the virgin birth. But he was the son of God, if only His adopted son. He had been resurrected, but the Moslem holy book, the Koran, denied that he had even died on the cross.

The main obstacle to conversion was becoming a Jew. Mohammed, in his struggles to found his religion, had been betrayed by some desert Jewish tribes, composed mainly of converted Arabs, and so the foundation of prejudice against Jews had been established early. Yet the Prophet had included Jews among the People of the Book, the Old Testament, which he revered. The more tolerant Moslem chiefs of the dark and medieval ages, especially in Iberia, had let the Jews worship as they pleased and even appointed them as viziers of their states. Jewish philosophers and scholars were highly regarded. But the Palestinian issue, Zionism, and the birth of the Israeli nation had hardened and sharpened the conflict. It was as much political, economic, and national as religious, but to most Moslems the conflict was religious. Shirazi was an Iranian, not an Arab, and his country had not until recently been directly involved in the war against Israel. Nevertheless, many Iranians sympathized with their fellow Moslems, and to be a Moslem was to loathe the Jew.

Shirazi had had no difficulty in becoming Bronski's friend. He was highly educated and sceptical of the literary validity of the Koran. In Iran, he had been wise enough to keep these opinions to himself except when with like-minded friends. Eventually, though, he had to flee Iran because he couldn't any longer endure the suppression of free speech and the jailing of some of his friends for their lack of discretion.

Shirazi could be a good friend of individual Jews, but the profound antipathy to their religion itself lived in him. He would admit that this attitude was emotionally based, but his conditioned reflexes were so strong they overcame his rationality. He knew that, yet had been unable to do anything about it. He was a Moslem confronted with undeniable evidence that Judaism was the true religion. It had to be if it could produce the living Jesus, whom, despite the Koran, he had thought of as mouldering bones in a rock tomb, awaiting the resurrection of all the dead in the last days. Thus, though he admitted that Jesus was whom he claimed to be, he was still torn. The battle inside him was as fierce as that in Danton though the elements of conflict were different.

Orme was having his own civil war. The solution to peace within himself seemed clear. All he had to do was to go to the nearest rabbi and say that he wished to convert. Rationally, emotionally, he desired to do this. But there was something in him that was fighting this, a deep strong counter-current. What it was, he did not know. Perhaps it was all that he'd heard about the Antichrist, the false Christ who would appear in the days before the Last Judgement. He'd read about him in the Bible, he'd heard many sermons preached about him, and his parents had talked much of him.

The Antichrist would seem to many to be the true Christ. Was this Jesus that man?

Orme didn't know, and he had no way of proving or disproving the truth. He would have to rely on his faith or, to put it another way, his intuition. If he were a true Christian, he should be able to see through the façade, determine whether the real or the false Jesus was behind it.

Perhaps that was the trouble. He wasn't a genuine Christian. He may have been giving to his religion more than lip-service, but it still wasn't enough.

The silence continued. Suddenly, he rose.

'I'm going for a walk. It's too much like a funeral here. I want to see some live people.'

Bronski also stood up. 'I'm going home. Sorry about this, Madeleine. Thanks for the supper, anyway.'

'I think we're all going crazy,' she said. 'Why not? We're in an irrational environment.'

Orme thanked her for the supper and left. Bronski followed him to the middle of the street.

'You want to come along?' Orme said.

'No. I have some thinking to do. Or some feeling. I don't know which. Whatever it is, I hope it comes to a head.'

'Well, if we're confused and upset,' Orme said, 'we have company. I imagine that there are billions like us on Earth.'

'They can't be as disturbed as us. After all, we've lived this, and they're only seeing something on TV. It's the difference between being actually shot at and viewing an actor in a film dodging bullets.'

They said goodnight, and Orme walked on down the street. The only light was that from the windows of houses and the 'moon'. The latter, however, was at least a fourth brighter than Earth's full moon. A sliver of darkness edged the globe, emulating the waning of Earth's satellite. When he'd first seen this, Orme had wondered why it was being done. He was told that it followed the same pattern of phases as the moon as seen from Palestine. The ancient festivals and holy days that had been scheduled according to the real moon were still followed, but with some modifications. There were three harvest seasons here, and so the necessary adjustments had been made.

The 'sun', of course, was always at noon, and so the Terrestrial ceremonies based on the solstices could not follow it. But the Martians were on the Earthly annual calendar just as their day was Earth's. Passover and Yom Kippur were celebrated once a year; the Festival of the Booths, three times a year.

He thought that it would be much more practical just to pretend that the moon had phases. This would give the land more illumination. Sha'ul had replied that this was true, but they didn't need the light. Most people stayed at home after dark except during festivals. If they went out, they could use electrical lanterns or searchlights.

Now, as he went along streets in no way mean, he found himself almost alone. A few bicyclists, a couple in a horse-drawn buggy, two pedestrians, and a group in an automobile were all he came across in an hour's walk.

He was about to turn back when he saw a municipal car park. Why not take a drive? He picked the nearest vehicle, a long one with three rows of seats. A minute later, he was barrelling along the superhighway, the bright headlights probing ahead. After fifteen minutes of this, he turned off on to a road that led directly to a village. Since he could see well in the moonlight, and he was not going over ten miles an hour, he turned the headlights off. It was pleasant cruising along like a phantom past the rows of tall trees bordering the street, moving past houses from whose open windows came snatches of song, bursts of laughter, and animated conversation. Once he saw a huge bulk ahead and slowed, but it was only a cow crossing the street. Some farmer had been careless and left a gate open. He found this reassuring. Sometimes, he thought of these people as perfect, and so he was discouraged about his own imperfections. This was not Utopia, the Martians were just as human as he, though they'd achieved more of the human potentiality for good, and they could be forgetful or neglectful.

A little later, he passed a house from which loud angry voices issued. He glimpsed a man and a woman standing by the window, shaking their fingers at each other.

One more item to remind him that they were not perfect, not robots. The difference here was that, most probably, the argument wasn't going to end in a beating or murder. If it was a serious argument which they couldn't settle themselves

162

privately, then they would go to the neighbourhood arbiter, and he or she would settle the matter. Custom demanded it, and here custom had its way.

The good thing about the Martians was that they kept the good custom and abandoned the bad. Whatever worked was right – if it didn't conflict with good morality. Usually, anyway.

But could this system work on Earth?

It went well here because they had the man in the sun, and the man in the moon, too, and he closely observed them and they knew it. In practice, though not in theory, a god was their head of state and of family.

Earth had no Jesus. No living Jesus, anyway.

After leaving the village, he increased his speed and tore down the country roads, if you could call thirty-five mph tearing. The moonlight fell in between the trees and formed a black-and-white pattern. Darkness, light, darkness, light. A symbol of his life here. On Earth, too. Would there be a great white light surpassing all lights at the end of the road?

There was. It wasn't a blinding but enlightening light, but it was certainly the brightest, except for the moon, he'd seen since he'd started his wandering journey. It came from a large long house set well back from the road, surrounded on three sides by massive trees. Large lamps hanging underneath the overhang of the roof lit up a parking space in front. This contained at least twenty cars, six bicycles, and two buggies.

There were no windows, and the single tall door was closed. Orme stopped the car. It looked as if a party was going on. Should he drop in? He'd been assured that he'd be welcome wherever he went, except for certain government buildings. He was suddenly tired of being alone. The walk and the drive had not resulted in finding a solution to his problem. In fact, he had not even thought much about it. It had been his intention to do so, but something in him had clamped down.

While he was hesitating, he saw the door swing out. Music

and laughter blasted out, and the breeze brought him the odour of wine and something stronger. A man was silhouetted against the frame. Behind him were tables at which men and women sat, and beyond them were couples dancing.

The man stepped out under the overhead lights.

Orme called out, 'Philemon?'

The man started, then walked across the lot to the road. Here the moonlight fell upon Orme's black face. Philemon stopped and ran his hand through his curly red hair. He said something under his breath. Then, 'Richard Orme! How did you find this place?'

'By accident. I was just driving along, and when I saw all those cars and cycles, I thought maybe there might be a party here. I was feeling lonely, so . . .'

Philemon stepped out past the car and looked up and down the road.

'Are you sure that nobody's following you?'

'No. Why should they?'

'Never mind. Drive up and park it near the door.'

The young athlete got into the seat beside Orme's. He leaned close and breathed alcohol into Orme's nostrils.

'I would have brought you here before, but you're too noticeable, what with your black skin and kinky hair. Besides, I wasn't too sure of your reaction.'

Orme turned the car into the lot. 'What are you talking about?'

'Never mind. Just follow me.'

Orme, wondering where Philemon had got strong spirits, which he hadn't even known were made here, went into the building. The young man closed the door after him. The music smote his ears, and the odour of wine and the liquor and sweaty bodies assailed his nostrils. He wasn't offended; it was like being in a disco on Earth, except for the lack of tobacco smoke, and he liked that.

As people caught sight of him, they stopped talking. The band, however, except for a brief miss in the beat, seemed

164

unperturbed. Philemon waved his hand to indicate that nothing was wrong, and the conversation started up again. Orme suspected that it was now mainly about him. He followed the athlete to a small round table with narrow chairs around it. Three were empty; the fourth was occupied by a dark lovely woman. Philemon sat down, invited Orme to take a chair, and introduced his companion.

'Debhorah bat-El'azar. She knows who you are, of course.'

She seemed unsurprised. Her glazed eyes and aroma of liquor indicated that at this time there was very little she would react to.

Philemon, noticing Orme's expression, chuckled. 'She's had far too much; she always does.'

Orme found it difficult to accept that such a place could exist. He was in the equivalent of a 1930s speakeasy.

Philemon bellowed an order to the bartender, and shortly a barmaid, clad in a diaphanous robe, brought two drinks. The dark woman protested, though weakly and slurringly, that she wanted another glass. Philemon told her she'd had enough, and she subsided into a stupor. A moment later she was sleeping, her head on the table.

Orme tasted the purplish liquor. It was like bourbon whisky in pomegranate juice with a dash of tonic water.

'Where do you get this?' he said.

'It's made from wheat and various other ingredients by our esteemed proprietor. Drink up; it's fabulous stuff.'

Orme didn't like the first swallow, but after that the liquor went down easily. His stomach warmed, and presently he began to feel both numb and exhilarated.

'Wow!'

'That's an excellent exclamation,' Philemon said. 'Wow!'

'I don't get this,' Orme said, waving his hand to indicate the entire place. 'Isn't it unlawful?'

'Well, yes. But it's this way, my kinky-haired friend from far-off and iniquitous Earth. You see, we feel repressed or frustrated from time to time, some of us all the time, and so we come to this place or some other place, there are a dozen in this cavern alone, and we get drunk and we do some other things that our elders would frown upon. More than scowl at, I'm afraid.'

Orme took another drink and pointed at a couple at a table in a distant corner. Each had a hand under the other's robe and their mouths pressed together.

'Like that?'

Philemon turned his head and blinked owlishly.

'That and more.'

He was trying to speak precisely, though his words were drawled out.

Orme drank another mouthful, and he said, 'Those two will be married soon?'

'Not neshe-cessarily.'

'Then you young rebels just come here to blow off steam? But I thought you were very temperate. How do you stay in shape for your running?'

Philemon finished his glass and shouted for another round.

'There won't be another contest until two months from now. I jusht – just – come here to relax. Plenty of time to get in shape – sape – I mean, shape, for it.'

Orme shook his head. 'I'm flabbergasted. I've been naive. I really believed that everybody behaved as they're expected to. But this . . . what happens if you get caught?'

The barmaid put down two more glasses. Debhorah suddenly raised her head, looked blearily down, reached for a glass and had her hand pushed away by Philemon. She went back to sleep.

He gulped down half of the glass and said, 'Public humiliashun for all of ush – us. Houshe – damn it! – house arrest. Lotsh of lecturesh. I wouldn' be able to compete for a year, and when I could appear in public, I'd have to wear ass-sh earsh for a month. But it'sh worth it. I think. Look at that drunken Debhorah. She passes out every time. How can we make love?'

166

'So,' Orme said, 'there's a fly in the balm of Gilead.'

'You know,' Philemon said solemnly, 'I've never seen a fly. Read about them, of courshe, sheen picturesh of them. But I don' really know what a fly ish – is.'

'If you come to Earth you'll find out. I'll introduce you.'

The exhilaration was fading away, disappointment replacing it. He told himself that he shouldn't feel this way. The Martians were not angels, they were human. They couldn't all be expected to live up to the high ethical standards they professed. Nevertheless, living as they did under the very eye of the Messiah, knowing that he was indeed what he claimed, and probably much more, having him as an example, how could they act in this manner? How could they want to do so?

Of course, every barrel had its rotten apples. Though these patrons of the Martian speakeasy were not really rotten. What they were doing would be regarded as only normal on Earth, except for some puritanical citizens. It wasn't that they were bad or vicious. What bothered him was their attitude in comparison with that which he had been observing among the majority of the population.

The music stopped. The wildly hopping and gyrating dancers, some of whom had fallen down, walked, staggered, or crawled off the floor. The players stepped down off the platform at the far end of the bar. For the first time he saw the flutist, who had until then been partially hidden by the other musicians.

He rose so abruptly that the table tipped. Philemon's glass toppled and fell on to the floor. Debhorah slid off also and thumped on to the wood.

Orme goggled for a moment, then cried, 'Gulthilo!'

17

'I couldn't believe my eyes when you came in,' she said.

She signalled for a drink and sat down. The barmaid brought over a glass of the liquor for her and a refill for Orme. Philemon, looking indignant, rose unsteadily and went to the bar.

'It was pure accident that I stopped here,' Orme said. 'Are you an habitué of this place?'

'No, but I come occasionally. Of course, there are other places.'

'Why?' he said.

'Why are there other places?'

'No. You know what I mean.'

She took his right hand and kissed it.

'Because we like to come to places like this and degrade ourselves. It's fun to get roaring drunk and flirt and sometimes make love. It makes us feel better, for a while anyway. And we . . . ah, like to get away with an escapade now and then . . .'

'That's childish.'

'Is it? Well, as Yeshua' has said, "Blessed are the children."'

She lifted her glass. 'A toast to the children and confusion to him.'

Orme was scandalized. 'You don't mean that?'

'Look at you, sitting there, drinking *krreebrht*, enjoying the company of the Sons and Daughters of the Grey. You don't look as if you planned to report us.'

'The Grey?'

She swallowed more, said, 'Ooh!' and fanned her open mouth.

'Burns, doesn't it? Yes, the Sons and Daughters of the Grey. We're not the Sons of the Darkness, you know. We're really not evil. We're just having a good time, though I know plenty who would question that it's *good*. So, though we may not be behaving exactly like the Sons of Light, we aren't behaving like the Sons of Darkness, either. We're the Grey. The inbetweens. When we're here, anyway. The rest of the time . . .'

'Butter wouldn't melt in your mouth.'

She laughed and said, 'That must be an Earth expression. Yes, that's right.'

Orme sighed and took another drink.

'Dissidence and discontent in Heaven,' he said.

He felt a draught and turned around. A Krsh male and female had entered and were going to a table at a far corner. They had obviously been drinking on the way.

'The Krsh, too,' he said.

'Why not?' Gulthilo said. 'They're sentient, therefore human. Look, we're not evil, just moderately bad. Our sins are little ones. He'll forgive us. That is, he will if he ever catches us.'

'And if you're caught? You have to go through that horrible humiliation.'

She drank again. 'I think that the difference between us sinners and you of Earth is that we're willing to pay the price. From what I've heard, you aren't very responsible.'

'I haven't heard anybody talk about sin and sinners since I left my parents' house,' he said. 'It is refreshing, in a way.'

Gulthilo put her hand on his arm. 'Well, what about it? Have you made up your mind yet?'

He thrilled at the touch but moved his hand away. Almost automatically, he raised his glass for another drink, then he put it down. The liquor was drowning his inhibitions. A few more swallows and he'd ask her to go out into the bushes with him. And that would be the same as a proposal of marriage. Or would it? What had she said about making love?

'Listen,' he said fiercely, 'have you just been keeping yourself pure, with me, that is, so I'd marry you? You haven't been having lovers all the time you've been telling me how much you love me and how much you want to marry me?'

She laughed and said, 'I told you I was bold and brash. What I'm not going to tell you is whether or not I've had lovers. That has nothing to do with my love for you. Anyway, even if I'd had lovers, I would be faithful to you if we got married. But, again, you've evaded answering me.'

He said nothing. She drank again, laughed again, and said, 'You're jealous!'

'All right, so I am. So what?'

There was a long silence between them. A tall brown-bearded man come to the table.

'The break is almost over, Gulthilo. Ah'hab says he wants to close early. Three more pieces and we quit.'

'Can you get along without me?' Gulthilo said. 'We're talking about getting married.'

The bandleader looked surprised, but he nodded, and left.

'Now,' Gulthilo said, 'maybe we can thrash out the obstacles you think exist.'

'We've already gone over . . .'

He stopped. Two men were standing across from each other at a nearby table and bellowing insults and threats. The apparent cause of this locking of horns, a busty redhead, was trying to calm the two but without success. Suddenly, one of the men, broad-shouldered, black-bearded, and green-eyed, reached across the table and grabbed the other by the robe. This man, taller but slimmer, blond, and blue-eyed, struck the aggressor in the face. The woman shrieked and fell off her chair. The table was overturned as the two males rolled on the floor.

Orme got out of his chair and backed away. A man hurrying to aid one of the fighters, or to break it up, bumped hard into Orme and sent him sprawling. He rolled over and looked up just in time to see Gulthilo kick the man in the ribs. He went sideways, flying further than he would have in Earth's gravity, and collided with the bartender just as he leaped over the bar.

A dark-haired woman, screeching, attacked Gulthilo with clawing hands. The blonde rammed a fist into the pit of the brunette's stomach, and the stricken woman vomited on to Gulthilo. Another woman, undoubtedly one of the brunette's friends, hooked her arm around Gulthilo's neck from the back and, her knee against the blonde's spine, pulled her back.

Orme came off the floor like a grasshopper, soared, landed just behind the brunette, and seized her. Immediately, some-one slammed a fist against the side of his head. Stunned, he fell down, but he managed to kick the legs of his attacker from under him. Yowling with pain, the man started to get to his feet. Orme kicked him on the chin, and he was out of the fight for a while.

'No violence! No violence!' the bartender shouted. His nose was bleeding; one ear looked as if it had been chewed on. His opponent, just as bloody as he, was crawling on the floor, shaking his head.

Nobody paid any attention to him. It was doubtful that anyone heard him but Orme. The entire place had erupted into a scratch-or-slugfest. Orme got up unsteadily and looked for Gulthilo. It took him a minute to locate her in the melee. She was straddling the chest of the brunette and banging her head on the floor.

Orme started towards her. A woman bit his calf. He drove the butt of his palm against the top of her head and she opened her mouth; he kicked her away.

It wasn't easy to drag Gulthilo off her now half-senseless victim. She screamed and writhed and clawed backward, raking his face, before she realized who he was.

'Let's get out of here!' he shouted, and he started to propel her towards the door.

'Why should I?' she yelled, still struggling. 'This is fun!'

'Somebody's going to get badly hurt or even killed!' he shouted.

She shrilled, 'Yooow!' and reached out and yanked savagely on the ear of a man wrestling with another. The man clapped a hand to his ear, at which the other took advantage of the opening and hit him in the throat with his fist.

Angry, Orme shoved Gulthilo ahead of him. She stumbled and fell on her knees. Two cursing men fell over her. She grabbed one by the testicles and squeezed. He screamed and, writhing, rolled away. The other man lacked gratitude. He slapped her across the face so hard that she crumpled onto one side of the floor. Orme kicked him in the chin.

Gulthilo was knocked half out of her wits, enabling Orme to get her to her feet without protest. He was close to the door when the blast of a trumpet cut through the uproar. This was followed by a rapid ratatatat on a drum. A voice bellowed, 'Stop it! The police are here!'

Silence except for some moans and groans and a whimper.

Whistles were shrilling outside. Then, a banging on the door.

'Open up in the name of the law!'

The bartender, Ah'hab, staggered to the door and shot a massive wooden bolt across it. Turning, he shouted, 'Everybody follow me! Pick up the wounded!'

He ran to the door to one side of the bandstand, paused in the frame, and gestured to the crowd. Orme helped Gulthilo to her feet. Supporting her, he got her to the door. For a minute there was a jam as everybody tried to get through at the same time. Then it broke, and he got her through into a wide but short hallway. The proprietor did something around the edges of the wall at the end, and the wall slid downward. Beyond was a narrow stairway. This led spiralling through a passageway cut out of the stone.

Orme helped Gulthilo down it into a large room. At the other end was the opening to a tunnel.

Ah'hab had not come down. From the top of the staircase,

he yelled, 'Follow the tunnel, and when you come out, run! I'm staying! They're probably already at my house, so there's no way I'm going to get out of this! Don't worry! I won't tell them your names!'

Those who were able to do so cheered, feebly. The wall slid back up.

The bandleader said, 'All right. Do as he said. I'll turn the lights off after you're out, and I'll close the tunnel door.'

By now Gulthilo was able to walk on her own. She went ahead of Orme through the lighted tunnel. After about a hundred yards, the tunnel began curving upward. Soon it ended in a trapdoor above a short flight of steps. The big burly man who had started the brawl put his back against the trapdoor and heaved. It rose slowly, dirt falling around it on to him, and then it was open.

Orme came out into the shadow of a big tree. He seemed to be in the middle of a wood. Nearby, a small creek gleamed where the moonlight fell through the branches. An owl hooted, and a tiny creature ran out from the darkness. The owl swooped down, struck, and lifted with the little animal in its talons.

'That's us,' Gulthilo whispered. 'The owl's the police.'

'How'd you get here?' he said. 'In a car or bicycle?'

'In a car with some friends. Fortunately, we took the precaution of wearing gloves so we wouldn't leave fingerprints if there was a raid. But the police will know which lots the cars came from. They'll be questioning everybody in the neighbourhood.'

Orme groaned. 'My prints are on the wheel of my car.'

'Just tell them you stopped off to eat and you knew nobody here. You'll be questioned, but it'll be all right if you stick to your story. Poor Ah'hab! He'll suffer, his family will be so ashamed.'

'He knew what could happen.'

The group, which had at first huddled closely together under the tree, began to disperse. Whistles began sounding.

The police were spreading out and would soon be beating the woods. Orme and Gulthilo took a wide curve through the trees, and after some floundering around came out on a road. She said that this was the same road that ran in front of the inn. They walked along it, occasionally trotting, ready to run into the trees if they saw any light.

'Here's where we part,' she said. 'I have to take the left road. You continue ahead until you come to the highway. Go left on it, and you'll soon come to familiar territory.' She paused. 'Unless you want to come home with me.'

'No. It's not that I don't want to. But they'll have my fingerprints. If they should find me with you, they'll know you were at Ah'hab's.'

'Well?'

He didn't have to ask her what she meant.

He took her in her arms and kissed her passionately. Releasing her, he said, 'Very well. We'll get married.'

She smiled, but she said, 'You love me?'

'I either love you or I'm crazy. I'm not sure which.'

'You're crazy with love.'

She kissed him lightly, and said, 'This is a very strange place and situation for a marriage proposal. But I love it. *Shalom*, Richard.'

He turned at once and began trotting. After a while he resumed a slower pace. The moon was beginning to brighten into the sun. He'd be caught in full daylight before long. Walking was silly, so he started looking for a car. After ten minutes he found one parked in front of a farm house. He climbed in and drove off hastily because a dog was barking inside the house. Not more than ten minutes had passed when he felt a touch on his right shoulder. That startled him so much he drove off the road and almost into a tree. He looked around, saw a man sitting in the seat just back of him, and he slammed on the brakes. The car slid sideways, coming to a stop on the brakes. The car slid sideways, coming to a stop with its front wheels near a ditch.

'Jesus! You startled me!'

Then, 'How in . . . *She'ol* . . . did you get on?'

The man in the blue robe climbed over the back into the seat beside him.

'That's a stupid question. I'm sorry I startled you, but it *was* funny.'

'You might have got us both killed.'

'Not me. Drive on.'

Orme's heart was hammering, and he was shaking. Nevertheless, he backed on to the road without mishap.

After a while, Jesus said, 'The police would have picked you up, both of you, a long time ago, but I asked them not to.'

'Thanks,' Orme said. He tried to sound casual, but his voice quivered.

'May I ask why?'

'You may. Nobody is going to be arrested. Ah'hab ben-Ram will be questioned severely and then released. He may be frightened enough to close up his place or ensure that it's used only for legitimate purposes. Some of his patrons will just go to other places like this. Most, I hope, will see the folly of their ways and settle down.

'You must understand that the police are aware of these places and have been since their establishment. In fact, not one has ever gone long undetected in the past fifteen hundred years. But the police are very tolerant. These places are a sort of safety valve for the rebellious youth. They get drunk, and they tell each other their rebellious thoughts. Sometimes, they even plan some wild action, but these plans are seldom carried out. If they are, they're quickly squashed. The participants pay a high price.'

'May I ask what the price is?'

'You may. The hard-necked culprits are sent to a certain cavern where they stay until the police are sure that they have truly repented. I examine these professors of repentance myself. That way, there is no deceit possible.'

Jesus's cold tone chilled Orme.

'And what happens to those who don't repent?'

'It's best not to ask. However, only a very slight percentage of the young ever get there. You must realize, Richard, that there is such a thing as true evil. From what I've been told, you of the social democracies have abandoned the concept of good and evil. Now it's a matter of the disadvantaged, of bad social and economic conditions, of bad parents, of incorrect conditioning. The communists believe that incorrect thoughts and acts are the result of misapplied economics and wrong political thinking. Am I right?'

'It's much more complicated than that. In essence you're right.'

Jesus said, 'You know that here on Mars there are no disadvantaged, no bad social, political or economic conditions. Family life is generally a joy, and the harsh or unjust parent is quickly reprimanded by his relatives. If that doesn't help the situation, then the neighbourhood steps in.

'We've been able to form this situation because we started out as a very small community. The human members came from many races and nations, but it only took three generations to make one race. Then they had but one religion and language, and of course the early humans had as an example the Krsh, who were more advanced.'

He paused. 'And they also had me.'

He paused again. 'Earth will have me, too, in the near future.'

Orme said, 'If I may be so bold, Rabbi, Earth is a much bigger place than Mars. You have a million only to watch over. But we number ten billion, and Earth has a tremendous variety of tongues, races, nations, customs, and institutions.'

'You may be so bold. Quit being so uneasy, so humble. Relax.'

'I can't.'

'Because of who I am. Despite my great powers, I've never been able to get anybody to relax completely in my presence – except for one person. That is the price I pay for being the

Messiah, the Merciful One's adopted son.'

Orme summoned up his courage.

'May . . . who is that one person?'

'My wife. Ah, here we are. My house. Just beyond that house with the onion-shaped roof. Stop in front of it. I could levitate from the car, but I don't like these tricks in my own neighbourhood.'

Orme was so astonished that he almost drove past the indicated building. His passengers got out, said 'Shalom,' and walked up to the front door. It was a large house, though modest for the Messiah and God's adopted son. There were no police in sight and probably none were hidden.

Orme could not restrain his curiosity. He called, 'Rabbi, if it's no trouble. A word with you?'

Smiling, Jesus said, 'Certainly.'

Orme got out of the car and ran up to the porch.

'You flabbergasted me, Rabbi. I never heard of you having a wife. It's . . . unimaginable! Please don't be offended. But—'

'That is because you Christians have thought of me as The Spirit of Holiness's divinely conceived son and also as Him. You've also taken over the Christian idea that I would be defiling myself if I had intercourse with a woman. That, from what I've been told, derives primarily from the man you call Saint Paul. It was his idea that a man shouldn't marry unless he "burned", to use his quaint phrase, and just had to have sexual satisfaction. He thought that the second coming would be within his lifetime and so there was no sense in getting married and having children.

'I can't blame him for that idea, since I was responsible for it. I, too, thought – erroneously – that the day of supreme wrath was near, and I promised my disciples that some of them would still be living when it came. As for my Terrestrial celibacy, well, a wife would have hindered me, and she would have been unhappy and in grave danger.

'But, though the Messiah, I am a man and therefore subject to error. Not to mention sexual desire.'

He opened the door and said, 'Why don't you come in and have breakfast with me? We can talk a little longer. I'd planned to talk to all four of you in the near future about certain matters. But you can relay the information to them.'

Numb, his head bent, looking up from under his brows, Orme entered. The living room was well-furnished but no more than in any other house he'd been in.

Jesus called, 'Miryam!' A moment later a tall dark woman in a blue-and-scarlet robe came in. Her face was beautiful, though Orme had seen those that surpassed it. Her figure was Junoesque: big-busted, narrow-waisted, very wide-hipped, and, judging by the ankles, the legs and thighs were thick.

She kissed Jesus, and he said, 'Miryam, we have a guest for breakfast. He knows who you are and you, of course, could not mistake him for anyone else.'

'I'm happy to meet you,' she said. 'May you be in good health. I'll have breakfast ready in five minutes.'

Jesus chuckled and said, 'You still aren't able to accept the idea. Richard, I am a man, and while I could be celibate – and chaste – on Earth because I was there for such a short time, I cannot be celibate, though I'm chaste, here. Besides, the good women of my flock would criticize me – behind my back, of course – if I did not marry. They *are* Jewish. A home is happy only if a happy woman is under the roof. When I was on Earth, I had no home. I was a wanderer dedicated to spreading my message.'

'But . . . children?'

'I've foregone them. I am only home for a few days every month, and children should have a father who is with them every day. Miryam appeases her maternal feelings by teaching in a school. She understood when we married that we could have no offspring. She also knew that I would be able to see her only occasionally, but she thought it well worth it. The ecstasy of being with me for those short periods more than makes up for my absences. And I am happy with her.

'And now, let us wash our hands and faces. It's not good to

sit down to partake of the Creator's bounty with dirty hands, though there are times when it's permissible.'

Orme said, 'Yes, I've read your words on that subject.'

18

It was strange to be served food by Jesus, but the ancient custom that the host should do this for his guests was honoured even in this house. The breakfast was ample and tasty: a muskmelon, grapes, bread, honey, mutton, beef, and wine. Though the Martians had coffee bean bushes in their cryonic vaults, still potentially viable, they had never grown any. Orme had spoken to Hfathon about their use, and the Krsh had said he'd see what he could do about it. So far, Orme had heard nothing of any progress in the matter.

Miryam ate with them, but she served herself. She ate quickly and sparingly and left to shop in the market before the men were halfway through their meal.

While eating bread and honey, Jesus said, 'I had expected that all four of you would have asked that you be admitted into the Fellowship of the Sons of Light. That is, as Hebrews. But so far you have made no request. What is it that holds you back? Hardness of heart?'

He chewed, swallowed, then said, 'Or is it that you are still unconvinced that I am indeed the Messiah? And that my powers are only seeming, that, in fact, I am tricking you?'

The food in Orme's stomach seemed to transmute into a lump of iron. He wished that that serious subject could have been avoided so that he could enjoy the meal. There was, however, no way to avoid this. He didn't have the courage to tell Jesus that he would prefer another time for this subject.

'Three of us are firmly convinced that your demonstration was valid,' he said. 'One is still trying to rationalize, but . . .'

'That is the woman, Madeleine Danton.'

It was not a question.

'Yes. May I ask how you know?'

'I know the souls of all of you.'

'Then,' Orme said, greatly daring, 'you shouldn't have to ask what hinders us.'

'I know your souls, that is, your characters, but I cannot, or will not, read minds.'

'I think,' Orme said slowly, 'that we've hesitated because we've been raised in different religions. None of which have prepared us for what we've found here. In fact, what we were taught to believe is so different, so contrary to the situation here, that . . . uh . . . we find it hard to accept. It'd be easier, I think, to accept something totally alien to our beliefs. But here . . . some things are exactly what our religions said they would be. But, others . . . well, they contradict . . . if you see what I mean.'

'They shouldn't. Hfathon says that Bronski told him that your scholars have known for a long time that your holy texts are full of interpolations, of pious frauds, and that many of your dogmas are based on misinterpretations, deliberate or otherwise. That your holy texts contain contradictions that can only be reconciled by the most desperate and illogical rationalizations.'

'Yes, but very few people know of these. Or want to know. I'll have to admit that I was one of them.'

'And still are,' Jesus said.

He sipped on his wine, then said, 'Bronski has also spoken of the Antichrist. Perhaps that worries you. I don't understand the references fully, so we've requested an Earth government, your Canada, to transmit to us the full text of this book you call the New Testament. In the original Greek, of course.'

Orme thought, what a sensation that must've made! Jesus Christ asking for a copy of the Gospels!

'We've also requested that the nation of Israel transmit to us the full text of the sacred writing of the Jews. We will compare these to ours.'

A cat, russet-coloured, long-legged, long-eared, and with

181

some tiger markings on face, legs, and tail, strolled in. It meowed, then jumped up on Jesus's lap. He stroked it while, purring, it fixed its golden eyes upon Orme.

Jesus smiled as if he was enjoying a private joke, and he said, 'Of course, it is possible that I am not what I claim to be. I could be this Antichrist whom the man you call John the Divine wrote about. By the way, could he be that Yokhanan who was one of my twelve disciples?'

Orme cleared his throat. 'It is generally believed that he was. But Bronski said that there is no proof.'

'It doesn't matter. From the quotations given by Bronski, it's a superbly poetic apocalyptic vision. John was obviously symbolizing the Roman Empire when he talked about the seven-headed beast and the great whore of Babylon. And he just as obviously expected the coming of the Messiah and the days of judgement in his own lifetime. But then so did I.

'However, that is beside the point, though interesting. What about this Antichrist? If I should be he, then there also has to be a Christ, a Messiah. Do you believe that there is indeed a Christ? Or do you, in your heart of hearts, think that he, too, is a myth?'

'No,' Orme said huskily, 'I don't believe that. I do believe in Jesus Christ, my saviour, mankind's redeemer.'

'Good. So . . . I could be his great antagonist.'

Jesus was smiling as if he was enjoying this dialogue immensely.

'Let us consider other possibilities. Is the Antichrist this devil, this Satan, to which the New Testament refers so often, according to Bronski?'

Orme cleared his throat and drank some more wine to relieve the dryness.

'Not as I understand it. The Antichrist will be a mere man, but he will be directed by the Devil.'

'This Devil, as I understand it, is a fallen angel, whose name was Lucifer in English. The word is derived from Latin and means Light-Bringer or Light-Bearer. Correct?'

'Yes.'

'The Hebrew holy writings include the Book of Job. In this, Lucifer is only one of the angels, though a chief one, and he is not evil. He's a temporary prosecuting attorney chosen to argue against Job's case. It is you so-called Christians who have made him into a fallen angel, a being with horns and hoofs and a tail.'

'That's an old folk legend,' Orme said. 'Nobody nowadays really believes that he has horns and all that.'

'The point is that you Christians had to have an evil force which was almost as powerful as God. That's an idea which was probably borrowed from the Persians, by the way. Thus, much of the evil in the world could be attributed to him. But it is obvious that man does not have to be influenced by a spirit to be evil. His evil is sufficient unto himself. There are spirits, angels, but these are not evil.

'Suppose, though, that I *am* Satan. What would I be doing on Mars? Why, I would be preparing an evil force to invade Earth and completely subdue it. Thus, evil would reign there, my enemies would be slain, and I would have established a worldwide kingdom which worships only evil. Although, from what I've heard of Earth, I'm not sure that Satan doesn't rule there now.'

Jesus laughed, startling the cat on his lap. He soothed it with a few strokes between its ears.

'Look about you. Can you truly believe that the Martians are an evil people and that I am Satan?

'Of course, I could still be the Antichrist, and the goodness here is only a façade, a reasonable facsimile.

'But there are other possibilities. Let's imagine some of them. What about something that could, scientifically speaking, possibly exist? Nothing of the supernatural about it, though it can't be proved, at this time, that it is in the realm of the natural. As if the Creator wasn't natural, though he is at the same time outside of Nature.

'Let us say that, during its interstellar exploring, the Krsh spaceship stopped on a planet that seemed to hold no life. This was somewhat larger than Earth, and its sun was considerably larger than Sol. A blue giant. In fact, the Krsh did land on such a planet.

'Let us say that, though there was no life as we know it on this planet, the Krsh instruments did detect strange electromagnetic phenomena. These roamed the surface of the planet in seemingly random pattern. In actuality, they were moved by winds. The electromagnetic winds from the blue giant.

'Let us say that the Krsh never knew the true nature of these phenomena. They tried to capture some but were unable.

'Let us imagine that these electromagnetic phenomena were actually sentient beings. They were composed of pure energy fields which were as complex as human beings and just as intelligent. In some respects, they were more intelligent. They did not have a society as we know it, but they had one. They communicated with each other, they had a language, the words would be transceived modulated pulses of electromagnetic frequency.

'Let us say that one of these was possessed of immense curiosity. Instead of fleeing the strange forms of life that had landed on its planet, it investigated. And it found, through experimentation, that it could possess the body of one of the strangers, or not so much possess it as integrate with it. This led to its being able not only to share its intellect and its emotions but to become, in effect, its host. And it was able to take over control of the host without the host being aware of it.'

Jesus laughed again and took another sip of wine.

'Interesting speculation, isn't it? So, it also discovered that it could mutate its own energy fields so that it could resemble exactly any of the strangers. Its companions would not be able to tell the difference. To them, the facsimile was no different from the rest of them or any different than he had been before.

'Of course, the facsimile or the possessed would have to

exhibit the same limitations as any person. He couldn't walk on water or float throught the air or repair damaged cells with a touch of the finger. Or bring life back to the dead. If he did that, he might raise questions, cause doubts, and initiate an investigation. The Krsh were not your ignorant superstitious men of Earth of that time. They wouldn't accept these strange powers as suddenly given by the Creator. They might have suspected the truth. If they had, they would have used their delicate instruments and found a troubling electromagnetism that no Krsh would have radiated.

'However, before long the possessor learned this, and it was able to confine the radiation so that there would be no chance of detection.

'But why not reveal itself to the Krsh? Would they harm it? It didn't seem likely, since the Krsh were a peaceful folk. They would allow it to spend time in the atomic reactor that provided the fuel for the drive of the ship. You see, this energy being was like every other living thing. It had to have food, and it got this from radioactivity. It could absorb, or digest, but it did not have to excrete. It used one hundred per cent of the energy taken in.'

Orme muttered, 'The sun.'

'You mean the globe that floats in this cavern. Yes, it is fuelled by an atomic reactor, though it is used much more efficiently than those on your world. This would explain why I spend so much time in the sun. I am renewing my being in more ways than one. That is, it would explain it if I were indeed this being. But this is, of course, pure speculation. I am amusing myself and, I hope, you, too.

'Let's say that this being decided not to reveal itself yet. It had to know the strangers much better before it took a chance. So, it left its host from time to time to reside in the reactor of the ship. And it occupied all the Krsh, one by one, before the ship had reached Earth. It came to know its hosts well, better than they knew themselves. It was able eventually to read the unconscious minds of the Krsh.

185

'Just as I, if I were indeed that being, could read your unconscious. But I, if I were this thing, wouldn't do so now. You see, becoming my hosts, I also became human. And I find the trip into the unconscious very disturbing. It's a nasty place down there, my son. Of course, I'm still imagining this; I'm speaking as if I were indeed this hypothetical creature.

'Now, on to the adventures of this pure energy-being that became human. Fortunately, or perhaps unfortunately, this being developed a human conscience. It couldn't escape it, since it became a man. All the Krsh were highly ethical and so it, too, became highly ethical. Moral problems, which not only never had been its concern but which it never had heard of before, now occupied its thoughts.

'Was it moral to occupy the body of another sentient being and control it? The answer was that it was not. Was it moral to just live in a host and leave the free will actions up to its host? The answer was that it was moral. But as a guest in another's body, it was a parasite and a very bored one. It wished to control the body, to direct it so it, too, could act as a free-will agent. But it couldn't because that would be evil.

'Nor would it momentarily convert its energy into matter and so assume the likeness of one of the Krsh. To reveal its presence now would cause all sorts of consternation. And if the Krsh found that it had been taking over their bodies and minds, they might decide that it was too dangerous. And, being intelligent and highly scientific, they could find means to destroy it. Or if not, to hurl it into space and leave it behind.'

Jesus, still smiling, paused. 'You don't seem to be enjoying your meal. Miryam is an excellent cook, so it can't be the food.'

Orme said, 'It's very good. I was so fascinated that I forgot to eat.'

He cut a slice of mutton and began chewing. But the meat seemed to have lost its taste.

Jesus said, 'And then the ship came to Earth. As you know,

it was there for three years. The energy-being thought about staying there and letting the Krsh go on without it. But it really was a horrible place from the viewpoint of the Krsh and from mine, since I was now a Krsh. The terrible plagues: leprosy, gonorrhea, smallpox, and the rest. The horrible conditions in which most people lived. The wars, the massacres, the stupid laws, the hatreds, the plight of the children, need I go on?

'And yet I grieved for them and would have liked to change their condition. The Krsh themselves had plans for coming back some day and introducing their science, their technology, and their society. But there were those who said that to give these bloodthirsty savages the means of making weapons would result only in more horrors.

'Finally, the electromagnetic being decided to return with the Krsh to their native planet. It would become a Krsh and live among them as one. This wouldn't be easy, since the Krsh had records of every citizen, and the sudden appearance of an unaccounted one would cause an investigation. Perhaps it could form the body of a just-dead Krsh, get rid of it, a thing easily done, and take his or her place.

'The ship finally left Earth. Among those humans on it were Matthias and some of his fellow Hebrews. They talked much of this Yeshua' the Messiah, the Anointed of the Merciful One. The Hebrews were successful in converting their fellow Terrestrials to their religion, but they didn't get any place with the Krsh.

'And then an idea came to the being. It would form a body which exactly mimicked that of the dead Jesus. And, as Jesus, it would announce that he had decided to go with the Krsh to their world and preach there. And some day he would return to Earth, to Jerusalem itself, and establish the new state of Zion as foretold, though somewhat ambiguously, in the book you call the Old Testament and the New Testament.'

Orme cleared his throat again and said, 'Pardon me, Rabbi, but wouldn't this be unethical?'

187

Jesus chewed on a piece of bread and honey for a moment.

'Yes, in one sense. But this being saw a way to make the people of Earth healthy and happy. So, the higher ethics, the higher law, won.'

'I've heard that before,' Orme murmured.

'Ah, you mean evil people talk about the higher law to justify their evil actions? That is true, but there is no doubt about the validity of this particular reasoning. Nor would the thing, as Jesus, have used force and violence to bring about this Land of Beulah on Earth. These would, unfortunately, result in war. But then, as I once said, "I bring a sword, not peace." The peace comes later.'

'And then?' Orme said. 'I mean, what happened then on the ship?'

'You have seen what happened. The Sons of Darkness trailed the Krsh vessel, and the Krsh had to dig into Mars. The rest you know.'

'Not entirely, Rabbi,' Orme said. 'There is much that I've not been told. Perhaps much that has been deliberately concealed. Anyway, why have you waited so long for the . . . uh, millennium? To return to Earth? Surely, after a hundred years or maybe even before, the Krsh could have gone back to Earth?'

'Yes. But they did not number many. And the humans had to integrate with the Krsh, and the faith had to be well established. Besides, a quick return would have found the Earth people in the same situation as when the Krsh left them. But the Krsh said that in time the Terrestrials would advance in science and perhaps in humane institutions. They would be at a stage where the Martian science and technology and institutions could be both readily understood and assimilated.

'Then, too, they did what this being who called himself Jesus told them to do. He said that when the time to return came, they would know it. That time, as foretold by Matthias, would be when the Earthmen came to Mars.

'It is possible that the being named Jesus hinted to Matthias what he should predict.'

There was silence for a while. Jesus finished his breakfast, and then he said, 'Let us give thanksgiving to our Creator for this food.'

Orme scarcely listened to the Hebrew prayer. Was this man putting him on? Was he just having fun? Or . . .?

Jesus rose and said, 'We can talk a little more. Then I must ask you to leave since I have business to attend to.'

They went into the front room. Jesus sat down in a large overstuffed chair. Orme took a seat on a sofa.

Jesus church-steepled his fingers, and said, 'There are other speculations, too. Suppose, for instance, that it was not an energy-being that possessed a Krsh when they were on the planet of the blue star. Suppose that, when they were on the planet of the hominids, some other creature possessed a Krsh. This would not be an energy being but some strange form of parasitical life, a loathsome slug. This creature has the ability to infiltrate the body of another being, to reside within its tissues much like a worm. But it can take over the brain of a sentient being and become, in a sense, sentient itself. And this creature has then followed much the same route that I outlined for the energy being, though perhaps with evil intent.'

'But that theory wouldn't account for its powers.'

'I suggest that this sluglike thing also had the ability to tap the potentialities of a human being, potentialities that human beings don't themselves realize they have. Not as yet, anyway. I keep telling them, and they refuse to believe.'

'Which of these stories is true, Rabbi?'

Jesus, his dark eyes seeming to blaze as if they were glass windows of a hot furnace, spoke loudly.

'You have heard the truth, and you have seen it! I tell you, son of man, that this son of man has revealed everything needful to you! You do not have much time to decide the path to salvation!'

Orme quailed before the fire and the thunder.

Jesus rose, and the stern forceful expression was replaced by the smile.

'You may go now. Peace and the blessing of the Merciful One shower upon your head.'

He held out his hand. Orme rose, went to him, and kissed the hand. He could feel the power flowing into him.

19

'What I'm doing,' Bronski said, 'is writing an unauthorized biography of Jesus.'

He looked across the piles of papers and recording machines on his desk at his captain. Orme was pacing back and forth across the room.

'Actually, it'll be a short book, since it's more an outline than a massive detailed life. But I want to have it ready by the time we return to Earth. Possibly I can get it done early enough to have it transmitted before the takeoff.'

The day before, the Marsnauts had been informed that they would be passengers on the Martian ship. It had come as no great surprise; they'd expected to be used as eyewitnesses and to validate that they had not been lying because of pressure by their hosts.

Orme had told the others of his conversation with Jesus at breakfast. Madeleine Danton had immediately seized upon the story of the energy-being as the true one.

'He's playing with us,' she'd said. 'He's telling us the truth, knowing that we won't believe it.'

'But *you* do,' Nadir had said. 'Personally, I think you're very confused and upset. Otherwise, you'd never give any credence to such a fantastic tale. It's pure science-fiction.'

'I'd rather believe that than that he is indeed Jesus Christ!' she'd cried.

'Why not?' Bronski said. And during the heated discussion that followed, in which they kept interrupting each other with increasingly higher-pitched voices, Bronski had stopped them cold. He'd told them that he intended to convert. The arrangements had been made with the neighbourhood rabbi. An hour later, the rabbi called back. Excitedly, the rabbi told

Bronski that he had wonderful news. The Messiah himself would conduct the ceremony.

'That's real class,' Orme had said. 'I'm jealous.'

The jest concealed a genuine seriousness. He *was* jealous, and he hated himself for being so. Last night, he'd prayed in the living room while Bronski slept.

'Lord, show me the truth. Tell me whether or not this man is indeed Jesus Christ, Your son, or the anti-Christ. Or . . . could he be that energy-being? Give me light. Don't allow me to make the most grievous error in the world. I'm one of Your children, and surely it would not be too much to show me the true path. I beseech You, Father. Please. Amen.'

He had not really expected that a great light would flood the room or a thunderous voice speak. Nevertheless, he was disappointed when nothing occurred. Not even his weak inner voice spoke or his own feeble light glowed. He stood up, tensed, whirled, and then let out a long sigh. For a few seconds he'd had the feeling that someone was standing behind him. It was the same sensation as when he'd awakened in the night knowing that someone had been standing by his bed.

Who was it? What was it? The result of overwrought nerves? The dim consciousness of God Himself? Or had the real Jesus allowed his presence to be felt so that he, Orme, would realize that he was not alone? But which Jesus had it been? The one he'd been taught about when he was a child, or this Jesus, the living man, the Messiah of the Jews, and eventually of all peoples? Or was there any difference between them? Were the Christians really in error? Or was this Jesus really the energy-being?

If Orme had not thought that it would be sacrilegious, he would have cursed Jesus for having told him that story. It had given him grave doubts, though that had not been Jesus's intention. Or had it? Perhaps he was testing Orme's sincerity.

This morning, Orme was still wrestling with himself. To strive with your own being, he thought, is harder than wrestling with an angel. Jacob had it easy compared to me.

He stopped pacing to look through the window.

'Here comes Nadir,' he said. 'He looks as if he's been through hell.'

A moment later the Iranian entered. His face was pale and drawn, and his eyes were edged in black, his hands shook.

'Madeleine's leaving me,' he said in a strained voice. 'I told her this morning that I'd decided to become a Jew. She screamed at me and told me to get out. I tried to reason with her, but she was crazy. It was useless to argue, she threatened to kill me if I didn't stay out of her way, and she mocked me because I, a Moslem, was becoming a Jew.'

Orme looked across the street at the Shirazis' home but could not see anyone through its window.

Bronski said, 'I'm deeply sorry about Madeleine. But I am glad that you've made this decision. Perhaps Madeleine will calm down. I think that she knows what the path is, but she just can't force herself to take it.'

Orme was worried about Danton, too. However, the news that the Iranian was also going to convert rocked him. What made them change their minds? And why couldn't he change his?

'I would have had to leave her anyway,' Nadir said. 'She's a pagan, and the People of the Covenant aren't allowed to marry pagans. We'll be divorced, though we probably would have been in any event. She's impossible to live with.'

There was no way of knowing why, at this moment, hearing these words, Orme made his decision. No great light bloomed, no trumpets blared. It happened as quietly as the birth of a mouse in a dark cupboard.

Shaking with excitement, he said, 'I'll see you later.'

They stared at him. As he went out the door, he heard Bronski call after him. 'Where are you going?'

'You'll find out!'

An hour later, having first found out where she was, he stopped his car outside the school where Gulthilo taught.

Alerted by his call, she was waiting for him in an office near the entrance. Today she was dressed in a robe printed with blue and red flowers. He could smell her musky perfume. Her hair was a golden cataract down her back. Her blue eyes glowed; her smile seemed wide enough to take him in.

'You wouldn't say why it was so important that I see you at once,' she said. 'But I think I know. You want to marry me?'

'Right,' he said, and he took her in his arms. Behind him he heard some small girls giggle from just outside the office door.

The initiation ceremony into the faith was short but impressive. There was a huge crowd, an estimated one hundred and fifty thousand. The onlookers were there partly because of the historic importance, since this was the first time in two thousand years that the ritual had been used. The other attraction was the presence of the Messiah.

Jesus arrived in a ground car, probably much to the disappointment of those who hoped that he would levitate. He wore a sky-blue robe and the *tephillin* or phylacteries, two little leather cases, each holding four passages of the Law and worn on the forehead and left arm. He also carried his *tallith*, the prayer shawl. According to the law, a Jew was to wrap himself in the shawl and wear the *tephillin* during prayer, but when Orme had breakfasted with Jesus, his host had not done this. But as the Messiah, he was given a certain freedom. But this time he was apparelled as the chief rabbi should be.

His wife, Miryam, was making one of her rare public appearances. She came in another car, and when she got out to enter the synagogue, the people closest to her tried to touch her robe. If unable to do this, they touched those who had succeeded. It was as if they thought the power was transmitted to her from her husband and could even be felt at fourth-hand. Or perhaps it was just an exhibition of the public's affection for her.

Orme, Bronski, and Shirazi waited on the steps of the *beth kinneseth*, the synagogue. From inside it came music by an orchestra of a hundred. Gulthilo was among them; she had winked at Orme as she passed by him. There was no repressing her.

With a blare of trumpets and a crash of cymbals Jesus entered, and the converts and notables followed him. Orme was numb throughout the vows, the symbolic circumcision necessary because they had had their prepuces removed at birth, the prayers, and then the meal eaten afterward in a large room at the university. His happiness was alloyed with a doubt. Was he really doing the right thing? Wasn't he being swept along by pure emotion? But then, in these matters, it was always the heart that dictated after the mind had pondered.

The next day he went through a ceremony almost as numbing but one in which he forgot his uncertainty. He and Gulthilo were married by Jesus himself. The *mistitha* or wedding was solemn, but the celebrating afterwards was very lively. *Mistitha* was an Aramaic word orginally meaning 'carouse', and this certainly was one. He believed that it would have been even wilder if Jesus had not been there. No one was going to tell jokes about a bride and bridegroom on their wedding night or drink themselves into a stupor while he was around. After he had left, the party exploded, but the newlyweds did not stay long. Gulthilo's mother wanted to talk more to Orme about her daughter. Gulthilo said, 'He knows all about me, mother,' kissed her, and they fled.

They drove to a little lodge on the shore of a lake in the adjoining cavern and wasted no time in getting into bed. At six in the morning an exhausted Orme was wakened by the shrilling of the TV. He dragged himself off the bed and staggered to the set. Nadir Shirazi's image appeared.

Before he heard the Iranian, Orme knew that he was the bearer of bad news. Grief had cut even deeper lines into his face.

'Madeleine called me about an hour ago. She said she was going to kill herself. I begged her not to, but she cut me off. Before I could get to the house – I was staying with Bronski, you know – she had driven a knife deep into her heart. I'm sorry to call you so early in the morning, but . . . I thought . . . you should know.'

He began weeping. Orme waited until the deep racking sobs had subsided, then said, 'We'll be there as soon as possible. But it's a long drive . . .'

'That's all right, Hfathon will send an airboat for you.'

Gulthilo and Orme arrived at the hospital fifteen minutes later. Bronski, Shirazi, Hfathon, and a Krsh doctor, Dawidh ben-Yishaq, were in the waiting room.

'I thought you said she was dead!' Orme said.

'She was,' Nadir said. 'But they repaired the wounds, got the heart working again, and now she lives.'

'But the oxygen supply to her brain . . . she'd been dead how long before they got her to the hospital?'

'Ten minutes. And she was dead at least half an hour. But the ambulance men had her in a cryonics chamber as soon as they arrived. Even so . . .'

Orme thought that she would be an idiot, a vegetable. Why bother? Then he thought of Jesus Christ. Couldn't he restore the cells to their original condition?

He took Bronski aside and asked him this. The Frenchman said, 'It wasn't necessary to ask him to come. In the first place, all restoration that could be done, even by him, was done at once. You forget, Richard, that their medical science is far ahead of ours. As for her brain, well, some irreversible damage occurred. Not even he could help her. There are certain things lost that only the Creator could restore.'

'What do you mean?'

'Her memory. Many of the cells storing this must have decayed. They can be restored, but their contents will be gone forever. They'll be empty containers, waiting to be filled.'

'Yes, but what about Lazarus? He'd been dead three days, and when he was raised by Jesus, he was as good as ever.'

Bronski smiled sadly. 'You still aren't able to distinguish between the Jesus of the Gospels and the historical one. No one could revivify a corpse that had been rotting for three days in that hot climate. That's a story that originated after Jesus had died or perhaps even when he was living. It's just one of the wild tales that collected about extraordinary people in those days.'

That was true. Madeleine did live, and her body was healthy, and her intelligence was as high as before. But she spoke believing herself to be twelve years old and in her parents' house in the city of Montreal. Prepared for something like this, the doctors had heavily sedated her to ease the shock. It would be a long time, if ever, before she would be able to understand what had happened to her.

20

What had Orme learned about Mars? Very little of what he had expected to discover, which wasn't much anyway, and far more than he could possibly have anticipated in imagination.

Even when he'd learned that the Martians were Jewish, he'd had daily experiences that surprised and sometimes upset him.

One reason for this was his firm preconception of what a Jew was. But the more time he spent on Mars, the more he realized that though he'd prided himself on his lack of prejudice, he had had far more than he'd thought possible. Or perhaps it was not so much prejudice as ignorance. Though it was hard to draw the line between them.

Also, the Martian Jew was not, could not be, identical with the Terran Jew, though there was a basic similarity. Two thousand years ago, the two had been separated. Those left on Earth had had intimate involvement with many hundreds of different Gentile societies. Their Gentile neighbours had made a cultural impact upon the Jews among them no matter how the Jews had struggled to keep intact their identity, physical, mental, and spiritual.

'The Jews who settled in China in olden times,' Bronski said, 'eventually became indistinguishable, physically speaking, from the Mongolian *goyim*. They also lost most of their Jewish heritage. On the other hand, the Jews in the Rome ghetto, though they preserved their religion, were Italian in many respects. That is, they could not escape adopting many cultural attitudes. This was to be expected. The Jews have always done this wherever they settled, and indeed, they could not have survived without doing so. But the Roman-ghetto Jews ended up looking like Italians.

'I've had explanations from various Jews as to why so many Italian Jews look Italian and Dutch Jews look Dutch and Sephardic Jews look Spanish or Portuguese and the Yemenite Jews look Arabic. They ascribe this to a sort of protective mimetism. That's a ridiculous, nonscientific explanation. It's based on their unwillingness to admit that somehow, no matter how hard they've tried to keep the "racial" strain pure, Gentile genes have entered it. Rape can account for a certain amount of this, but adultery is the main cause. Of course, the genetic flow has gone the other way, too, and many an anti-Semite has a Jewish forefather.

'The Jews, especially the devout, don't or won't admit this explanation into consideration. I don't know why. Throughout their history, their prophets have raved about the whoring of their people with the *goyim*. Or, to use a less emotional and more accurate word, miscegenation. You've read the Bible. You have. You know what I'm talking about.'

Bronski said, however, that this was no real danger to the preservation of Jewish identity, which was not based on 'racial' purity but on religious purity. Anyway, any child born to a Jewish woman was regarded, by Jewish law, as a Jew and was raised as such. However, it usually had to endure shame and reproach and would not be admitted to the Temple to worship.

'This was no big deal,' Bronski said, 'since there has been no Temple after 70 AD nor was there one during the Babylonian captivity. But I digress, as usual. Why not? The digressions are as interesting as the aspects of the main argument.'

All ethnic groups underwent acculturation because of contact with other groups. But what was to most Gentile groups acculturation was to orthodox Jews backsliding – contamination, pollution, evil.

'From their viewpoint, they were absolutely correct. How could they be Jewish, continue to be God's Chosen People, if they ceased to cling to the religion, if they abandoned any of the laws of Moses? To give up or alter even an iota of the basic commandments was to let the snake get his foot into the door.'

He smiled, saying, 'That is, if a snake has feet. His nose, anyway. However, the Martian Jew has been isolated from both his brother Jew on Earth and the Gentile community. He has not suffered the horrible persecutions of his Terrestrial kin nor has he been tempted to adopt Gentile ways, since he knows no Gentile. He's completely unaware of the nuances, the emotional associations, of the word "Jew" as uttered by too many Gentiles and by too many Jews themselves.

'Here, after the Krsh and the Terrestrials had worked out their cultural differences, which was made much easier by the Krsh becoming Jewish, the society became a homogeneous unit unaffected by non-Jewish contacts. In the beginning, there was a certain amount of friction, but none of it violent.'

For over two thousand years Mars had known no wars, no mass migrations impelled by fear, no riots. The only civil disturbances had been an occasional peaceful demonstration. There had been brawls among individuals or small groups and some murders. But these were so few that Bronski had said that he sometimes wondered if the Martians were truly human.

He would quickly add, however, that he, like Mark Twain, had some prejudice against the human race. What the Martian society demonstrated was the potentiality of the human for peaceful cooperation. It also demonstrated that *Homo sapiens* (and Homo Krsh) was not a born killer. Or, if he was, the Martian society had certainly repressed or diminished considerably any instinctual drive for murder and war.

'Yes,' Orme had said, 'but note that, now that there is going to be contact with the foreigner, the Martian is embarking on war.'

'No. He's not declaring war. He won't fight unless he's

attacked. He'd be insane or very stupid if he wasn't prepared for war. He knows the history of Earth and its present situation. He has to expect attack.'

'Which the Martians know full well will happen. The point is that they could avoid war if they stayed on Mars. Or if they did not try to proselytize on Earth. They know that, yet they are going to try to convert the entire population of Earth. They know that this will result in war. Millions, maybe billions, will die, will suffer terribly.

'In a sense, the Martians *are* belligerents, the aggressors.'

Bronski smiled wryly.

'You keep saying *they*, not *us*. You forget that you and I are among the *they*. You're not really a full-fledged Martian yet – if you ever will be.'

'How about you? You were calling them *they*.'

Bronski shrugged. 'It takes time. I can no more forget Earth than the ancient Jews of the Babylonian captivity could forget Jerusalem.'

One of the things Bronski could not help speculating about was the fitness of the Martians for war.

'What do they know about the horrors of war? It's an alien concept to them, something they've read about but which they've never experienced. Two thousand years of peace have made a psychic atmosphere we of Earth can't possibly imagine.

'It's true that every generation has trained for war, but it's all play – so far. What will their reaction be when they have to kill and be killed? Will two millennia of peace ruin them for war?'

'The red-eyed ape that slumbers in all of us will be awakened and let loose from his cage.'

'If there is such a creature in us.'

'But *he* says that this must be done, that it is right,' Orme said.

'If it was anyone but *he*, I'd question that.'

Both knew that the other still had reservations about what

was going to happen, still had doubts and questions. But they'd told themselves, and each other, that they had not yet overcome their Terrestrial conditioned reflexes. Surely, the time would come when they would be able to dissolve these, be as Martian as the natives. In the meantime, they were suffering. Orme was in a worse state than he would admit to Bronski, than, most of the time, he would admit to himself.

Another thing that made the Martians different from their Terran coreligionists was the initial influence of the Krsh. In the beginning, their impact had been tremendous. They were at least 2500 years ahead of their captives in science and technology. They had regarded the Earth people as culturally retarded and with good reason. Indeed, if it had not been for Yeshua', whose powers were undeniable and irresistible, they would have made the Terrans, or their children at least, into Krsh, in mind though not in body.

Instead, the totally unpredictable and highly improbable had happened. Under the only circumstances which could bring about such a turning around, the Krsh had been converted.

Though the first generation of Krsh accepted the Law whole-heartedly, still, they were Krsh. And so the inevitable changes in the interpretation of the Law and in the mode of life of the human Jews took place swiftly. It was recorded, in sound, living colour, and three dimensions that Matthias and his Libyan Jewish disciples objected to many of the changes. But Yeshua' himself did not, in fact, he blessed them, and so there were no more objections, openly, at least.

In any event, a difference about interpretation and a steady evolution towards the humanitarian spirit of the law had always been a feature of Judaism. And in no way was there any lessening of emphasis on the basics of the religion.

The Krsh and the humans became thoroughly integrated; they lived side by side, their children played together; they worshipped together. The Krsh were only different in that none of them could ever be priests or the temple servants of the priests. The blood of Aaron and Levi did not flow through them.

One of the changes that would have shocked an orthodox Jew was a minor change in the morning prayer of every adult male. For thousands of years the men had said the Three Benedictions:

'Blessed art Thou, O Lord, our God, King of the Universe, Who hast not made me a heathen.

'Blessed art Thou, O Lord, our God, King of the Universe, Who hast not made me a slave.

'Blessed art Thou, O Lord, our God, King of the Universe, Who hast not made me a woman.'

There were no heathens on Mars and very little chance that any Jew would become one. Yet there were many on Earth, and one day the Martians would go to Earth and encounter them. So the first passage was kept, though it meant little to the prayers.

There were no slaves. Though the worshipper had been taught what the word meant, he had not suffered slavery and had never seen a slave, so this, too, had no emotional impact. But there had been many on Earth when the Krsh ship left it, and for all the Martians knew, there still were. So this passage was kept unchanged.

While the first generation lived, the third benediction was unaltered. But then, under the urging of the Krsh and of the human women, affected by the Krsh views, the third passage became: 'Blessed art Thou, O Lord, Our God, King of the Universe, Who hast not made me a beast.'

Because the room for an expanding population was so limited, the first commandment of God, to be fruitful and multiply, had to be kept within bounds. Every couple was allowed three children only. But, when they became ninety years old, they were permitted, if they so wished, to have two more. At one hundred and eighty, they could have another two.

Once the children left home, the parents were free to

divorce. Still, it was considered socially incorrect, a matter for gossip, and reprimand by relatives. But when a new coupling occurred, it was usually sanctified by marriage before or shortly after the fact.

To a Terran Jew the Martian society would be strange at first. There were many things to approve of; but there were also so many disconcerting things. Yet, after a while, unless he was ultraorthodox, he could become comfortable. Whatever exotic or unexpected features life here had, it was thoroughly Jewish. Here the thought of God permeated the populace. Everything that could possibly be so was based on the worship of God. The people lived in an ocean of divinity. Yet, unlike the fish who were unaware of the element they swam through, the Martian was always being reminded of this Creator and of the ancient covenants He had made with their ancestors and so with them.

21

'Were you the one who stood by my bed at night and watched me?' Orme said.

'I am with every one of my flock by day or night,' Jesus said, and he would speak no more on the subject.

Orme was puzzled and also a little angry. What kind of an answer was that? Why couldn't Jesus say yes or no? This reply was too much like the one he'd given when the Pharisees had asked him if it was permissible to pay the poll-tax to Caesar. He had said to them, 'Render then to Caesar what is Caesar's and to God what is God's.'

This was much quoted during the next two millennia and the basis of thousands of interpretations of proper allegiance to one's government and to one's religion. Yet there had never been unanimous agreement on the distinction between what was Caesar's and what was God's.

And there was his answer to the Sadducees' question about the resurrection of the dead, 'He is not God of the dead but God of the living.'

At the same time Jesus had made it clear that there would be a resurrection. But there would be no marrying or giving in marriage; the resurrected would be as the angels in Heaven. What did that mean? That there was a perfect sexual freedom with men and women coupling when they wished with anyone they wished? Or did it mean, as the churches said, that men and women would be sexless and, therefore, no longer men and women? Whenever Orme had thought about this, which wasn't often, he had a strange feeling in his genitals, a shrinking, as if a castrator with a big knife was about to sever them.

Orme had many questions, and when he had learned that

Jesus lived and was available for questioning, he had thought that now, at last, he would get all the answers. But this Jesus, like the one in the books he'd read, was still giving ambiguous replies. Perhaps, as Bronski said, these were amplified and clarified in the many recordings of Jesus's statements made on Mars. But there was no time to go through these now. He was leaving for Earth.

On this fateful day, all three Terrestrials were in a huge cube-shaped level near the surface of the planet. Around them were seven spaceships, six cylindrical, the seventh three times as large as any of the others, a hemisphere from which projected six long cylinders each tipped with an enormous globe. Into each ship was filing a double line of men. They no longer wore their ankle-length robes and sandals; they were soldiers uniformed for war, though they hoped that war would not be necessary. They wore calf-high blue boots, baggy red trousers, hip-long white tunics, and round brimless black plastic hats. Metal insignia of Krsh origin, denoting service and rank, were on their chests, shoulders, and hats. Many wore belts supporting holsters containing pistol-shaped weapons. Some of these were lasers which could kill a man at three miles and cut through steel three feet thick half a mile away.

Of the twenty thousand men, only four were not in uniform. Jesus wore his sky-blue robe, and the Earthmen were dressed in their IASA uniforms. The Messiah had thought that it would not be good for them to appear to be part of the Martian space navy.

'You are with us and of us and so beloved by us. But the people of Earth may regard you as traitors. It is better that you appear first as converts only. You will be of the Kingdom of the Presence and hence His soldiers. But the Sons of Darkness will be filled with suspicion, fear, and trembling. They must not identify you as one of us. You must still be Terrestrials, not Martians. Thus, you will be a bridge between us, a means of communication and reassurance.

Later, you can wear the garments of the Sons of Light.

'The Kingdom of the Presence cannot be brought about by force. We do not go to destroy and slay. We will effect the rule of the Messiah by example, by love, by gifts. Of course, there may be war, but we will not be the first to attack.

'You see,' he said, smiling, 'this man whom you call Saint John the Revelator, the writer of the *Apocalypse*, was a poet. He cast the coming of the Messiah in vivid imagery, in hyperbole, in blazing symbols. And he based his visions upon the supernatural. But the establishment of the Messiah and the Kingdom of the Presence and the laying of the foundations of the New Jerusalem will not come about as he said. The sky may be rolled up like a scroll, and the four horsemen may ride, and the seven-headed beast burst from the sea, but these things will not happen except symbolically.

'Much of the conquest will come about because of science and technology. This will cause what you call cultural shock. For instance, we will announce, and it will be true, that just recently our scientists have gone beyond ensuring a long delay of old age. We can now tell the peoples of Earth that we can give them immortality. Barring, of course, homicide, accident and suicide.'

Orme gasped. Then he said, 'Master, is that true? No, forgive me, I don't doubt you. It is so staggering.'

Bronski said, 'But if very few die, there soon will be no room on Earth for children.'

Hfathon, who was standing nearby said in a low voice, 'Do not bother the Messiah with obvious matters.'

Jesus, however, said, 'I did not say that only a few will die. There will be plenty of room in the beginning. Afterward, when the Earth has been filled again, provisions will be made for the children.'

Orme felt sick. There would be war, the most terrible that mankind had ever suffered. Or did Jesus's words hold another meaning which only time would reveal?

'It does not matter,' Jesus said. 'In eternity, five hundred years are as long, and as short, as a million. Our plan takes time. How much does not matter. We can be as patient as a loving mother with her troublesome children. In time everybody who deserves to be resurrected will be. Our scientists are convinced that we will someday be able to raise the dead. The recordings of things past and gone exist in the substratum of the universe. Or, to put it another way, in the body of the Creator. The scientists refer to it as the ether, a concept which I understand your scientists reject. But they are, in this respect, as ignorant as the wise men of ancient Earth were of other matters.

'In time, the dead will be raised. Five hundred years, a thousand, what does it matter to those who sleep?'

'Master,' Orme said, 'will this, too, be revealed to the people of Earth?'

'You will see. Ponder this. All things are done by the Merciful One, but He often uses men as his hands. This applies to the rising of the dead as well as to the restoration of the Kingdom of the Messiah.'

Jesus turned away then to speak to a group of officers. Orme, feeling slightly stunned, walked away. Bronski said something, but it could not have been urgent since he spoke softly and did not repeat it. Though Orme had already said farewell to Gulthilo, he walked across the vast space until he came to a metal fence. Behind this stood the families of the crews and near a gate was his wife. She had been told the day before that she was pregnant. This news had caused both joy and dismay, since he had to leave the next day and there was no telling when he would return. Even if she had not been with child, she could not have accompanied him. No women were on the ships since there might be war. Later, if all went well, women would be sent to Earth as teachers and administrators. But she would not be going even then because she had a child to raise.

Gulthilo, seeing him, smiled, though not as bravely as when they had parted an hour ago. 'What's wrong, Richard?'

208

'Nothing, except that I'm overwhelmed. I just heard that the scientists have announced that they expect to raise the dead some day.'

She put a hand through the wide mesh and took his. 'That's nothing to be surprised about. Jesus has always said that it will come about, and so we've expected it. I didn't know that the scientists, who've been working on it for a thousand years, had discovered something substantial. They must be confident that they can actually do this. Otherwise, the Messiah would not have told you that it was so. Probably, the news will be announced on TV soon. It'll be an occasion for great rejoicing. Perhaps a new annual festival will be established.'

'Give me another kiss,' he said, and he put his lips against hers, the wires pressing against his flesh. The contact with her flesh reassured him, gave him the sense that this world had not suddenly become misty, immaterial, far away. It was as solid and warm again as her body and the entity in her womb.

'May the Creator be with you,' she said softly. 'I will also assuredly be with you. And you will return before the baby is born. If it is at all possible, you will be with me then. The Law ensures that, and the Messiah is merciful.'

'Until then, my love,' he said, and he walked away. But he was not as certain as she. Only One knew what reception the Sons of Light would get from the Sons of Darkness.

22

Among the many things Orme hadn't understood was how a spacefleet could set forth without a long training of its personnel. He was told that simulation-training had been going on for the last fifty years in anticipation of this day. Thus, when the ships were built there were skilled crews to run them.

The personnel had fasted and prayed. Those who had from one cause or another become ritually unclean had been cleansed. All was ready.

The upper-level cube was cleared of people, and the entrances were blocked by massive metal doors. At one end of the hollow, from the ceiling, the bottom of a Brobdingnagian plug, a monolith of granite, slowly descended. Though it was a quarter of a mile high and half a mile in diameter, and though it had no visible attachments, it came down as lightly as a toy balloon slowly losing its air, and entered a cavity prepared for it.

First, the flagship, the *Maranatha* (Aramaic for 'Our Master, come!'), rose through the exit. One by one the others followed. Last was the giant hemispherical *Zara*, or 'seed', and when it was a quarter of a mile above the surface, it stopped. In ten minutes the top of the monolith had replugged the hole. Then, from one of the globe-tipped cylinders sticking from the *Zara*, an orange ray shot forth, and the rock about the plug and the plug melted together.

No surveyor satellite from Earth would record and transmit this event. The two presently operating had been shut off by the Martians. And since it was night on this side of Mars, by the time the spot came into range of Earth's delicate instruments, it would have been cooled off. When the *Zara* returned, it would disintegrate the thin crust of lava so that the plug could move down again.

The flagship, accelerating at three-fifths of Terrestrial gravity per second, rose into the thin atmosphere of the red planet. The others followed in Indian file, the *Zara* bringing up the rear.

Hfathon, standing by the three who were no longer Earthmen but naturalized Martians, spoke.

'The *Zara*'s pet name is "The Weathermaker". It can tap the power of the sun directly at the surface and transmit it in modulated form to Earth. It can create droughts or a deluge. It can warm up an arctic region or cool off a tropic one. Over a large area, it can affect temperature in five months by raising or lowering it five or six degrees for a considerable time. When the energy is concentrated on a small area, the effect is quickly noticeable. The *Zara* also has other capabilities. May the King of Heaven spare us from having to use it.'

'May He indeed,' Orme said. Imagining what could happen on Earth, he was sad. But had not the Messiah said that he came not with peace but with a sword? On the other hand, he had also said that he came to preserve men's lives, not to destroy them.

What would be would be, and no matter what the interim results, the intentions and the end were good. However, that philosophy had been used – misused and abused – by so many people and with such evil means that it was discredited. But this was a holy war, ordered by God and initiated by His adopted son. Winning the war could only result in great good, the greatest possible good, for mankind forever.

Why, then, was his heart so heavy and tears so close to his eyes?

Bronski and Shirazi seemed to be happy. They had no doubts. Like all the other men of the crew of the *Maranatha*, they went around smiling, singing songs in Krsh and Hebrew, some joyous folk songs, others devout prayers.

Except for the hours after the evening meal, Orme did not

have much time to think of other than official matters. He was kept busy conferring with the chiefs of the state and the higher officials of the fleet. Occasionally, Jesus sat in on the details of the broad plans outlined for Earth. Orme was to be the chief administrator for the North American area. Shirazi was to be the main consultant in the dealings with the Moslem states. Bronski would be the head of the liaison department handling the affairs of Western Europe and Israel. He was also to be head of the department which dealt with the non-Moslem Communist nations.

In addition, Orme was taking short lessons in the Hebrew language, so he'd understand the liturgies thoroughly. By the time he went to bed, he was very tired. But his dreams were lively. Too much so, since his nightmares were hideous, and he woke more than once sweating and whimpering. Usually, a dim figure in the crouching darkness pointed an accusing finger at him, and it glided towards him without moving its legs until Orme was just about to recognize the face. Then he would start awake, and sometimes Nadir and Avram would call from their bunks, asking what the trouble was.

Once, in the day-watch, he told them. Bronski said, 'I think, Richard, that you conversion was not complete. You still haven't accepted with a whole heart what your mouth has acknowledged.'

'Don't say that,' Orme said. 'Of course, I believe that he is the Messiah, the true Jesus Christ. How could any man who's seen what I've seen believe otherwise?'

'Allow me to remind you of the parable Jesus once told about Lazarus and the rich man,' Bronski said. 'Remember? The rich man feasted while Lazarus, the beggar, lay at his gate. Lazarus was covered with ulcers which the dogs licked. And the rich man would not even bother to cleanse and feed the beggar. He ignored him. Then both died, and the beggar went to heaven and the rich man to the flames of Hell. So the rich man appealed to Abraham for succour but was told it was impossible to get him out of Hell or even to bring him water to cool his burning tongue. Then the rich man asked that Lazarus be sent to his five brothers to warn them that they too might go to Hell if they did not mend their ways. But Abraham said, "If they won't heed Moses and the Prophets, they won't be convinced if someone should rise from the dead." That applies to you also. You have seen far more than a man raised from the dead, yet you still have doubts.'

'But you don't?'

'No. Perhaps you should go to Jesus and tell him you're troubled. I'm sure that he could settle your doubts.'

Orme thought about this. Then, having summoned up his courage, he sent word through Azzur ben-Asa, the Messiah's chief secretary, that he would like an audience. Azzur replied that the Messiah was available to no one at this time.

'He will be residing with his Father for three days.'

For a moment, Orme didn't understand this. Then he said, 'Oh, you mean he is in the ship's nuclear reactor?'

'That is one way of putting it,' ben-Asa said.

Orme thanked him and turned off the intercom. There it was, that which was at the basis of his misgivings. How could any man, even Jesus Christ, go into an atomic furnace and come out unaffected? More significant, why should he?

If only Jesus had not told him that story about the energy-being. That story and the others were supposed to be speculations, made up on the moment to show Orme what absurd rationalizations could be created by unbelievers. Jesus had seemed to be having a good time doing it. He was not the always-serious person that a reader of the Gospels might take him for. But could he, under the guise of fantasy, have been telling Orme the truth? Was he playing cat to Orme's mouse and enjoying it? Or was he just testing the depth of his disciple's convictions?

His thoughts returned to the reactor. Jesus retired there and also to the deadly furnace inside the globe that acted as the sun for the Martian cavern. If he was indeed only a man, could he survive for more than a microsecond in it? No, he couldn't. But the Martians regarded him as both a man like themselves and more than a man. He could perform miracles and not just by hearsay. They were awed by his ability to live within that reactor, but they thought it was natural. Nothing was unnatural to the Son of Man who was also God's adopted Son. And what more natural than that Jesus should go into a place where no other man could enter and talk to God? Did Jesus ever see God? Not according to the Martians, who quoted the Old Testament. 'No one has ever seen God.' That is, no living person.

But – oh, damn him for telling it! – there was the story of the energy-being. Was Jesus indeed in that atomic Holy of Holies with the Presence? Or was he restoring his strength, eating, as it were, the raging radiations?

On that day, Orme prayed three times with the others. When he'd gone to his bunk and the breathing of his two companions assured him they were sleeping, he climbed out. Getting down upon his knees, he prayed in a very low voice that he be shown the light.

'Oh, God, let me know the truth! I am in despair, in a hell of uncertainty. Cleanse me of this. Let my soul be firm, unshakeable, riveted with the truth. I beseech you, Father. Amen.'

He could hear nothing except the wind of Shirazi's and Bronski's breaths, see nothing but the darkness. He got back into the bunk and lay there for a long while before he fell into troubled sleep.

In his dream someone was telling him that Jesus had warned against three types of people: the man who loved to display his piety in public, the faultfinder, and the false prophet.

'Now, which is he?' the deep voice said.

'Who is he?' Orme said.

'You know,' the voice said.

'But . . . I don't know,' Orme said, and he groaned. Then, as the voice did not speak, 'The false prophet?'

'You have said it.'

Orme came up out of the deep, and as he swam just below the surface of wakefulness, he felt that familiar, and now somehow comforting, awareness that someone was standing by his bed. He opened his eyes. A man was standing by him, a man who shed a bright light. He wore a black robe, and his hair and beard were reddish. His face was aquiline and very handsome, though his eyes looked as if he had suffered much.

Orme did not try to rise. He lay on his back with his head turned towards the man, his heart beating hard, his hands clutching the sheets. This man looked as he had imagined Jesus Christ did; even in his fright he thought that he resembled the conventional pictures of Jesus hung on the walls of his parents' house.

The glowing man held up a hand and made a sign as if to bless him. Then he glided backward, and as he did so, the light began to fade. It was gone and with it the figure.

The whole event had taken perhaps ten seconds.

He thought that that man was not the Jesus whom he had first seen coming from the sun in the cavern. This was the man who had come to his bedside from time to time, the true Jesus Christ. He had been watching over him. And now, in his disciple's crisis of despair, he had appeared to him. The light had come, that light which shone from him. No words had been needed; his presence was enough.

Or it should have been. In previous ages the beholder of such a vision would have accepted it literally. The figure would have been what it seemed to be. There was no other explanation. But he was born in a less naive, more knowledgeable time. Could this shining figure be just one of those phenomena that occasionally happened to people when they were in a half-awake, half-asleep state? Orme had never experienced such things before, but he had read about them. He had known a man who sometimes experienced these visions. His friend had said that the things scared him, they seemed to truly exist, and he would swear that he had been wide awake when he saw them. But he admitted that he may just have thought he was fully conscious and that the phenomena were probably exteriorizations, projected subjectivities of his unconscious.

Orme, thinking of this, had to admit that the figure he'd seen might be the same. After all, he was an engineer, he'd had rigorous scientific training, and he should choose the most probable explanation. Use Occam's razor. Let it cut no matter what the pain.

However, it did not matter whether or not the true Jesus had appeared. What had manifested itself was what he believed. 'I am the Way.' That vision was the gate through which he saw to the deepest part of his mind. Or, to be oldfashioned but nevertheless just as valid, to the deeps of his soul.

Assured by this revelation, he should have been able to go to sleep. But there were other problems to consider. And so, while his bunkmates slept, he considered what he should do and what he was able to do. As always, the difference was great.

23

Halfway to Earth, the fleet began decelerating. But when the ships took up orbit around the planet, the crews did not find themselves in free fall. Gravicle generators maintained a field equivalent to that of Mars within each vessel.

The *Maranatha* went into a stationary orbit just above Jerusalem. Two ships took circumpolar orbits in opposite paths. Two others went into equatorial orbits. The sixth angled over Earth at forth-five degrees to the equatorial line. The seventh, the giant *Zara*, prowled around the planet at a distance of 200,000 miles, changing its line of travel every other day.

No attention was paid to the communications and weather-survey satellites nor to the two space-colony satellites. But the 'space junk', pieces of satellites and the complete ones in decaying orbits, were disintegrated by the *Zara*. This cleaning up did two things. It made sure that no manmade falling objects would strike the surface and perhaps kill people. And it impressed Earth mightily with the power of the *Zara*.

The day after this event, Jesus himself asked for permission to land the *Maranatha* in a field outside Jerusalem. It was denied, though very politely and with many excuses. The Israeli parliament, the Knesset, was still hotly debating whether Jesus should be allowed to land as the political head of the Martian nation or as the Messiah. Since Jesus insisted that he was the Messiah, and the political head of the state was the Chief Judge, a Krsh named Eliakim ben-Yoktan, the issue seemed unsolvable. In fact, the Knesset was putting off its decision as long as possible. Israel was being torn apart, brother against brother, father against son. A tiny superorthodox group, so reactionary that it still refused to recognize Israel as a state because it was not religious enough, flatly rejected Jesus as the Messiah. The orthodox were divided, some ecstatic because the Messiah had finally come, others raging that he was not a true Jew, let alone the descendant of David called the Anointed. A large part of the population was agnostic or atheist or of the reformed branch of Judaism. Many unpractitioners of the faith, though calling themselves Jews, had been swept away and now were as devout as the most orthodox of the orthodox and calling loudly for the government to allow Jesus to come down and so begin the messianic era.

The whole nation was paralysed; business and the mundane duties of daily living were ignored as much as possible. The citizens were glued before their TV sets or arguing with relatives, neighbours, strangers in the streets. The air burned and quivered with quotations from the Prophets and the Talmud, each being used both to contradict and to prove.

Equalling the turmoil in Israel was that in all other nations. Despite great efforts in the communist countries to suppress the details of Jesus's messages, they had failed. Through underground channels and the radio, the news had got to the populaces, though often in distorted form. The socialist democracies had also tried, though not nearly as vigorously, to censor part of the news. There were even citizens' groups that demanded that the messages be heavily restricted, especially excluding all religious content.

In Rome the Pope appeared on TV and denounced the Messiah as the Antichrist. The Patriarch of the Greek Orthodox Church repeated the accusation an hour later. The Archbishop of Canterbury stated that the Church of England would at this time neither confirm nor deny the status of the claimant. More study of the messages and comparison of them with the theology derived from the Scriptures would have to be done. This was simply putting off the inevitable.

Even the layman with a cursory knowledge of the Bible (which included most church members) could see at once that there was no reconciling most of the teachings of the Anglican Church with the claims of the Martian.

The Baptist churches, Southern and otherwise, had officially rejected this Jesus. But their constituents were divided, and already splinter movements had formed with various names.

The official heads of the Hindus, Moslems, and Buddhists had scorned Jesus. But, again, their flocks were divided. Everywhere, there were bitter words often followed by violence. Mass demonstrations, riots, and a revolution in Uganda, had occurred.

On the third day of the fleet's orbiting, the radios and TVs of the world were taken over. No matter what the channel, the broadcast from the communications room in the *Maranatha* came through. When some governments turned off the electrical power so that their citizens could not hear, the sets continued to operate. This threw the officials into a panic. How could the Martians do this? And if they could do this, what else could they do?

All nations protested, of course, but Jesus replied that it was necessary and for the good of the people.

For twenty-four hours the *Maranatha* sent down a stream of programmes. These consisted of histories of the Krsh before coming to Earth, films of the Terrestrials of 50 AD, the taking of the captives from Earth, the preachings of Matthias and their effect upon the captives and the Krsh, the conversions, the first appearance of Jesus, and many sections dealing both with Martian life and Jesus's place in this. Also transmitted, in case they had been suppressed the first time, were the programmes in which the Marsnauts had participated.

The various governments protested angrily and many made veiled threats. But no atomic-bomb-tipped missiles were sent up against the ships.

219

In the final programme, an hour and a half long, Jesus himself proclaimed that the Martians could cure any disease and prevent any recurrence. All disease would be wiped out forever. These included mental diseases of a genetic or metabolic origin, and old age.

Also, if the governments would permit, two hundred small machines would be landed at various spots. From these would flow 'manna'. This would be a soft white substance which contained all the elements needed for healthy nutrition and was quite tasty. The manna would flow from each machine at the rate of one hundred cubic feet per hour. It could be transported to the hungry of Earth, of whom there were many, and be given at no cost – at this time – to the recipients.

Orme was shocked when he heard this. Until Jesus had spoken of it, he'd had no inkling that there was such a thing. When he'd recovered somewhat from his emotional upset, he was able to see the implications of this. If the governments refused to transport the food, they would have serious riots on their hands. In any event, the slaughter during suppression would be enormous.

'Do not make excuses about lack of transportation or the expense involved!' Jesus said. 'And do not try to make a profit from the manna or withhold it from those in disfavour with your governments! Woe to the man or woman who is responsible for this wickedness and to the one who carries out the orders of the person above him! Woe to all who do this! They shall suffer!'

More protests about interfering with the rights of the sovereign states. No reply to the protests.

Jesus then announced what seemed to his audience to be the ultimate, the climax. That was that physical immortality could be and would be theirs. The only requisite for receiving this was that the recipient must be a believer in the true religion and in himself as the Messiah.

'But I promise woe to the hypocrites who say they believe only to gain this gift of life! They will be found out, and they will be cast into the outer darkness!'

When he threatened, he lost the expression of kindness and in his wrath the light of promised hell shone from his eyes.

'I say, woe to you, you vipers! You cannot hope to deceive me long! You will be found out!

'The Father has given you all the good things of life, and you have made them bad! The Father gives, but He does not give for nothing! Nothing is free! You must give to get!'

Orme, sitting in his cabin and watching the TV, could imagine what the effect of promised physical immortality would have on the viewers. Of course, many had heard this before, since some governments had allowed this to be known when the previous programmes were transmitted to them. But the majority belonged to states which had suppressed this news.

At this point, the viewer on Earth might have expected that this would be the end of the programme. What else could be offered? It was then that Jesus told them of the hopes for the resurrection of all the dead. He did not promise that this could be achieved within a hundred years or two. But it was a certainty.

That does it, Orme thought. Everybody will be rushing to sign up. They'll do anything to get immortality. Most of them, anyway. The New World, the Kingdom of Heaven, the reign of the Messiah, has begun. It may take some time before it's established, but it's started, and nothing can stop it.

Can't they see that the devil would make the same promises? Only . . . this man can deliver. But the devil could probably deliver also. And the devil would think of himself as a good man. Who that is evil believes that he is? All think of themselves as good. No doubt Hitler and Stalin and Mao, Napoleon and Alexander the Great and Julius Caesar, Attila the Hun and Nebuchadnezzar, all thought of themselves as being on the side of good.

The only difference between them and Jesus is that Jesus can do good. But it's an insidious good that will lead directly

221

but subtly to subtle evil.

Nothing could stop him. Unless . . . but how could he, one man, do anything?

The next day, the *Zara* performed a deed that, in the minds of most, could only be a good one. All over Earth, all the missiles and cannons with atomic warheads and all cannons with atomic shells were melted. Again, the radio and TV stations were overridden, and the news was sent from the *Maranatha*.

'Surely,' Jesus said, 'this will cause great rejoicing among all but those who hate men and love war. I would have done an evil thing if I had melted only the missiles of some nations and not of others. But I am impartial, and I do not choose sides, saying this one is evil and that good. Vipers, spawn of wicked generations, you are all guilty! Repent, therefore, and praise the Lord with all your hearts because He has seen fit to guard you against yourselves!'

There were protests, of course, but these got no reply.

Again, Jesus requested permission to land outside Jerusalem. Again, this was refused. The Knesset could not make up its mind, and the state of Israel had proclaimed a curfew. The police and soldiers were patrolling the streets to enforce the regulation. Nor was it the only nation in a state of martial emergency.

The fourth day, the morning sky over the near East became blood-red. Then the sun grew dim and almost entirely black for several hours. And the moon turned as red as blood.

Bronski, watching this on TV, said, 'The *Zara* is doing that, of course. Can you imagine the power that takes or the means to control and direct that power? Surely, the Lord of our fathers is with us!'

Orme said nothing. He was beginning to wonder if he was wrong. And then he thought of the glowing figure by his bedside, and he became stronger.

The fifth day, Jesus again asked for permission to land.

'Oh, you men of little mind and even less faith! Why must

222

you harden your hearts? What must I do to convince you that I am indeed the Anointed of Heaven?

'Whoever believes in me does not believe in me but in Him who sent me. And he who sees me sees Him who has sent me. I have come as a light to the world that everyone who believes in me should not remain in darkness. You Children of Darkness, you can become Sons and Daughters of Light. But you must unstiffen your necks and soften your hearts!'

All of his talks had been in English, delivered with no trace of Krsh or Hebrew pronunciation. The accent was Orme's Toronto Canadian, undoubtedly learned from recordings of his speech while he was on Mars. Millions of non-English speakers would be able to understand him, but for those who wouldn't subtitles or verbal translations were provided in the languages which Bronski and Shirazi knew: Hebrew, Arabic, Hindustani, Mandarin Chinese, Swahili, Spanish, French, German, Italian, Farsi, Russian, Polish, Greek and Portuguese.

Even in the remote villages, at least one person would be able to translate the English for his fellows.

English was still the world lingua Franca, but Orme knew that it was an interim tool. In time, Krsh would be the international language. And in time, after the inevitable period of bloody troubles, the Krsh and the Martian humans, as elder brothers, would lead Israel, the elder brother of the nations of Earth, to instruct, to change, to modify, to form. In time, the whole planet would be much like Mars, except that there would be ethnic and national racial differences. Though Russia would still be Russia and North America still North America and China still China, there would be no national boundaries with their customs houses, import tariffs, and armed guards. A woman would be able to walk through dark streets without fear of being robbed, beaten, or raped. Children would not be afraid to speak to strangers. The cannons and the machine-guns would be melted and made into ploughs. The oceans and the rivers and the brooks would be cleansed. And in time the Kingdom of Heaven would be established, although there still would be contrariness and evil-wishing 'human nature' in some people. But, though Earth wouldn't be Utopia, it would be as close to it as human nature allowed.

This image of the future was very attractive. Why then did Orme feel heavy of heart? Was it because the Kingdom was being forced on Earth and, though the end was desirable, the means meant bloody strife and suffering for many? The people of Earth had gone through strife and anguish and violent death ever since the first man had walked over the veldt or prowled through the jungle. There seemed to be no way of ending all this until now, and if it wasn't for Jesus and his people there would be no end. Surely, the end, in this case, did justify the means.

But if this Jesus was the Antichrist, then the ends would not be what they were supposed to be.

Orme sent up a silent prayer to the real Jesus.

'Help me, Lord. Rid me of my weaknesses, make me strong.'

Two hours later, word was received from Jerusalem. A mob had stormed the Knesset and demanded that the Messiah be allowed to land. In the mob were many police and soldiers who had thrown down their arms and joined their fellows. The prime minister and half of his cabinet and a third of the parliament had resigned. Despite the illegitimacy of the procedure, the rest of the Knesset had issued the invitation. However, an extension of time was asked for. Many heads of states wished to be on hand when the ship arrived, but it would take time to fly to Jerusalem. Also, the necessary security couldn't be set up until tomorrow. Would that be permitted?

Jesus graciously said that he would wait one more day.

'But I will not forget that there are many among you who have hardened their hearts against me. And there are many who have not said that they are against me or for me. Whoever

224

does not declare himself for me is against me. Woe to the hard of heart and the neutrals!'

That night Orme prayed again, hoping that his Lord would show himself once more. But He did not.

24

The *Maranatha* was to land at noon. Early in the morning, however, Rabbi Ram Weisinger, the prime minister pro tem, called the ship. Under his black hat he was sweating.

'Master, we beg you to wait for still another day. The crowds are so great that we must call in more troops. We can't guarantee your safety. Many evil men, Moslem, Christian, and Jewish, have sworn to kill you. There is no way we can screen all of them out, though we've made many arrests.'

'Do not worry about them,' Jesus said. 'I cannot be killed.'

Weisinger's eyes widened, and his expression was strange. But he did not protest.

At 10:00, the three Marsnauts received instructions from Hfathon on their part in the day's activities after landing. Orme asked no questions, and when he was dismissed, went at once to his cabin. Shirazi and Bronski did not come with him.

At 11:30 he was supposed to be in the large room next to the central starboard lock. The instructions had ended at 10:30, giving him a little less than an hour to do what he hoped he would have the courage to do. He got down on his knees and prayed for guidance. When he rose, his heart was still beating hard and his stomach was clenched.

He sat down on the edge of his bunk and placed a large copy of a Krsh translation of the Holy Writings on his knees. Using this as a desk, he wrote quickly a three-page letter, making no corrections. He signed and dated all three pages and placed on each his right-hand fingerprints. After the ink was dry, he folded the letter into a compact bundle and stuck it in an inside pocket of his uniform.

At 10:45, he left the cabin. Instead of heading towards the

middle-level main lounge, where his compatriots and many off-duty officers were, he walked towards the aft. At approximately 10:55, he found his victim, a private coming out of a room he shared with nine others. It was empty, the soldier was alone, and there was no one else in sight. Orme, disliking intensely the violence he was subjecting the man to, slugged him with his fist on the side of the head, punched him in the belly as he staggered back, and then gave him a judo chop across the neck. After dragging the unconscious private outside the room, he removed his laser gun from his holster.

At 11:05 he left the room. The soldier was still senseless, his mouth gagged and taped, his legs and hands taped, lying on the floor under a bunk. His sergeant would note that he wasn't present, but it was doubtful that he'd send someone after him. He'd note down his name for punishment afterwards. Still, it was best to make sure that no one would investigate. Having learned the soldier's name, rank and unit from his insignia, Orme located his sergeant through the intercom.

'Private Yokhanan ben-Obed has been assigned to me,' Orme told him. 'It was decided that I should have a Hebrew interpreter with me, and so I picked him.'

'Very well, sir,' the sergeant said.

The Martian army was just like any other. You didn't question the orders of a higher-up.

At 11:15 Orme entered the designated room. Jesus had exchanged his blue robe for a scarlet. Since this was the first time Orme had seen him in this colour, he wondered why the switch had been made. Then he recalled that, shortly before Jesus had been crucified, he had been dressed in a scarlet robe by the authorities. He must have chosen this colour to remind the Earthmen of this. He also could have put on a crown of thorns and carried a cane, which the Roman soldiers had first given him and then taken away to strike him over the head. But that would be too theatrical even for this dramatic man.

Jesus, who was talking with some officers, gave Orme a

strange look as he entered. Orme sweated even more heavily. Could he detect that his disciple was nervous? Or could he even know all? He'd once said that he could read minds, though he never permitted himself to do so. In this instance, noting Orme's expression, though Orme was trying to look normal, perhaps registering the emotions inside him – by the electrical fields on Orme's skin? – had Jesus broken his rule?

If so, all was lost. But since Jesus said nothing to him or to the officers, he must not think anything was gravely wrong. After all, everybody here, except the Messiah, was nervous. They were also feeling fatigued, since the Martian gravity field had been cut off, and they were subject to that of Earth. It would take them a long time to get accustomed to their increased weight, three-fifths more than that of their native planet. However, they would soon ride in vehicles enclosed in a field equivalent to that of Mars, and all, except the Master, wore a belt to which was attached an adjustable gravity unit. When the strain got too much for them, they would switch that on.

That device alone was worth a fortune here, Orme thought, and he smiled wryly. Even now, he was speculating on the fortunes to be made from the sale of Martian artifacts.

'Ah, Lord, forgive me.'

The lock swung open. Bright, harsh sunlight, hot air, and the roar of a mob poured in. Jesus stepped out first and paused a moment. Those behind halted. He lifted up a hand and said, loudly, 'May the Creator, our Father, bless you, children of Earth and Mars alike!'

Awaiting him were a regiment of soldiers, squads of policemen, an honour guard, many TV crews, and perhaps five hundred dignitaries. Around the field and lining the road from it, people covered the low hills and the roofs of houses. They roared as he stepped out, roared so loudly that they could not have heard his greeting. But the microphones of the TV men must have picked them up.

Orme came out with the others then. There was much

confusion for a while. Jesus had to meet and exchange a few words with the assembled heads of state. He held out his hand, not to be shaken but to be kissed. Sheila Pal, the president of the NAC, did not hesitate, though she must have been aware that millions of her constituents would be enraged. Neither did the Italian ambassador, though the Pope had denounced the Messiah and his government was officially Communist. To kiss Jesus's hand would, theoretically, offend the majority of the populace, still devout Roman Catholic, and also the officially atheistic high-state officials. But the government had announced that its ambassador was sent only to greet the head of a foreign state, Mars. The Messiah's religion had nothing to do with political protocol.

Most of the other Communist nations and many of the socialist democracies had adopted this line. China and the southeastern Asiatic nations had sent no representative, but India, though Communist, was represented by its president and prime minister. The Soviet ambassador to Israel had been given instructions, obviously, to follow the example of Italy. Hand-kissing was excepted, since no self-respecting atheistic Marxian would emulate this capitalistic opiate-of-the-masses custom. But when Anatoly Shevchenko extended his hand to grip Jesus's, the Russian was not only kissing his hand, he was down on his knees.

Speaking English, he said, 'Master, forgive me! I doubted, but now I know that you are indeed the Messiah and that there is a God! Forgive me my sins, which are many, and allow me to take sanctuary with you!'

Jesus said, 'You are forgiven, and you will hereafter be at my right side. Though you are not of the seed of Abraham, you are a son of those with whom the Creator made a covenant in the time of Noah. Rise, and from now on bend your knees only when you pray to the Presence.'

Orme was as shocked as the others, though not so much that he could not imagine the effect of this unexpected conversion behind the Iron Curtain. Or, for that matter, on this side of it. Every TV set was showing this; what a sensation it must be causing!

Surely the ambassador, though probably a third-generation Marxist atheist, had had some doubts. He may have been as unaware of them as St Paul was when he was persecuting the Christians. But, like Paul, he had been overwhelmed without warning. Paul had his road to Damascus; the ambassador, his road to Jerusalem.

Or, and here Orme cursed himself for his everpresent suspicions, had the ambassador been given instructions by his government to pretend to this conversion? Then he could spy on Jesus. But the Soviets would be aware of the tremendous impact this public defection would make on the world. Would they dare to risk this just to plant an agent? It didn't seem likely.

Orme felt even more doubtful and weakened, physically and emotionally. This man, or being, spoke and acted as if with authority from God Himself. Yet, the Antichrist would seem to be good, to be, in fact, Christ Himself. Only by its fruit could you judge the tree. The Antichrist must be judged by the long-term results of his actions. But, so far, the Martian Jesus had done nothing the the real Jesus would not do.

In time, the fruit would be ripe for the plucking. Then anyone with a good heart might see who was who, what was what.

Orme wondered if he should wait, should put off what he'd planned for this day. He hadn't given the so-called Messiah enough time to reveal the evil behind the seeming good. The seed should be allowed to grow until, instead of food, the harvest was weeds.

'Oh, Lord,' Orme thought, 'let me not take the road to the right nor to the left. Let me go straight ahead on the road that leads to Your beloved city.'

He looked around, and, seeing a familiar face, felt joy. Was this man's presence here a sign from God? It was Jack

Tarlatti, a well-known TV-documentary producer and newsman.

Orme strolled over to him, aware that two Martian soldiers were watching him. But they would be doing so only to ensure his security. He grabbed Tarlatti by the hand and said, 'Jack, my old drinking buddy, my blessing and my cross! There were times I thought I'd never see you again! How are you?'

Tarlatti, feeling the compactly bundled letter in his hand, quit smiling.

Orme said, 'Just take it. Put it in your pocket when no one's looking. Read it after you get back to your hotel. It's self-explanatory. Do as I say, please, Jack. It'll be the biggest scoop you ever had.'

Tarlatti, trying to smile as widely as before, said, 'Sure. Anything you say, Dick. How about an interview right now?'

Orme looked around. Azzur, Jesus's secretary, was gesturing at him to come immediately. Obviously, he was wanted for the greeting of the dignitaries.

Orme clapped Tarlatti on the shoulder. 'Sorry, I'm too busy right now. Sure good to see you, Jack. Have to run now.'

As he walked away he hoped that Tarlatti's curiosity would not overcome him. He must not read that letter until what had to be done had been done.

After what seemed to Orme an interminable time, the greetings and the diplomatic compliments ended. From the *Maranatha* issued thirty large canoelike vessels. Into these the Martians and a number of honoured Terrestrial guests seated themselves. The lead vehicle contained the pilot, Jesus, the Russian ambassador, the Israeli prime minister, the three Marsnauts, the fleet admiral, Jesus's secretary, and the presidents of the NAC, Uganda, and West Germany. Orme thought that the selection of the last three was curious, but he didn't doubt that Jesus knew exactly what he was doing.

The procession started with squads of motorcycle police and an armoured car leading. Behind them was a car with a TV crew and three cars of Israeli secret service men. Then

231

Jesus's vehicle, two cars of more secret service personnel, then the Martian vehicles, then the cars with the Israeli and visiting dignitaries and behind them more secret service men, uniformed policemen, and soldiers. On both sides of the parade soldiers kept the crowd from pressing in or attempted to do so. The heat and the tumult were almost overwhelming. So great was the noise that Orme could not hear Bronski when he shouted something at him.

The plan was that the procession would go first to the Wailing Wall. There Jesus would pray for a few minutes. After that, he would to go the Knesset and make a short televised speech, and then to the new King David Hotel which would be occupied only by the Martians and several hundred security men.

Orme felt the butt of the laser under his baggy uniform. When he got to the Wailing Wall and Jesus got out, he would use the weapon. The whole world would see Richard Orme, captain of the Marsnauts, a recent convert to the Jesus of Mars, draw the laser and shoot the ray into him. Orme did not expect to live long afterwards. Nor was he sure that Jesus would be hurt. If he was indeed the energy-being, he would absorb the energy of the laser beam. If he were not the energy-being but the Antichrist – though they might be one and the same – he still might be invulnerable. A man who could walk in an atomic reactor, as Shadrach, Meshach, and Abednego had walked in the furnace, would not be touched even by the ravening fire of a laser. On the other hand, if he were just a man, he might not have entered the reactor. He might have just pretended to do so.

In any event, the whole world, Earth and Mars, would see Richard Orme try to kill the Messiah. It might even hear his words of denunciation, though there was little likelihood of this. But Jack Tarlatti would produce his letter, and then everybody would know the truth. Whether they chose to believe it or not was in the hands of God.

At least, he, Richard Orme, would have done what God

would want him to do. He would die a martyr for the true faith. The world would see, though it might not fully understand until later, that a man who had walked and talked with this Jesus did not believe that he was the true Jesus. And the man who did not believe this was an Earthman. Therefore, other people of Earth might conclude that one of their own knew the truth and, knowing it, had acted as his conscience told him to act.

Or would his act be misinterpreted? Would he be called a Judas Iscariot?

It did not matter. He had to do what was right.

Gulthilo would be very hurt and very ashamed when she saw this. Perhaps she and their child would be disgraced, even though they had no blame. He grieved because of this, but he still must act.

He was thinking of this when the vehicle came over the top of a hill and the sprawling city of Jerusalem was in view. There it is, he thought. How differently I feel now. On Mars I had been in ecstasy envisioning the return of Jesus to the city that had crucified him. But then I did not know that the Jesus who was nailed to the cross was not the Jesus who returned two thousand years later in triumph.

At that moment there was a flurry on his right side, men and women and children caught in a human whirlpool. The soldiers halted and the procession with it.

'What's going on?' Orme shouted to no one in particular.

Suddenly, there were pistol shots. A soldier staggered and fell, and a man, tall, lean, bearded, wild-eyed, burst from the melee. He raised a pistol in his left hand and pointed it at Jesus. Shots from at least a dozen soldiers struck him; others must have missed, since four spectators fell to the ground.

But this man was only a diversion. From the other side of the street a woman stepped out and threw a small round object. A grenade!

It arched up and down, the end of its trajectory Jesus, standing up in the front of the vehicle in his scarlet robe, seemingly unaware of the second attacker.

Orme shouted a warning.

He did not have time to think of the irony of his trying to warn the man whom he was planning to kill. Nor did he have time to think that when the bomb went off, he, too, would be killed.

He rose from the seat and leaped out, passing from the insular field of Martian gravity into Earth's. As a result, he started out as if he would jump twenty feet from a standing start but the arc he'd intended to make through the air curved abruptly downward at almost a right angle. Nevertheless, his left hand, reaching out, smacked into the hard metal object. He struck the ground, holding the grenade with both hands to his belly, his face and knees sliding on the pavement.

There was no time to think about the irony of this. He would die a martyr but not for the true Jesus – for the false.

25

There was time after all.

'Why did I do it?' he mumbled.

He was in the midst of a vast roar. The hot sun was blazing in his eyes. Then a head moved between him and the glaring light, and he saw the smiling face of Jesus.

'It didn't explode?' Orme said.

'It did,' Jesus said. 'You died. Your belly and genitals and legs were blown from your trunk. Your hands and the lower parts of your arms were shredded.'

He bent down and touched Orme on the forehead. Much of Orme's numbness, feeling of unreality, and weakness faded.

'There. That should take care of it.'

Orme sat up. His body was intact. It was also naked. Nearby were some shreds of his uniform. By the side of the vehicle from which he had leaped was his laser-gun. Where was the blood? Dissipated by Jesus as he had boiled away the blood of the ram on Mars? Of course!

But a few feet away soldiers were putting into plastic sacks the bloodied remnants of flesh and bone. He thought he was going to vomit, but Jesus touched him again and the nausea flowed away.

Bronski and Shirazi and the Russian ambassador were standing to one side, all as pale as if they, not he, had become corpses. The TV crews were working away, some cameras pointed at him, some at Jesus, some at the crowd.

He thought, the blast of the grenade should have made me deaf, too. But Jesus would have restored my sense of hearing.

A Krsh soldier came up bearing a large blanket.

'Rise, man, and cover your nakedness,' Jesus said.

Orme obeyed and wrapped the blanket around him.

Jesus turned and walked to the car and picked up the laser-gun. Returning, he extended it to Orme.

'You should have had it in a holster instead of concealing it under your uniform. How did you expect to get it out quickly if you had to use it?'

Orme shook his head. 'I can't carry that and keep the blanket up, too. Besides . . .'

The large black eyes and the slightly crooked smile of Jesus showed that he knew. He *knew*!

Jesus said, 'Out of nothing I made flesh and restored your body. This was recorded, and now the whole world has seen. Will there be any unbelievers left on the face of this planet? Yes, there will. But millions who did not believe until a few moments ago will now believe. The others are still the lost sheep.'

'Master,' Orme murmured, 'am I forgiven?'

Jesus indicated a man and a woman. One was he who had shot at Jesus, and probably hit him, and the woman was the one who had thrown the grenade. They were unwounded, but holes in their clothing showed where bullets had penetrated. Though surrounded by police, they were not handcuffed.

'They, too, are forgiven,' Jesus said. 'I raised them from the dead so that the whole world might know that I can be merciful. Now they will probably be among my most devoted disciples. If not, they will at least be witnesses.'

Jesus put his mouth close to Orme's ear.

'Doubt no more. But if you do, you'll betray yourself to me before you can betray me. I don't think that you will doubt again. However, I will not be merciful the next time. It is not fitting to tempt the Holy One too many times. Or the Son of Man.

'Now, tell me, do you know why you chose at the last moment, when you thought there would be no more moments, to sacrifice your life to save me, who does not need saving?'

'I don't know,' Orme said. 'Perhaps it was because,

somewhere deep in my mind, was the thought that it made no difference if you were this energy-being and not the original Jesus. The Father uses many hands to do His work, and He sometimes works in a subtle circuitous manner. If He chose a nonhuman creature from a faroff planet to be the Messiah, just as He chose the Krsh to be among the People of the Covenant, then . . . But are you truly . . . !'

Jesus raised his hand to indicate that Orme should stop.

'The true Messiah is the one the Father chooses to be the Messiah. Now, let us go into the holy city.'

'But, Master, I gave a man a letter telling what I planned to do. It will do you great harm if it's published.'

Jesus kissed Orme on his lips, and said, 'Let it be made public. The world saw what you did. Tomorrow, we will be rested, and we will advance the work of the Father one more pace. There is great evil to overcome. The days will be dark and the nights darker. But, in the end, there is the light that all the Children of Light Seek.' ·

THE WORLD'S GREATEST SCIENCE FICTION AUTHORS
NOW AVAILABLE IN PANTHER SCIENCE FICTION

E E 'Doc' Smith

Classic Lensman series

Masters of the Vortex	£1.25 ☐
Children of the Lens	£1.50 ☐
Second Stage Lensman	£1.25 ☐
Grey Lensman	95p ☐
Galactic Patrol	95p ☐
First Lensman	£1.25 ☐
Triplanetary	£1.25 ☐

Skylark series

The Skylark of Space	£1.25 ☐
Skylark Three	£1.25 ☐
The Skylark of Valeron	£1.25 ☐
Skylark Duquesne	£1.25 ☐

Family D'Alembert series (with Stephen Goldin)

The Imperial Stars	£1.25 ☐
Stranglers' Moon	£1.25 ☐
The Clockwork Traitor	85p ☐
Getaway World	£1.25 ☐
The Bloodstar Conspiracy	85p ☐
The Purity Plot	£1.25 ☐
Planet of Treachery	£1.25 ☐

Other Titles

Subspace Explorers	£1.25 ☐
Galaxy Primes	95p ☐
Spacehounds of IPC	£1.25 ☐

SF1081

THE WORLD'S GREATEST SCIENCE FICTION AUTHORS
NOW AVAILABLE IN PANTHER SCIENCE FICTION

Philip José Farmer

The *Riverworld* Saga

To Your Scattered Bodies Go	£1.25 ☐
The Fabulous Riverboat	£1.25 ☐
The Dark Design	£1.50 ☐
The Magic Labyrinth	£1.95 ☐

Other Titles

Riverworld and other stories	£1.50 ☐
The Stone God Awakens	80p ☐
Time's Last Gift	85p ☐
Traitor to the Living	85p ☐

All these books are available at your local bookshop or newsagent, or can be ordered direct from the publisher. Just tick the titles you want and fill in the form below.

Name _____

Address _____

_____

Write to Granada Cash Sales
PO Box 11, Falmouth, Cornwall TR10 9EN.

Please enclose remittance to the value of the cover price plus:

UK 40p for the first book, 18p for the second book plus 13p per copy for each additional book ordered to a maximum charge of £1.49.

BFPO and Eire 40p for the first book, 18p for the second book plus 13p per copy for the next 7 books, thereafter 7p per book.

Overseas 60p for the first book and 18p for each additional book.

Granada Publishing reserve the right to show new retail prices on covers, which may differ from those previously advertised in the text or elsewhere.

SF281